Return to Me—
A LOVE LOST
IN TIME

JANE MARIA

outskirts press

Outskirts Press, Inc.
http://www.outskirtspress.com

ISBN: 978-1-4787-8065-6

Library of Congress Control Number: 2016913445

Outskirts Press and the "OP" logo are trademarks belonging to Outskirts Press, Inc.

PRINTED IN THE UNITED STATES OF AMERICA

PROLOGUE:

"We have what we seek. It is there all the time, and if we give it some time…It will make itself known to us."
Thomas Merton

I was eight years old when my father told me, "Marisa, be careful what you tell people—what you reveal of yourself," as he broke his gaze from afar for just a moment to look at me.

"I mean all the things I've taught and shared with you about our friends out there. People won't always understand you, or even try. They may label you, turn away, and well—it's just best to keep these secrets to yourself for the most part."

As my father and I continued to gaze up at the life beyond and outside our realm, I broke our mutual ritual for a moment and looked at him. "Dad, why is that again? Why can't I just be me and say what I want to say?" I, myself, did not call them secrets as my father did. I called them "knowings" as a child. My father and I just knew stuff that maybe only a few did.

That particular night had dominated a clear unobstructed sky. Except for a few childlike questions from me, we both basked without any interruption in our viewing of inexhaustible counts of divinely fixed bodies of light, who so proudly boasted of their penetrating luminosity. Those bodies were akin to us. They were our own. They belonged to us and we belonged to them. We knew this to be true.

My father was given the gift of these "knowings" when he was a child. As an astronomy professor, he would be the one to introduce and bestow truths to me of intrinsic as well as extrinsic mysteries of those worlds above and beyond. From the earliest time that I could remember, he had presented me to our friends, the constellations, and their own collective domains of various inheritances. It made me feel special, yet isolated much of the time.

After that time of being eight years of age, I began venturing through my higher self. I became awakened to higher grounds, so to speak, ever soaring more and more as time passed by.

I was my father's daughter indeed. I was one of his kind who possessed these "knowings." I was also the one whom he had chosen to be introduced to his best friend shortly after my birth and likewise, she would become my best friend also. She was not of this world, though. She resided elsewhere.

As he continued to reiterate the necessity of being "careful" throughout my childhood, I would reassure him. I divulged to only a few along the way and more so to my friend, Caroline, who would become my earthly best friend at the age of nine. Otherwise, I kept quiet. So I came to be, well—the one whom I was meant to be.

As my journeys continued into adulthood, I would be lifted and escorted into the abodes of the night skies comprised of endless esoteric mysteries. These journeys would lead me to the knowings of the Great Liquid who retained from us sentenced humans the secrets and sins that had been hidden for eons. Though I would possess great reverence of this massive liquid, I would also possess an unexplained lifelong fear of it, and thus I would continue to hope for the day of reasoning of this lingering fear.

In time, I would also be taken to a forgotten earthly period where a former lover would yearn to be reunited again with me in the present. Thus, the word "familiar" would come forefront in endless successions consuming my thoughts and rousings.

My best friend from elsewhere would be the very one to propagate those journeys and have me enter into those worlds of unveiling what is hidden…what is hidden in liquid.

Chapter 1

AND SO I CAME TO BE

"It beckons, drenches, and cleanses us,
and then drowns us in its sweet delights...."

*I*t was not quite twilight yet, but I felt assured this evening would be engulfed with promises of hope and maybe a smidgen of magic. I was forty years of age now and it was mid-spring of 2009. Driving down the coastal highway along the North Carolina coast, I had the top down on my Lexus convertible. With my hair having permission to blow in any direction as it pleased, I was happy. I believe I was the happiest I had been in quite a long time.

Medleys of my parents' songs of the 1970s were blaring out their lyrics that I had never tired of, for these songs belonged to those who were kindred to romantic moonlit evenings full of their enchanting dances, as they were shared with all the deserving who were predestined as myself. So as loud as I could get my sound system to play, they were appropriate on this early evening of my best friend's expected affirmation of what was yet to come. Yes, I was happy.

I lifted my hands from the steering wheel for a moment, waving them wildly while catching the wind in gratitude for its promise of good luck. As I was singing along, there was nothing that could have countered this ecstatic moment. This evening was magical. I knew it. I could feel it. I could taste it.

My hair took an unexpected sudden wisp of flight to my left and upward, so as to make my head jolt a bit. I looked up toward my right, and in an instant a collection of whimsical lights had strewn themselves across the early sunset horizon. They began to dance their dance. I began to feel those familiar electrical currents as the vibrations of my soul's existence were rising. "This is one of those pivotal moments, as I knew it would be," I heard myself say. The premonition I had expected was about to become a disclosure of what I had already felt and known.

I was close. I would be arriving at the property that I was considering buying. A realtor friend of mine had been encouraging me to settle in this area. Even though this particular property had been uninhabited for several years, I felt that I was being pulled to go check out this abandoned dwelling. I already knew who had been pulling me. So somehow, I already knew it was a done deal.

The house for sale was located on a beach where I had always dreamed of living and taking refuge, so to speak, along the North Carolina coastline. Since childhood, I had longed for this. Besides, my best friend resided just right above this home-to-be.

She had promised me during my childhood that she would always be there and never leave, if I would just say "yes" to her proposal of residing "at the place where you are meant to be some day," she would always say.

Suddenly, an imposing bolt of light burst majestically over the horizon, causing the whimsical lights to vanish. Then there she was in all her glory. My best friend had appointed and bestowed herself so elegantly across the horizon just for my sake. How delighted and somewhat surprised I had felt.

As the songs continued, she came forth in full view, radiating a glowlight more forceful and vivid than I had ever seen from her before. Her face appeared within her spherical light, and as she ever so smoothly gave me a wink, her lips pursed and blew me that delicate kiss of her blessing...the kiss that settled everything and assured my destiny. I reciprocated the kiss, and with a smile I bowed my head.

I saw Stan's car parked as I drove up along the road and up the hill. I did not recall parking and getting out of my car. I must had been in some sort of trance that my best friend had concocted for me. So I assumed I had greeted and spoken with Stan already, for I was standing next to him in an almost-frozen state before the lonely, worn and forgotten two-story house.

Stan had informed me that this house had been vacant for three years now. It had been a rental when last it was occupied. The owner, who had been down on his luck, was planning to tear it down in a couple of months and sell the lot. He had to do that anyway because the appearance of the abandoned house was having an effect on the property value here, not to mention how the neighbors had complained.

I was saddened, as I could see how the unwelcome cold winters and smoldering summers had not been a friend to the house. She was enveloped with old weathered and peeling dirty dull paint, along with beaten and splintered shutters. An unkempt distressed yard enclosed her and had kept her captive to a life of loneliness. But even so, I felt something magical and mysterious, as well as haunting. Stan had used this description of "haunting" when I first inquired about this house.

As I continued my desiring fixed gaze upon this dwelling, I suddenly began to possess a strong vibrant affinity for this dull, dilapidated house. I knew I was being pulled from the moment I saw her. She had summoned me and her spell had been cast.

"How could anyone discard you when I can feel your beauty so strongly and so powerfully?" I said aloud, as the melancholy for this strange yet magical abandoned abode consumed me.

I felt blessed that my best friend from above had saved this treasure for the past three years just for me until the time came. I would learn later that she was the one who would "haunt" this house, so others would not partake of its true essence. This odd and captivating house would be kept waiting and yearning just for me, for this house had appeared in my childhood dreams many times. We had already met.

Then just as quickly, I cheered up. "I will fix her up. She will be most beautiful, all-consuming and all-compelling to those who come to see her. I will stay with her. I will be at home with her and will keep company with her. Never will she be abandoned again."

I had actually said this out loud as Stan stood before this haphazard house scrutinizing her presence. Stan looked at me with jaw-dropped puzzlement and said, "You like her? You're not really interested, right? You're kidding, right?"

Stan continued to give me that "you're crazy" look. "I'm glad I told you how she looked before you drove up as a courtesy beforehand, but I'm rather dumbfounded about your hasty decision. She's haunted. I'm telling you again, Marisa. That's why she is what you see. There have also been numerous complaints of strange lights with colors, movements, and shit."

He stood there waiting for a reply, but I continued my trance. I continued to stare, as if starstruck, at this soon-to-be-delightful abode.

"It's haunted, Marisa!" Stan grabbed my arm to break the trance.

We both chuckled. I had known Stan for quite some time, for he had sold a couple of homes to me in the past. He and his wife had moved here several years ago and started a new realty business. He was the one who convinced me to move to this charming beach town, but not before my best friend had given me her take on it and had assured me.

Stan could joke about anything with me, and even though he found the house quite displeasing, he knew it was my choice. Besides, he knew I was rather on the strange side anyway. I was always "charmed at anything that was remotely haunted," as he would say.

Then I remembered what my dad had reminded me many times: "Many don't understand or accept…keep your secrets…until they are ready." I knew that telling anyone was hardly ever to happen, for to only a few people in this life of mine did I ever dare to reveal my secrets, or should I say my knowings.

Without looking at him, I continued to gaze on this old familiar house. "Oh boy, Stan, there is something or someone telling me that she's the one." I took a moment to look over at my sister friend.

Stan stood staring and puzzled again for a bit and finally said, "You haven't even checked out the inside of this house to see how much repair or renovation she needs. As far as the outside—well, look at this debacle. There are better ones along the way up the hill as I've told you, but if you insist, hey, she's all yours. Why again, please tell me, did you want to see this one?"

"Oh Stan, I know you. You just want me to spend a pile of money, don't ya?" As I said, we could joke about anything.

I did not answer his question, nor did Stan answer mine. I knew, the moment that she blew me that kiss from her heavenly abode, this was it. This shunned and forgotten dwelling would become my home, my sanctuary. From this place, my friend would come to me in twilight's arrivals. She would teach me mysteries I had yet to know, and she would reveal to me what I needed revealed. She was the one who led me here, you see.

I suddenly spoke inwardly to myself. "Who is she, you ask? She is MoonGlow, my illumined sister friend who sets herself high within a starlit tapestry of night-time delights as she shines her glowlight across our earthly realm as well as many others."

I continued to walk about this lonely home. I would glance up at my sister friend, the moon herself, every now and then. Since the time shortly after my birth, she had personified herself as a blessing from our Creator to be my sentinel, to reveal a specified set of secrets and mysteries throughout my lifetime here. But most of all she was to be my sister friend, my best friend, companion, and teacher. And I would thank her by naming this sanctuary after her. I would call her the name that I gave her at five years of age. My abode would be called MoonGlow.

I replied to Stan with a few words already forgotten. We then proceeded to enter this "familiar" abode. From this first encounter I felt the tranquility and lightness that she possessed for no, no— she was not heavy. She was my home to be... "Yes, my home," as I had said to Stan. The spell had been cast. It could and would not be broken now. I was destined.

And then it came to mind, my travel a couple of nights ago into the "Nights of Lights and Mysteries," as I called it. I said to myself, "It is all because of MoonGlow that I go and that I find."

As Stan and I walked back out to the front porch, I continued my smiles and finally was able to look back at him and with confidence and decision. "Well, there you go." Or should I have said, "Well, there I go"? Noticing Stan's bewildered look, I ended saying, "I'll definitely take her," and just continued the smiles.

We began wrapping things up for the evening. It was nightfall now. As I looked over the ocean, I imagined how I would have a larger veranda built with a boardwalk leading to the beach, and to the Great Liquid.

As I was thinking of this massive liquid and peering out, his waves began to mount and surge upon the shore. He was showing off his power now and I could feel his intimidating presence. Yet I considered it a mutual invitation for I, Marisa, was ready for him to show me what MoonGlow had promised me so many years long ago.

MoonGlow then beckoned me to look her way. She was beautiful and full of her stunning glowlight. It was relayed to me once again in that magical state of my friend's mystical world, how she had promised me in my last encounter that my time had come to take me to a place somewhere in time and space. She would also partake with me in understanding my being in this present time and space as well. She would partake with me to having my endless bothersome questions unveiled. She would do so by taking me to flight at twilight into the night skies—to places and times I could not imagine.

"That is all for now," she relayed. "Go on your way."

Stan interrupted my visit with my friends, because he wanted to wait until I got in my car. He sensed something was keeping me from going, though. He asked, "Marisa, are you okay?"

"Don't you see her?" I replied with a question myself. "The full moon in all its glory?"

Stan looked up and with puzzlement, he said, "It's crescent."

I shook my head no to what Stan had replied. I wanted to dance the dance she had taught me some time ago. I took a finger, curling a strand of my hair, and started swaying while smiling up at my friend. She smiled and relayed, "Not just yet."

I finally came back down to earth, as they say. "I'm so sorry, Stan. I just got caught up in the moment. I really do want this house! Can you tell?"

He chuckled along with me, but I knew he was still dumbfounded about what just happened and why I would even consider buying this forlorn abode. *Oh well, whatever. He'll get over it. Wait until he sees her a few months from now*, I thought. We waved our goodbyes and I went off even more elated than ever.

As I drove off near the end of the town's entrance, my parents' songs were continuing to play. Then as I came upon an intersection, I noticed a man sitting in a truck who had stopped politely to have me pass. He was looking my way and gave me a wave. As I waved back, I could vaguely see a smile from the distance and he looked as though he could be quite attractive. I laughed for a moment, "Silly me," I said aloud. Was I, Marisa, feeling flirtatious?

I could not make out his face entirely, but as quickly as I sped, the words of the song playing had me tasting the potion that MoonGlow was having me drink, for as I said before, the spell had been cast. "Oh yes, she will send me on my way now, but it will soon be my time to go and play," I said aloud.

I started laughing and thoughts of the man in the truck chose to linger for a while. I took a strand of my hair and curled it around my finger. *There's something familiar about him*, I thought. My thoughts of him would dim after some time, for never did I see him again while MoonGlow was in renovation. Would he return again? Little did I know that soon enough when the time was right, my thoughts would be of him again.

The time passed by slowly, it seemed, I believe because I was beyond ecstatic about having my dream home at last. So, somehow I knew the time would creep along just to teach me patience—but then again, maybe it was just the jealousy that time itself possesses.

It was coming toward summer's end of 2010 now. It was the end of August now. My birthday had been in June, so I was forty-two.

It took longer than I had thought. It had taken slightly over a year for my house to be gloriously habitable. I had been caught up with my work and my writing, and with life's melodramas. Since I could not be there to supervise the goings-on because of my busy life, I had Stan go over and check on the renovation of the house a couple of times a week and consult with the remodeling team for me on matters. He was such a good friend. Even his wife, Paula, would come to check on the décor and aesthetics that I had chosen for my home. I was blessed to start a new place with such good friends who resided close by.

MoonGlow, my lovely abode, had to wait for me to make her acceptable. Besides, she needed to be in absolute splendor, and I was willing to wait, even with such impatience at times, so that this grand sanctuary was grand indeed.

Finally, in mid-August, my house had been completed and done just the way I wanted, and just the way I had always dreamed of such a home as this. "She's not haunted," I said to my cats. "She's mystical! That's why people are afraid of her."

I knew the cats, Charlie and Sugars, felt the same way. They seemed to love her too at first sight as they scurried around in amazement. Yes, they seemed to be quite at home and quite at peace in their new dwelling on their very first day.

Then one of those pivotal moments happened on my first night that my cats and I stayed in our newly painted, refurbished and peaceable home. The cats had settled themselves at the end of my bed. I had opened the window to allow the evening's cool breeze to come visit and soothe us for the night. The curtains on either side of the window were swaying together from left to right rather than opposite. I thought it was strange. I looked across the beach and noticed the Great Liquid was coming forth. Though I was conscious, I felt the vibrations conjuring up in me wanting to allow my escape. My soul was ready to take flight.

I was lifted and sent through a tunnel of bright yellow light which darkened as I traveled. I somehow knew I was being sent into the recesses of the Great Liquid I had seen ahead from my window. This would be the beginning of many travels such as this with High Tide, as I called him.

On this first travel, High Tide would suppress some of my memory of how this particular travel took place into his deep liquid. Maybe he knew I was apprehensive because of my lifelong fear of his massive liquid, or because my sister friend, MoonGlow, had not appeared to me beforehand to be present during this pivotal moment. *Why was that?* I thought. *Why wasn't she here?*

In time, I would come to know that a much-needed ample force of his strength would be propelled in order to go into these mystical states…for these states of mine would require the power of liquid. My MoonGlow would teach me. I would attain the knowledge that everything I would experience from henceforth would be hidden in liquid, revealed in liquid, and it would be in High Tide's liquid.

As the travel continued, I was then taken into a swift and spiraling liquid tunnel. I would feel only sprinklings of the liquid pelleting on my skin, as I would be taken deeper into the recesses of his bowels. I began to see faces—human, celestial, and alien. Voices unfamiliar to me were heard in whispers and mumblings. I saw volumes of books with their pages flapping not by the wind, but by the water and were of various sizes and density.

So many, so many of them, I thought. Was this some kind of life review? These lives seemed somehow to be intertwined and connected, but why and how? Whose lives, by the way? Who were these humans, or the souls of humans?

It was then relayed that many moons and many tides pass in our lives. The moons dance and lure us to the tides. The tides pull us into worlds of long ago ages that would reveal secrets of our beings…the lives of lovers and sinners.

Suddenly a formidable force snatched me and molded me into a fetal position as if in a cocoon of sorts. I was sped back from this tunnel with a feeling of being vacuumed. I had returned to my bedroom and on to my bed. I was clearly conscious as I looked about. All was calm and all was well, and so I slept with no memory of ever waking for even a moment during my first night at MoonGlow, until the Master Sun had decided to reign once more.

That was my first night at MoonGlow. "What a ride that was," I said as I called the cats to come closer to me the next morning. I looked up at the ceiling and read the words "Liquid Awakenings." I was not fearful, nor apprehensive. I felt at ease. Somehow I knew this was some sort of initiation into what was yet to come. And what was yet to come would be a ride indeed.

"Did you two feel all that? Were you there with me?" I smiled at my babies and left it at that.

As we spent time in our inviting and cheerful kitchen, I was certain now that the supernatural experience of last night was my initiation into adventures that I surely knew would be quite some amazing times. I smiled and started to play some music that would have the three of us engage in a delightful dance during this cheerful morning.

I glanced out the window and looked up toward my sister friend's home. I knew she would not be visible for me since the Master Sun had declared his usual day's reign, but I blew her a kiss anyway. "I know you had something to do with all that last night. I'm excited, my sweet MoonGlow. I can't wait until you show me more."

As soon as I had said that, my memory went back to the first night that I had arrived to see this lovely home when she was abandoned. I thought of the man I saw in the truck at the intersection. It had been some time since my thoughts had wandered back to him.

"I wonder who he was?" My thoughts had gone back to him again. "Oh well." I again took a strand of my hair and curled it around my finger, and continued my busy day.

My phone rang. It was Stan. He was checking up on me and wanted to know how the first night went. I told him this was home indeed, and I was where I was supposed to be.

He would say again, as he had said at least a hundred times already, I believe, "Marisa, I am still amazed and flabbergasted by how beautifully you transformed that piece of shit—forgive me, my dear—into the most beautiful house all along the North Carolina coast."

Of course, it was not the most beautiful, but I did know it was quite beautiful in her own right, and it was quite stunning to those who would peer over as they drove along the upper hills. How proud I was and how right I was to pick her. Oh my, I mean, how MoonGlow had picked her. "Forgive me, my love," I said, as I blew a kiss up her way.

So as evening came, I decided to send Caroline an email and write my "crazy-ass stuff" as she called it. It was time to invite her over and have her experience my lovely abode. *At last,* I thought, *my adventures can begin.* MoonGlow had promised they would. And High Tide, the Great Liquid, would be the one to incite the venturing along with the rest of us.

Hi Caroline (my best earthly friend):

Come visit me, dear friend, and stay a while. The beach house is ready now and yearns for a visit from you. It's been long time awaiting, but MoonGlow is definitely living up to its name in all its splendor. I know you will love it here as much as I do. Besides, you need a much-needed reprieve from your always frantic busy days. I have already told you of my plans for the evenings which, I believe, you do not fully comprehend, but nevertheless, I know from more youthful times, I always kept you guessing and delighted in my quirky, "crazy-ass ideas," as you say.

So come spend evenings with me on the veranda, sipping cocktails and reminiscing about our delightful memories of times gone by while patiently awaiting Sister Moon to come out and play, prancing her ever-seductive dance of summoning forth the Great Spirit of High Tide along her moonlit shore. And after bowing with reverence before his majestic presence, we will ever so humbly ask for permission to be thrust into the deepest secluded recesses of his ocean bowels. For there in his depths is the place where lay furrowed and anchored decades and centuries of suppressed and forgotten secrets of the souls who once walked upon these shores.

Because of these souls' obsessive delightful passions and melancholic despair, the Great Spirit of High Tide brought them here along with their secrets and despair to the place most compatible for them, only to be released and atoned for by the living who dare to know, dare to help, and dare to pray, no?

Shall we go, my friend, as we unabashedly delight in their secrets and then maybe aide these poor souls in their release? How fun and enticing that would be, don't you think?

Yeah, I know you're laughing now. I know you think I am the most bizarre friend and writing the most bizarre letter you have ever read. Thank you for the compliment.

Nevertheless, come dance with me, Caroline! We shall dance the dance alongside Sister Moon during these enchanted summer evenings as she illumines MoonGlow, my new abode. I promise to keep you safe and near to me, as we engulf ourselves into Great Spirit's enticing world…for in his possession are volumes of the stories, secrets and despair of discarnate souls. Let's taste the bittersweet ferment of what seems to be a soul's arduous pining for healing and release. Come visit your childhood friend, Marisa. Let's get crazy for a bit.

Love ya dearly….

Me

I signed my name "me" and sent the email to my friend, Caroline, who lives in South Carolina, a two and a half hour drive from me now. Caroline had always enjoyed my communicating this way. She would always say I had a way with words and it made her smile and even laugh when they were via pen.

Caroline and I had been friends since we were nine years old. We met in the fourth grade when she and her parents had moved to South Carolina. We were neighbors, and over time, I had opened up to her about my strange celestial beliefs and how I had always been obsessed about the ocean and all its glorious mysteries at a very early age. She just took everything in stride, never definitely agreeing or disagreeing. She just accepted me for what I am and what I had to say. The same was due to her also.

We ended up the very best of earthly friends. Her family and mine were neighbors and shared many times together. We went to Catholic school, and yes, we were what you called "good Catholic girls" until, well, you know, the ever-unpredictable antics of puberty, and suddenly getting curious and intrigued about those strange mysterious creatures called "boys".

Caroline and I could not be more different in many ways, especially in our looks. I am Marisa Marie Bordeaux-Landon (Marisa is of Latin origin meaning "of the sea"), but I am of French/Irish origin. Landon was my married name. How befitting my name, Marisa, is though, since I was born with bewildering and powerful love of the great waters. With long thick bouncy blonde hair, big blue eyes, and pale skin, yeah, I think I'm pretty on a really good day.

My friend's name is Caroline Anne Mardas. She has long thick wavy raven hair, and hypnotizing doll-eyes of dark brown with specks of crystal green. Never had I seen eyes like that. She is of Greek/Latin origin. Her skin is of light olive complexion and purely flawless. Even now in her forties, she could pass for late twenties, and she is so absolutely beautiful that yes, I'm jealous just a bit.

Caroline and I always laughed and joked about how our names should had been switched. I was definitely more of a "Caroline" and she was more of a "Marisa." Anyway, I truly believed she and I were either sisters or best friends in another lifetime. It had to be. We were too connected and too akin to each other.

And so it came to be that I believed the ocean held secrets. I felt this Great Liquid, High Tide, as I would come to name him, held the secrets of all the souls who had left their allotted time as incarnates on earth and had either moved on to another realm, or had ended up staying in their disincarnate states wandering endlessly.

The exact reasoning was unknown to me, but I wanted desperately to possess that state of knowing. Since I had become consumed in the mysteries of everything that was beyond the veil of our earthly plane, I somehow sensed the Great Liquid was akin to these mysteries that were earthly bound. My plan was to find the key to unlock the door to all that had been kept at bay for decades.

My journey would begin when MoonGlow, a few nights from now, would beckon High Tide to come forth, and then patiently sit to watch Caroline and me flirt our way into his domain, the ever- deep enigmatic world beneath his mighty persona.

As for MoonGlow, as I had said, she had been the one to inspire me to name my beautiful abode after her. Naturally, I would duly give reverence to the one who led me to come fall in love with the dwelling she had saved for me. Oh, my beloved glowlight who comes to all when evenings befall. The One who has captivated lovers and loners for centuries by her hypnotizing spells would be my sweet delight, indeed.

My father, who had presented me to MoonGlow shortly after my birth, was Robert Bordeaux, a professor in astronomy. He died about ten years ago. He was a very spiritual man who believed there were realms, dimensions, and beings other than ourselves throughout our vast and endless universe.

From a tender age, as my father held me during warm summer nights, he would point to the constellations attempting to keep my attention on them, but I would continuously stare starstruck at her, our beloved moon. For to me, she was the most beautiful, delightful creation there was to gaze upon in this massive space of the night skies. My father was not offended, though, for he was the one who had presented me to her at birth and she had been his best friend too. In turn, she would personify herself and forever appear to both us in her complete fullness.

Since I was raised in South Carolina, my family and I would take trips to Hilton Island. I always looked forward to our trips, and as I would long for them, I would frequently ask if we could move to the ocean. My yearnings of endless fascination and affinity for this massive water would eventually lead me to the present.

Though I had a great love and magnetic lure for this Great Liquid, at the same time, a great fear harbored me to stay at bay. Never knowing exactly the reasoning, I would live decades perplexed and frustrated. So much was my fear that I would never get into the water, nor even wade in it. I would sometimes reach out and ever so meticulously lightly touch this mysterious liquid, this captivating wet creation called the ocean.

So for me, my two great loves were the "moon" who belonged to the great universe out in the heavens, and the "ocean" who belonged to our earth.

Over time, I would come to know that my Sister Moon had chosen High Tide to be her lover many centuries ago. I knew she was the one who had chosen him before he could even consider the choice. For you know, who controls whom? Who entices, who flirts, who dances her whimsical and seductive light projections to draw forth as she summons, causing to rise in majestic power his own liquid projections?

It is Sister Moon. It is MoonGlow, herself, in all her clandestine splendor. She is the vixen with a true gypsy spirit. For one who possesses a gypsy spirit is always a free spirit of wonder and seduction, and in time, you will find that she has taught me oh so well to be one too.

Chapter 2

CAROLINE'S ARRIVAL

*Your beauty is ancient, yet ever new…and you say you saw that
same beauty in my own soul before you ever even met me.*

$\mathcal{I}$ had asked Caroline, when finalizing the plans for her visit, to arrive no later than Wednesday evening just to relax and get settled. That way, she would catch the first full moon the next evening on Thursday, and the plans that MoonGlow had in store for us would begin.

So late afternoon on Wednesday, my beautiful friend arrived. As she was pulling up to MoonGlow we caught each other's glance, but I realized she was more taken by the magnificent view of the house. I could tell by the glowing gaze on her face that she was truly delighted. I had not even sent pictures of MoonGlow, because I kept telling her I wanted her to be completely surprised, and surprised she was.

I ran up to the car as she almost immediately stepped out while putting the brakes on. "My sweet sweet Caroline, I have missed you so," I said as we embraced and gave each other double kisses on the cheeks as we always do.

"Ohh Marisa, how I have missed you too—and how beautiful and rested you look! The beach suits you well dahhling. It becomes you."

She knew for certain that I would be well suited, because I had always told her that I was "related" in some way, akin to this massive assembly of sea and sand. So yes, I belonged here.

Caroline stood before this magical massive structure after our greeting, and while bringing her jaw back to position and slowly taking baby steps around the front and back, she said, "Marisa, this is the most stunning beach house ever. Wow! What you have done is amazing!"

"And you haven't even seen the inside of it yet," I proudly boasted. "Yes, the beach does suit me, doesn't' it? And as you say too, this house is definitely stunning."

After showing Caroline around the house, she sighed quite audibly. "You did good, girl. You did really good. I cannot believe this is the same house as in those pictures. Those pictures of that old unbelievable ugly house. Sorry, I mean...."

"That's okay, my friend. That's okay—but take at a look at her now, eh?"

"And there's something about this house I can't quite figure out. It's like, like a feeling of adventure."

I just continued to smile and smile some more. *She has no idea yet*, I thought.

Caroline looked ravishing as always with her hair slightly pulled back; just a touch of mascara and lipstick was all she ever really needed—unlike me. Because of my light-colored eyebrows, lashes, and skin, I needed more color. Hell, I always needed more primping that she ever did.

Caroline and I had not seen each other for about six months, since I had been so busy with the beach house. When I bought MoonGlow in Spring 2009, I had gone to visit Caroline two months later after the purchase to catch up on life. As I told her all about the beach house and showed the "before" pictures, she would cringe as she intensely noticed how dilapidated it was. I do believe she thought I was crazy for having bought it, and I told her I would not show her any pictures until it was completed.

Oh, how her opinions on this beauty would change now that she was here! It was so good to share the miraculous transformation of my abode with Caroline now. The last six months had been the longest separation we had ever had. I had decided to resign from my nursing job to spend time sprucing up the house and had also started my new venture with writing. Caroline has been very busy with her own work and just with life itself. Even so, my best friend and I had always remained close.

I would want to pinch myself at times to wake up to reality. To end up living here in this beautiful abode, alongside my my sister friend and the mighty mass of the Great Liquid, had been a lifelong dream.

Finally, I had been bedded and surrounded by the existing worlds unseen to us mere humans, as I would dare to delve myself into their sequestered lives. As I had promised myself, I would welcome moments in time to come to this enchanting life here alongside me, as I would blend into its existence, becoming merged within those worlds.

Of course, along with my sister MoonGlow I would venture, for it was she who led me here. It was she who had promised me such a life. It was the sweet vixen, the effervescent moon, who would summon High Tide to take me into those enchanting, mystical, and hidden worlds.

The reason my lifelong dream came to be possible, unfortunately, was because of my husband's passing. Matthew had been killed in an automobile accident on the way from work two years ago in 2008. My son, Zachary, was 18 and was preparing to go to college in the fall. A year later, I decided it was my time now to allow a lifelong and destined dream come true.

As far as my childhood, it was lonely most of the time. I did not have, nor did I make very many friends. It always seemed to me that they had shunned me because I was different. I was pensive and contemplating just about everything most of the time.

Except for my parents, a few family members, and Caroline, I was on my own, rather troubled at times with life in general and always looking up…looking up and searching, hungering for a life somewhere other than here. Why was that? I often thought. Why could I never be content with what was right here where I stood? Even my marriage with Matthew had been troubled and unsatisfying. We had our good times, especially with our son, Zach. Though I missed him now, I never could quite experience that longing and need for a close bond with him in our marriage. Yes, it was troubled. I was troubled.

Caroline came out of the guest room with hair pulled back tightly in a hairband this time, tan flip-flops and tee-shirt, and the shortest of red shorts. Guess she's ready for the beach life!

She immediately ran up to my two cats, Charlie and Sugars. Charlie was an orange tabby and certainly in charge of the house. Sugars was younger black and white princess. She would follow me everywhere and anywhere.

"How in the world did I not ask about you two or even look for you as of yet? How rude am I?" We both laughed and all went downstairs.

She loved my cats and I loved her dogs. I had told her to bring them, Sam and Pookie, both maltipoos, but she said, "Helloooo, I want some relaxation and whatever craaaazy experiences you're planning, dahhhhling!"

Of course, I know dogs are a lot more work than cats. It's funny how she always seemed more suited to dogs and I to cats. Although, when my husband, Matthew, was alive and while Zach was living with us, we did have a black Labrador, named Sara, who died several years ago. None of us wanted a replacement and so the cats became our babies.

Caroline had been divorced for three years now and was still not seriously involved with anyone as of yet (I knew because I asked her all the time). "Just dating occasionally, but nothing serious, or ongoing," she would tell me. Her daughter, Samantha, twenty of age, was away in college just like my Zach.

She works as a nurse anesthetist presently just like I had. I say "had" because since my husband passed away two years ago, in addition to purchasing MoonGlow and living my life as I had always meant to live, I decided to go on a sabbatical from my work and embark on writing a novel. The novel would be about my new life here and the adventures that Caroline and I would embark on, as well as the adventures on my own. My Sister Moon and High Tide would lead the way and literally take me along. Somehow I knew it would be this way. How? I don't know...just a feeling, just a knowing. I had felt for a long time that it would come to be.

We spent the evening just eating some nachos and sipping our martinis. Hey, that is one of many things we have in common! We would much rather have the vodka than wine...hmmm interesting, but we would occasionally switch to the wine. It's good for whatever the experts say.

We reminisced of younger days and the missed opportunities along the way as everyone seems to have. As evening fell, we acknowledged Sister Moon as soon as she started peeking through the dark lit evening, showing her beauty in three-quarters to Caroline.

She came forth radiating her glowlight upon us, but especially upon my beach house dedicated to her and all her glory. We smiled at her and as my MoonGlow blew me a kiss, I would do the same back, and Caroline would reciprocate.

Caroline stood up in awe and walked toward the boardwalk as I followed. She seemed as if in a trance when she looked back to view what was the most beautiful of sights to behold...MoonGlow, my home which suddenly lit up as if the heavens had poured out the Light of all Lights...the Heavenly Light that held us spellbound for an unknown amount of time. Was it a forewarning for us? Were we being informed of something formidable forthcoming the next evening when Sister Moon would come to display her power and beauty before us as if never before? I had asked for it, I must say. I knew she and High Tide had secrets to share and I wanted to know them.

Caroline and I walked back to the veranda and sat for a while being quiet and being in our trance. We finally snapped out of it.

"What the hell was that?" Caroline chuckled. "That was definitely the liquor. Some strong shit that was." We held nothing back and as usual laughed hysterically until we had no more tears. Finally, as we both agreed we were totally blitzed and worn out, we called it a night.

"So Caroline, my dahhling, you need a good night's rest and a peaceful day tomorrow, because when the next evening comes forth, you and I will meet up with my vixen sister and her lover, and we will travel to a realm you will never forget."

Why had I just said that to Caroline, I thought? How would I know that and with such conviction I should say. Caroline, although she was rather lit, looked just for a moment a little bit dazed, maybe a little bit frightened? I could never quite tell, because she always just took me as I was and never questioned me. Well, we shall see. I do believe that Caroline was absolutely fascinated by what I just said. She always had been.

As I finally ended up in my room, I went over to the window to peer out.

There she was. Upward and to my right, my MoonGlow appeared. As her face immersed, she winked and lowered her eyes, and then blew me a kiss. I caught it and blew one back. I smiled with a long sigh. Oh, how I loved her.

I began to think how much I felt at home. Yes, I was home. This dwelling was called MoonGlow and she was mine.

MoonGlow, a two-story wooden structure of 3200 square feet, sat proudly on a hill enclosed with pure white picket rails around the entire abode. A newly built two car garage sat left to the house and that is where I secured my convertible Lexus and Jeep. Yes, I purchased a Jeep before moving in. That was a must for beach life and running errands. Of course, I kept my convertible for play, and I did intend to play eventually.

Along the front and back of the house were various native landscaped plants and gardens consisting of various summer flowers when appropriate, and then replanting for the winter flowers when that season comes along…quite lovely and inviting. The front yard also consisted of two sabal palms along with a couple of oaks. Two flowing fountains sat on either side the flagstone sidewalk leading up to the house.

MoonGlow would need visitors who were able to climb stairs when coming over to greet me, Sugars, and Charlie. Its front porch was perched high off the ground for viewing over the landscaped area. Two ceiling fans were evenly spaced on the porch for warm summer days, and of course, a porch swing was a must, along with wicker chairs and matching pillows to fill in its large, inviting space.

The back of the house boasted a huge veranda with matching wicker furniture very similar to the front porch. The veranda looked much like the front porch, but even larger, and had three ceiling fans for those ever-present warm summer days. An enclosed area on the left side was a cozy breakfast nook, where various ivy plants and several vases of fresh flowers had made their own little home. On the right side, the veranda wrapped around to a narrower porch.

Oh, and the windchimes, which I have always loved! Several suspended themselves in timelessness throughout the front and back. Each and every day they chose to sing and play their delightful melodies of old and new, ever ancient and ever new. I loved to believe that they assisted in harmonizing the mystical ambience of my abode.

On the right of the veranda, facing the ocean, a four-foot-wide boardwalk led out. As the descent started, surrounding were dunes of wild olive plants, marshes, and sand.

The weathered, splintered shutters were painted a light seafoam green and so were the porch and veranda. I had painted the house a luminescent pale yellow so that it would "glow" when my MoonGlow would come out to play and dance for the long evenings. She would immediately swing her glowlight to my house, and notice how I had chosen to continue to revere and love her, giving thanks for all she had done for me since birth.

I took pride in how she looked (and glowed), but I was also humbly thankful and grateful, for I had finally been blessed with what I had been patiently waiting for many many years. This once old worn, lonely and weathered house that no one wanted and that no one loved had become a most beautiful, delightful sanctuary that had become truly loved now and truly filled with love. Yes, a sanctuary it was, indeed, and it was all mine.

The next morning, I had awoken before Caroline. Sugars had spent the night with me, of course, but Charlie had cuddled up with Caroline. Charlie always wanted to flirt, snuggle, and show off with anyone who came to visit a while, especially if the person was a female. He was such a ladies' man.

I went ahead and prepared scrambled eggs and hash browns and was about to make some toast when Caroline and Charlie came in to greet us. Caroline was holding Charlie and caressing him so tenderly.

"Good morning, dahhlings," she said to me and Sugars.

"Well, good morning, Sunshine." We both chuckled and gave each other a big hug and kisses on both cheeks. It was a beautiful morning. Master Sun was pouring his smiley rays through the highly positioned windows in the kitchen. He was happy, and I think he knew about what his nocturnal friends had in plan for us. He wanted us to have a happy day, because tonight we just might discover secrets that would relay knowledge that we had not expected and just maybe had not intended.

We had breakfast out on the veranda. Caroline could not say enough about how much she absolutely, totally, and unequivocally loved this place.

"Can I move in already? I'll be good. I promise." She lowered her head and took a part of her hair to hide her face. Her sheepish look gave her away.

"Yeah, right, but you can come visit anytime, you know." I laughed along with my friend. Yes, the morning was beautiful and the rays of our Master Sun had been the one to sprinkle his own sunkisses upon us.

"I feel blessed so much, yet feel undeserving it seems." I knew Caroline was aware of my thoughts. Since the death of Matthew, the guilt of acquiring my long time dream did result in guilt, to some degree. I had tears in my eyes, and Caroline reciprocated with tears in her own eyes. She knew me well.

She took my hand, "Listen, in time you will get over it. You need to know you deserve this life. You deserve all of it."

———⟲———

Caroline and I hopped into the convertible and went for a morning ride. Having the top down gave a way for Master Sun to pour forth his rays upon our windblown hair and sunshine faces gleaming with all the SPF lotion we could pile on. Gotta keep that skin protected! We are over forty, you know.

I had not really made friends yet in this town besides Stan and Paula, because I had been so busy with renovating and getting the beach house in its glorious state. I had met a few acquaintances, I would say, and they seemed to be very friendly and welcoming. I thought the time would come soon when I could spend more time in town and get involved. But for now, I was happy that my friend Caroline was there. And always and forever my friends, MoonGlow and High Tide, would keep me company every day, actually. Oh, I must not forget my Charlie and Sugars of course, too.

Before having lunch in town, we stopped at a convenience store to fill up the gas tank. After doing so, I hopped into the passenger's seat. I was actually giving Caroline permission to drive the rest of way. Now, that is definitely a friend if I, Marisa, was going to let anyone at all drive my fairly new hot red Lexus convertible. Not surprisingly, she did so with absolutely no hesitation, not even for a millisecond.

As Caroline revved up the engine and started the music blaring, lo and behold, we both happened to look up and there he was! He was standing outside the store's door looking at his cell phone.

After Caroline and I had managed to close our mouths after a few seconds, we ever so simultaneously tilted down our sunglasses to get a better look. I finally heard Caroline say, "Whoa, Mr. Fine…."

"Specimen of a Man…." I finished her thoughts.

So while Caroline would tilt her head down a bit, wetting her lips, I would continue a wide-eyed stare while biting my lower lip. This would be so much like us whenever any hot guy would be spotted, at an instant's notice.

We continued our drooling as we watched him moving his fingers across his phone and ever so slightly moving his mouth. "Damn, look at that," of course Caroline would say. "He is so fine."

He broke his stance by moving away from his right hip, putting his weight on his left one. Now that was the sexiest move I had seen in quite some time, I must say.

Suddenly, he did something to break the spell he had concocted upon us. He looked over at us.

"Oh my goodness, he's loookkking! Go! Just go!" I looked away.

"Oh shit!" Caroline said as she put the car in reverse and began to speed off. "But wait. Isn't that a good thing that he's staring at us? And he's smiling, too."

"I would think we would want him to look at us. Why are we going?"

"Caroline, just go!" I kept crouching down.

Naturally, Caroline would do exactly just this—she suddenly turned the steering wheel and swerved around to drive back to where Mr. Fine Specimen of a Man was still standing. And naturally, she would be blowing the horn!

"What the hell are you doing?". I had started to laugh hysterically. "Oh shit!"

As Caroline finished her crazy antic, of course I could not help but take a look at him again. So I actually turned my body around to get one more good look as Caroline started to speed away again.

How could I not take another look at this fine specimen of a man? He was looking at me too as he smiled a crooked grin and gave a slight wave. I then did something that I would never before had thought to do. I smiled and waved back just like some silly sixteen-year-old.

"Caroline!" I shouted.

"What? What is it?"

"He looked at me! He smiled and waved too. Oh my God! What am I going to do? I think I'm in love." I looked over at her, waiting for her response.

"About time, girlfriend!" Caroline bellowed out her contagious laugh as we high-fived. *What a ride that was,* I thought, *even if it were only for just a second.*

Caroline continued echoing her loud contagious laugh that could make anyone immediately catch the fever and succumb to her delightful disease. I had not laughed like that in such a long time. It felt so good.

After we had calmed down in somewhat of a normal state, I remembered I had glanced over at a parked truck after I tore my dazed gaze from that fine specimen of a man. It looked familiar. Then I realized it was indeed the truck I had seen at the intersection that first night I had laid eyes on my home, MoonGlow.

I wondered if he was the man I saw vaguely in that truck? Of course he was. He had smiled and waved just like this guy we had just left behind.

"Go back! Quick, turn around!" I commanded Caroline. As soon as I explained to her the reason, no further discussion was needed.

We drove up to the convenience store, but we noticed the truck had gone. I continued to command Caroline to drive past the opposite direction from where we were heading, to see if we could find the truck.

Caroline was laughing hysterically again. She could not believe I, Marisa, was acting just like we used to do as young girls. "Interested in chasing this man, eh? Well, you just go, girl. You need some action. Hell, we both do."

We could not help ourselves again. We continued to laugh hysterically. After a few minutes, no such luck was to be had. *Of course—naturally,* I thought.

Caroline noticed my disappointment and said, "Let's go back to the store.

Surely someone would know who he was."

"That is oh so totally brilliant," I said with an agreeable nod. "Of course, though, you are a brunette."

We both practically ran into the store. We must have been a sight to see. Fortunately, no customer was at the register, so I let Caroline ask about the fine specimen who was here a few minutes ago. I was much too nervous.

The lady knew exactly who we were talking about. But of course she did. Who wouldn't?

"Oh yeah, who doesn't? That fine man is Nathan Rynn. He stays here a ways up whenever he's in town. He's some kind of real estate developer." As she finished, the two of us just kept quiet to see if she would continue and tell us some of the good stuff, like was he single? I did not dare ask and I was not sure why that was. What surprised me more was that Caroline did not ask. What the hell?

She finally said, "Don't worry ladies, you'll see him again. We all do." She gave us a wink. "And yes, we all just love seeing him again, whether he's walking toward us or walking away from us, if you know what I mean." She winked again as she flared her hands, saying goodbye as we walked away.

"I know his name. I know his name now, Caroline! That's a good start. Hey, I can ask Stan too if he knows him!" I suddenly thought how brilliant an idea that was. So I guess now I was just as brilliant as my friend.

"There you go! You just go, girl. Don't let this one get away. And he's all yours dahhling, since I don't live here anyway." She looked over at me and laughed. "You know I'm kidding, right? I know you're already sweet on him and that makes me happy, Marisa. About time, girlfriend, that you take an interest in a man. You need to get you some good loving going on…you need to get you some of that man there…you need to get you some fine…."

"Okay, that's enough. Whewwww."

We both continued to have fun going over what just happened. As Caroline drove toward the end of the beach for lunch, I decided to give Stan a call and ask if he knew Nathan.

"Yeah I know who he is from briefly meeting him at a couple of real estate gatherings. He's a nice guy, friendly. And ahh, he's single, Marisa."

My relief was evident, I do believe, as I let out a sigh. I went ahead and told Stan how I had vaguely run into him a couple of times and was just wondering. Oh hell, I just told him everything.

He laughed and said about the same thing that Caroline had been telling me. "Go for it. You need to get on with it, Marisa. And if you ever need any help in meeting him, getting you two set up, just let me know."

"I might need to, Stan. I'll let you know, though." I knew he could hear the excitement in my voice.

After having lunch in town and reminiscing about the past, we went back to the house and looked over some old albums of our lives. We laughed at all the changes in our looks, our clothes, our growing up from girls into womanhood.

After having our fill of too many laughs, we spent the afternoon walking the beach as I questioned and prodded Caroline as I usually did about her love affairs. "What did he look like, what did he do, why did you drop him—why, why, and why?" Yeah, I was living vicariously through her at the moment. She was beautiful and I knew she never had to wait when and if she was interested and ready for another…and another.

For myself, I knew I was attractive and would have no problem catching someone's eye, but since the death of my late husband, I had decided to delve into buying and renovating my dream home, writing ,and just taking care of stuff. Before moving in I had decided romance could and would wait, but then again, I slightly desired it occasionally.

Now since almost meeting Nathan, I should say, I did believe I was ready. Actually, I felt really ready. At the same time, I knew that would depend on Nathan. My feeling of lack of confidence in myself in catching such a man as Nathan crept up again, as always.

As Caroline and I continued our chatting, I felt happy to have had this day of showing off my home and town that had been chosen for me. This little charming world with which to spend peaceful and meaningful days, to write as I should, and to belong to the place where I was meant to be, was exactly what I had longed for a lifetime.

I wanted to be close to the "familiar." This familiarity was my family, Sister Moon and High Tide along with every creature, rock, seashell, tree, and marsh that came with this place…this place I would call home now. Even the discarnate souls that lingered here were family to me. I had felt their presence the moment I drove up in 2009. They were my sentinels, my watchmen. This was their home too. But why did I feel I belonged to them in a strange familial sense? What was I to them, and what were they to me?

Such a strong magnetic pulling to all those souls and their secrets always led me looking toward the Great Liquid. Were we all together in other lifetimes, and that was why we were still connected, still a part of each other? Were we still here on this sometimes bereft and forlorn planet because we did not love enough in our past lives? Was it because we did not learn enough, share enough, give enough of ourselves? Maybe our Creator would bless me with answers to my neverending questions, and maybe it would start tonight.

We would see, when evening falls and Sister Moon shows offer her beauty tonight, yes? I wonder what she had planned for us? She was such a vixen, alluring and beguiling…and I did love her so.

Chapter 3

WE SOUTHERN BELLES CAN SURELY BE HELL AT NIGHT

So many mansions….so many rooms…so many worlds

*E*vening was about to bestow itself and it was quite anxious to stir up its clever and enchanting antics. Caroline had taken a short nap and I could hear her and Charlie shifting and bopping about. I began to wonder how she was feeling about tonight.

"She must think I am totally nutso, crazzzzy and have really lost it this time!" I said to Sugars. Maybe I had. Oh well, I have always asked myself as well as others, "Do we walk, run or dance our way through this life?" My answer is unapologetically "Always shall I choose to dance!" Just as foolishly as I can and will, I will dance along this pebble-stoned, dirt-ridden path with every turn, twist, stumble and fall that I may have. That's me for sure. For I am definitely a southern belle.

Caroline and Charlie came down to greet me and Sugars. She gently gave Charlie a kiss and placed her with Sugars.

"So you said we'd have nachos again tonight, right Mari?" she asked.

"But of course, dahhhling. So glad you like my nachos! So do I."

We laughed and chatted nonsensically while preparing our appetizer and martinis for the evening. "We're gonna def need these, for sure! There's no telling what you've got up your sleeve, Marrr-isa. You know, I am a little nervous, yet very intrigued." She paused and looked at me with her crooked half smile, "It's gonna be okay, though…and fun, I think."

I believed she added on the last few words because of the look on my face. The look was one of "Maybe I shouldn't have planned this." Caroline always had a way of trusting me though, I think? Well, maybe she would eventually in this case.

The gray of evening began to come forth and ever so sweetly touched our souls with ease and feelings of what might be revealed to us. As we started walking down the boardwalk heading for the beach, it was quite obvious with our stance that we had for sure had a little too much to drink as Caroline pleaded, "Say it again, Marisa. You know, that southern belle thing you say about us, dahhhling."

After laughing for a bit, I straightened my stance. Well, at least I tried to do so.

While lifting one side of my hair up with one hand, a martini in the other, I said, "A true southern lady always sprinkles her plentiful politeness and hospitality. But now a true southern 'belle'…well now, she always adds a tad bit of flirtatiousness and a mighty pinch of sweet and sassy." We both snapped our fingers.

"I love it! I always do." Caroline attempted to swing around.

As Caroline and I continued the walk, for some reason we suddenly froze and ever so synchronizing, we both turned to our right and looked upward as we began to bask in her beauty and majesty. The ever so clever and mesmerizing Sister Moon, my sweet MoonGlow, came forth with such captivation—more so than I had ever seen her. Her moonlight illumined the entire sky and shoreline ever so brightly. It was as if at that moment, she drenched us with her moonshine, her own potion of total surrender and abandonment to her. Without any words, but maybe a few gasps, Caroline and I began walking off the boardwalk toward the moonlit sand where MoonGlow's lover awaited her, but also where her lover awaited both Caroline and me too. Yes, HideTide would be summoning us.

Caroline and I began dancing the dance….the dance that my Sister Moon had taught me many years ago. I had then taught Caroline the dance so as to pay it forward, I should say. I wanted her respects and be able to experience maybe a part of what was yet to come.

We had blaring from the veranda the 1970s songs of moonlight that my parents used to love and play. Yes, we southern belles are always ready for a moonlight trance. We are always ready to taste its potion.

The wind was forthcoming from MoonGlow's direction. We danced, we laughed and taunted our sweet sister with our flirty movements. We were even more intoxicated now with our sister's concocted potion that drenched our souls with silliness and surrender. Free wind blowing through our hair felt as if it were preparing us to take flight.

We stopped for a moment and turned to gaze at Sister Moon. "You look ready for a wet kiss to make your tide lover rise again for you, my sweet Sis." I knew MoonGlow was ever so ready to receive that wet kiss for another evening.

Mesmerized, we held hands, clenching as if for dear life as we turned again. Now looking as the waters rose in such majestic power ever growing higher than the sky itself, we gasped. It was High Tide! His coming forth was loud and obtrusive. His presence demanded duly deserved reverence as we trembled.

I nudged Caroline for the both of us to bow in veneration as we would ask permission to take us as planned, but I was not even breathing now. I most certainly was not moving.

His clamorous sounds ceased. Then the whispers came faintly. The words were incomprehensible. Where did they come from? There were many voices heard—male and female, child and adult. Who were they?

High Tide barrelled forth as his chest thrust itself upon us. His arms enveloped and held us ever so tightly, yet gently. As my head fell backward, my body went limp, as if he had suddenly become my lover. Then thoughts of a man that I had known, not in this lifetime, but somewhere in time and space, had come to me. I could not remember his name nor any events of our lives, except that we had been a part of each other's lives. We had been together, we loved, and we were one.

I surrendered to the moment, to this moment of High Tide taking me and thrusting me into his being and into the depths of his ocean's floor. Deeply, I was taken into its hidden life of its hidden souls and hidden secrets. I was so consumed with my own being of total surrender to this massive liquid that I was unaware of anything that Caroline was experiencing. I only thought for a moment that she would be all right.

Late 1800s – FIRST ENCOUNTER

My eyes opened. I was presented in a room standing on the inside of the doorway. The room was slightly darkened and cold. Anxiety about this unknown place was consuming me, until I noticed the kerosene lamp on a table beside a bed. I was relieved to see light and within a moment's time, the lamp began to illumine this darkened room and I could feel warmth enveloping me.

The bed was small, and sat rather high, I thought, much higher than beds usually do. The thick massive wooden bedposts at the four corners of the bed stood prominently and made me feel uncomfortable. The bedspread was a dark beige color with scattered lace. The walls were wallpapered with an unfamiliar paisley print. I noticed a small vanity table which held a couple of pictures of a man and a woman unfamiliar to me. One of the pictures showed a couple holding a baby. Then I noticed a third picture of a small girl.

I felt compelled to look back at the bed. A female who was sitting on the other side of the bed was looking away from me. I was startled and uncomfortable again, but ever so slowly she turned her hed slightly toward my direction. She appeared to be about sixteen years of age. She was wearing a long white nightgown, rather full and buttoned up to her lower neck. There was embroidery on the collar and upper shoulder areas. Her hair was long to her waistline, thick wavy light brown and loosely braided. A few ringlets of hair fell from her forehead and temples. No words or sounds I could hear. The silence was odd.

Her eyes then looked directly at mine. She then smiled a most beautiful sincere smile. She took her braided hair and swept it to her right side, letting it fall over her shoulder to her frontside. Then the sound of her giggles filled the room and I thought at first how relieved I was to hear the sound.

I thought, *What is so funny?* This beautiful young girl, or shall I say young lady, said nothing, but continued to giggle. I began to giggle too. I simply delighted in just joining in with her own enchantment, for she had transformed the ambience of the entire room to a more comfortable one now.

I could not take my eyes off of her. She had me mesmerized.

Is that me? I thought for some odd reason. *What is this place? Everything looks so Victorian as if from another century, 1800s maybe?* I asked this lovely girl, "Who are you?"

She only smiled as she lept off the bed and starting turning the covers down. She quickly hopped back up on the bed and stretched her arms toward me, beckoning me to come to her, still smiling. Without hesitation, I walked up to her and without thought, I proceeded to reach out to embrace this lovely gentle soul.

As we each reciprocated, the scent of jasmine and lavender perfumed her hair and clothes. *We have scent now*, I thought. As I looked into her eyes, I could see a light- blue hue with specks of crystal-clear lights dancing about. Yes, they were dancing. Beautiful crystal-blue dancing eyes that had me enveloped in a most comforting secure feeling of total surrendered love.

We kissed each other ever so gently on the lips as we said good night, and as quickly as we did, I sighed a most forceful reply, "You are my daughter, my sweet lovely daughter." She just continued to smile.

I then felt a force pulling me back as if falling with no control at all. I wondered why the time had been cut short. I wanted to see more, to experience more.

"No, no, I want to go back." I woke up in bed. I was at MoonGlow and it was early Friday morning. My eyes closed swiftly and I felt the cool breeze on my face from the window I always keep open at night. I heard the ever so faintly waves of low tide and early morning seagulls getting ready for their feed. My eyes opened slowly again and I immediately saw a name written across the ceiling: "Calissa."

I suddenly forced myself up, now fully awake and, of course, wondered, "Who is Calissa?" But then, just as quickly had I asked this question, it came to me that Calissa was my daughter's name. I remembered how Caroline and I had been swept away last evening by High Tide and I was taken back in time. Back in time would be to a place where my sweet lovely daughter resided, and her name was Calissa. "A most beautiful name," I said aloud.

I jumped up and ran over to Caroline's room. Her door was slightly open. I peeked in and saw her standing at the window with arms crossed and staring out towards the water.

"Caroline?" She looked toward me and slightly smiled. "Are you okay?"

"Yes, Sweetness, I am. How did we get here? Back at the house and in our beds? I don't remember anything." I told her that I didn't know and after a few exchanges I told her to meet me in the kitchen so we could talk more.

I quickly made some coffee and toast and sat down at the table in the kitchen and not in the breakfast nook out on the veranda. I thought maybe Caroline might think it a bit too much to have the ocean staring at us in the face after what happened last night. I did not know at this time what happened to Caroline, if anything. I know for myself, I actually felt good about what happened. I was taken to another time, another world, another life that I had lived so long ago. I wanted so much to find out more. Would Sister Moon, my dear old friend, along with High Tide, whom I have both loved so dearly all these years, take me back in time and tell me the secrets that they know lay hidden in High Tide's deep oceanic bowels? I could not wait until nightfall again.

Caroline came in half-smiling again hugging Charlie and sat with me. She immediately delved into the coffee.

I had to ask her, "Caroline, do you remember when we were dancing on the shoreline and then MoonGlow and High Tide appeared to us?"

"Yes, I do," she said.

"Do you remember anything else?"

She hesitated and then said, "I remember when the tide started rising and we were holding hands, and then I sort of fainted, I guess. The next thing, I awoke in my bed, remembering nothing of what happened between those time frames."

I hesitated too now, but then went ahead and told her about my experience and that I was so delighted about the encounter I had with my daughter. She seemed to be interested and rather delighted as I spoke, but then asked if I thought it might had been a dream.

"Oh no, no, no. Remember, I've told you before of how I experience out-of-body travels at times, so I know the difference between a dream and an actual visit or travel. On the other hand, I don't rightly recall a visit to another time dimension ever as I did last night, or that I can remember, anyway."

Caroline just accepted what I had said and thought it was very special that "something" so pleasant and unexpected had been experienced for me. I felt like she was hesitating about what really happened with her. Somehow I felt she, herself, had experienced "something" that she actually remembered, but maybe it had not been pleasant, or maybe the whole experience was confusing at this time. Maybe she needed time to collect her thoughts and sort things out. For whatever reason, I respect that, of course. I went on to tell her that if whatever happened last night was too much for her in any way, that she did not have to continue on with this crazy thing I had come up with.

She immediately responded in a rather positive way. Her response was unexpected, since she had been strangely evasive and maybe actually keeping something to herself. Either way, I told her how much I loved her and had always valued our friendship. I assured her how much it meant to me to have her here with me and share this adventure….this "craaaazy-ass adventure."

We spent the rest of the day with a drive into town, some shopping, a late lunch, and then back for an afternoon nap. As for myself, I couldn't nap. I just kept reminiscing about my own adventure. I kept picturing Calissa, my beautiful, crystal-blue-eyed daughter. I Googled her name to find out what was its origin, etc. Her name meant "fairest/most beautiful" and was of Latin/Greek origin. I wanted to see her so badly again, and I did believe MoonGlow and High Tide will reciprocate and grant me this delight, for I had loved them forever as they had loved me.

Forever? I suddenly realized why I thought "forever." I had definitely loved them forever. We, the trio, had been together for centuries. I had been here, just like them, for at least a few multitudes of centuries. And poor High Tide had been here in this prison we call the earthly realm way too long.

The secrets that he knew of us lowly human souls must be innumerable, boundless, and full of weighted-down despair. How many times he must have reclaimed such souls, the same souls over and over throughout the centuries. For I do believe the soul's never-ending healing and search for release may take many of earthly years.

For MoonGlow and High Tide, because of the fetters of us lowly humans, there remain too many years bound with endless sunrises and sunsets, and countless moonlit evenings of our lovely sister dancing her seductive dance to spend time with her High Tide. Will these two lovers ever be able to rest together and bask in each other's delights? Will they ever be free of us, the ones who keep them bound to our endless secrets?

Maybe now, High Tide would divulge my fetters and secrets of long ago which had been hidden from my present life. Oh, how I would love to know what secrets I have, what kind of karma has kept me chained and anchored here in this earthly realm for so so long. What had I done that was so bad? He would tell me! He would divulge to me. I would beg him to tell me. I would persuade Sister Moon to make him tell me. She would make him take me to times long gone, to times that caused my birth recycling to happen again and again. How excited I was to find out. Or should I not be? What if I were to find out something that I wished I had not, something that would cause me to relive unbearable pain again? Even so, I was choosing to know now, and I would.

The gray of evening started to fall again. Caroline had taken a very long and deep nap. She said earlier that she was feeling unusually tired after we had come back to MoonGlow. Of course, I understood because of what we had experienced last night. I still thought she had encountered something even though she stated no memory of anything. She must have. I most certainly did. Why would High Tide not accept her request to reveal some part of secrets from long ago? Surely he would have been gracious and ever so gentlemanly to do the same for Caroline. Or maybe Caroline did not make the request, come to think of it. Maybe she was too frightened and started praying, asking for the light of protection to keep her at bay instead of venturing out.

Even so, if she did encounter something and it was so unpleasant, I would wait until the right moment to prod it out of Caroline. It was too fresh and early right now.

Caroline and I changed up the menu this evening. We grilled up some chicken on the grill along with some veggies and added some toasted French bread to be shared with my delicious mix of Tuscan olive oil. Healthy? Yeah, along with a bottle of my finest Cabernet. We needed the wine—if not some hard liquor, as we did the last two nights—if we were going to embark on another unknown crazy adventure tonight, right? Well, actually, we both knew we definitely needed the wine, if not the vodka. We needed to relax and only some sort of "spirits" had to be ingested to be the soothing saving balm that we both needed.

After our first glass, Caroline and I started to relax. She seemed to be back to her cheerful, silly self. I prodded her to talk about her dating experiences and we made light and fun of her encounters.

It was time. Caroline looked at me with a telepathic look of just knowing. Without a word said and just a reciprocal smile, we stood up and pushed our chairs in underneath the table and proceeded to take our walk down the boardwalk to begin the evening of enchantment we had been planning all along. Another night of surprises, but hopefully delightful again for me, and hopefully something delightful for Caroline. Just something, please High Tide—if you have not already given her a portion as of yet, please do so this time? I do wonder.

I wanted High Tide through our sweet MoonGlow to have me delve more into that long-ago lifetime. I wanted to see Calissa again and get to know her. I wanted to know in what time period we had lived our lives, who was I, who were my mother and my father, who was my husband, what was my life like, what did we do, where did we grow up, and what did we experience? What in the world had we done so wrong that had us continue to be recycled in this karmic world? What had been our sins and misfortunes?

"Did I say we?" Was it possible that Calissa and my parents in that time were now here in this present lifetime with me? If not, where were they, then? Who were they now? So many questions I had. I needed to know, because I needed to heal!

And yet, what was revealed to me last night was just a snippet, a tiny portion, of just one lifetime…not much at all. Just thinking about what could possibly be revealed to me with High Tide's doings made me feel uneasy and nauseated now, yet giddy and delighted. Feelings of unrest and hauntings of long ago and perhaps centuries ago came upon me. "Who are these people, these souls who were before in another space and time?" I needed to know.

Caroline and I stopped again along the shoreline as I proceeded to turn on the music from my phone this time. I knew my sister, MoonGlow, loved my music and was honored by its reverence of her. As she lowered her eyelids and blew us her welcoming kiss, we girls were already feeling the intoxication of MoonGlow's potion. Caroline followed me as we each blew a kiss back to MoonGlow, as was appropriate.

We began the dance again, swirling and turning, laughing and singing. We were wild like gypsies, like the gypsy girls we really were. Like MoonGlow herself, we were a touch of crazy! We loved it. We loved being the women that we were. We loved being the vixens that we were…free and flowing…free and easy. Yes, my beautiful glowlight had taught me well, indeed. Now, I would be sharing this with Caroline.

I began to lift my hair, swirling and curling the strands in the summer's evening breeze. The sound of the currents began to increase its magnitude. The winds came.

"Well, High Tide, come on over," I said in a seductive voice that made even Caroline turn and look at me with slight surprise. His liquid projectiles rose up in their ever-prominent and foreboding presence. I quickly grabbed Caroline's hand as we both bowed, as was appropriate, in reverence and submission.

The whispers came from the Great Liquid, but continued to be incomprehensible. I was swept up in him again, but this time I was not frightened. I felt an ectasy never felt before. It was a "mystical" ectasy, more potent than any earthly one ever experienced.

"Be on your way." I knew the whisper this time was from MoonGlow. And so my sweet sister did exactly that. She sent us on our way with a kiss to a place that High Tide chose to send us again this time.

Late 1800s – SECOND ENCOUNTER

I was taken back to the same room. Everything was precisely the same, except this time I noticed my sweet Calissa walking into the room from the doorway. She smiled her lovely smile as she walked over to me for a motherly hug and kiss on the lips. I felt that incredible sense of love along with a sense of longing, a longing to actually be in this time again with her and to never leave her side ever again.

She quickly interrupted my senses by telepathically telling me how I had come to her in such a time as this. She wanted to relay our journey, our story, our lives, to help me progress in my spiritual journey. I needed to know not only because I desired this, but also so that I could "move on" to where I was supposedly expected to be when my present earthly time was over. I gasped at first, but of course, this was what I wanted, right? I wanted all my questions answered and I wanted to see Calissa again.

I was then taken. It appeared to me I was standing outside a clothing store, an unfamiliar place of long ago in another time, of course. I noticed that I was standing right beside a lady of color holding a small child about two years of age. The thought came to me that the child was actually me.

A woman who I suddenly recognized came out of the store. She was my mother. This was certain, I thought. She had on a satin dress of late-1800s style with matching gloves and hat, and dangling on her forearm was a cloth handbag which had a thick string on top to open and close. It was not my style, but of course, it was late 1800s. She walked with elegance and grace as if she had been bred of some fine quality. It was relayed to me the year was 1864. My mother was beautiful, and I knew that someday I would look just like her.

Calissa came to me and graciously started to impart information. She said in time, I would know everything and relive some parts about our lifetime together, but it would be in "doses," some for a short time, some for a longer time. She said that time did not exist in her world, so even if it seemed I had been gone for quite some time when I return to my body, it was not so, she told me.

She began to reveal that my mother had married a wealthy man who had practiced law and owned a massive plot of land outside of New Orleans and grew rice and cotton on several plantations nearby. We had a house in the city and lived there most of the time. My mother loved my father so dearly as he loved her. He was about twenty-three years older, than she and had been a widower, having had two children with his previous wife. His children were not fond of my mother. In fact, they had nothing to do with us and very little with their (my) father.

Sadly, my father had died when I was the young age of three. I had been his love and joy, just like my mother had been. After the death of my father, his children from his first marriage had managed to leave my mother and me penniless due to the son's wheeling and dealing with the legal professionals of the city. His son was an attorney himself, so it came to be that my mother ended up selling her fine jewelry, clothes, and personal belongings at different times to make ends meet. She took up sewing and tending to other people's household needs eventually when the money from her belongings had drained, but Calissa was hesitant to say any more.

Calissa knew and sensed I was wondering how we got by after my father's death, but she immediately transmitted that she would have me see for myself how things came about. This was the story she wanted to tell me, to show me, to have me experience for whatever reason. I knew she wanted me to write about it. Yes! That was what my sweet girl wanted me to do. She wanted me to write the story, our story of a past life once upon a time. But why? What was the message?

I was feeling so excited and so enthralled to find out the rest of our story. Was this story to allow me to comprehend the reasoning of karma and why we must live many many lives before we could move on? Maybe, she also wanted me to comprehend and accept why things happen the way they do and what we must overcome to rise up, to awaken, to evolve so that we can, pardon my french, "get the hell out of here."

I suddenly felt faint and a pulling sensation engulfed me as I felt my body flowing backward. I looked at Calissa and felt so saddened. She smiled and relayed, "In due time, Mother. In due time you will know everything you want and need to know."

Mother? I thought. I smiled. I was used to being called "Mom." Mother seemed so formal, but I guess in that time period that was the usual nomenclature.

I was taken back to my bedroom and into my body. Again, I did not know how I ended up in my bedroom. My thoughts were on Caroline and I wondered if she was in her bedroom now and had any encounters. Why is she keeping this secret from me? I was hoping that she had not experienced anything that was troubling or....

I was falling asleep again. I heard a sharp ringing in my left ear, indicating that someone from spirit had come to visit. I felt my soul ever so gently lifting up out of my body with no control of myself by two angelic-like beings. The feeling was one of never-before utmost peace and tranquility. I was taken by these two massive and majestic angelics, one on either side of me, toward the heavens. We were just beyond the fourth realm, maybe on the outskirts of the fifth dimension, if not actually inside its veil.

Place of Tears…

I was placed on a shore and began to walk. No sight of the two angelics could I see, as they had left me. As I started walking and feeling a slightly cool breeze, my eyes gazed up at the heavens above me, totally fixed and infatuated. There were galaxies meshed in various places above the transparent sky veil with their own planets, constellations, and peoples. There were several moons scattered about. I counted seven of them of differents sizes, but all in brilliant fullness. Constellations were vividly seen and more numerous than any human could see from the earthly plane. They were of all shapes and sizes, radiating their light in every direction.

Suddenly, the constellations were dancing in unison, dangled and dazzled, sprinkled with illuminating crystal-like iced projections. One star stood out, more magnificent, brighter and opulent than all the others. I thought, *That is Him, I AM.*

That was all I needed to know. I felt such incredible humility and unworthiness. I felt faint and tiny and insignificant. Suddenly I was forced to fall on my knees and bring my extremities closer and snug to the trunk of my body, like a fetus. I felt small.

I gasped and tried to take a breath. My eyes welled up with tears. The tears were massive and endless streams on my face, my chest, my arms and entire body as they drenched me in purifications while I sobbed uncontrollably. My tears became streams of a spring, then of a river ever flowing. They began to merge into the ocean before me, becoming one with the ocean's rhythmic flow, encompassing every turn of my body as I finally stood up and swirled around taking in its majesty.

I ever so humbly and with a permissive bow began to gaze about and knew my tears were part of the ocean, along with all the other souls before me who had come to this "Place of Tears," this place of cleansing, this place of purification. The ocean sprouted its liquid projectiles upward to the heavens, displaying its tiny and giant creatures who are all a part of this world and have been for infinity. The human souls curled in fetal positions bounced and floated alongside these oceanic creatures. All were bathed in the salty liquid of healing, "The Healing Salts" as relayed.

Some of the humans were smiling, some laughing, some crying with their voluminous tears that added to the volume of the ocean's liquid. As I could see the transparent sky veil above me, I heard a voice say, "You are not in the fifth realm. You are just below it in a purgatorial realm." It was relayed that this was a place where a soul goes when a soul is just about able or "worthy" to move further on.

I realized then that there are many heavenly realms, endless and innumerable realms that go beyond the fifth realm. We can choose to go there to the endless realms if the soul is ready and willing and worthy to do so. Was this a foretaste, a preface of what lay ahead for me? Could I possibly be worthy at some point in time to be able to actually make it?

I continued to shed my tears, for I knew and felt at that moment our God is a merciful God beyond anything we can imagine. I felt a love and peace shower over me which consisted of still more tears, the tears of God Himself. For I knew then for sure that He loved me and wanted me to enter and abide in His Realm someday....someday long from now, I thought.

I felt myself being pulled back. I was being pulled beyond any speed I had ever experienced. I saw lights and colors unimaginable in the earthly realm. I woke up, eyes open, but groggy. I smiled. I praised my Creator and his "light beings" for taking me to that special place. I felt humbled and so very grateful. I pondered for a short time what I had seen and thought of Jesus' quote in the Bible, "In my Father's house, there are many mansions." Yes, I had been given the knowledge that there are many mansions, many rooms, many realms, and many worlds out there—so many, so many. Where had I been all these centuries? Where all had I gone? Where all had I lived? So many mansions…so many rooms…so many worlds…then gently I fell asleep.

Chapter 4

NATHAN

We should live only to love and
we should die only to love again.

*A*s I woke up again this second time, I realized it was Saturday now. We had just had our second encounter.

What in the world? What the hell was that about with those people floating in the water? I thought. Did this strange and mesmerizing place in time and space actually exist? Was it a dream? "No, no, no," I said. It was real. It was as real as I am here in my bedroom reminiscing about the most amazing and inexplicable experience of the night. "Forgive me, God, for doubting."

I then remembered meeting Calissa again and the information she had telepathically imparted to me. I was bewildered, confused, and dazed, but you know what? I was ecstatic and elated at the same time, because I had embraced this adventure, this very strange and bizarre adventure of a life that existed elsewhere… beyond time and space…just for me. "I love you, my sweet Calissa," I said aloud.

As I looked out the window and gazed upon High Tide's abode, my head began to spin as a warm calming light draped itself upon me. "Return to me…it is written."

I pulled myself out of the trance. "Return to whom?" I did not recall, nor did I understand the message. I felt as if it had been a man's voice.

Since it was Saturday morning, I decided to leave a note on the kitchen counter for Caroline. I would take a ride into town while she and Charlie were still sleeping, as I had presumed. I didn't know for sure, but nothing was stirring about that I could hear.

I stopped by the coffee shop to pick up some pastry goodies for breakfast, maybe some egg croissants, I thought. I didn't feel like cooking after last night. I just wanted to sit back with Caroline in the breakfast nook and scope out her situation this time to see if she was really okay. Maybe she would tell me something of what she had encountered these last two nights. Please God, let her open up and tell me!

I sat over in a corner to sip some coffee while checking my email on my phone. I needed some time to just be by myself.

I happened to look up over to the pastry area and there he was. He was probably in his forties, like myself. He was about 5-11," medium build (quite perfectly built if I can say). Just a slight profile that I could see from the distance showed his hair was thick dark brown, combed back and cut short around his ears. His day-old beard made him look even more manly and handsome.

My heart fluttered a bit and my mouth opened. I was staring at this fine-looking specimen of a man. Wow! I unexpectedly felt a "familiarity," as if I already knew him. I realized he was Nathan Rynn, just from his distant profile. I felt I was instantly in another space and time for a moment—or for a while at least. Why was that? I then snapped out of it and remembered what a fool I had made of myself when I had turned around in the car, smiling and waving at him as if I were some schoolgirl.. Good grief!

My heart skipped a beat this time. He looked over at me as if he knew someone was watching him...staring at him. It was definitely him. The man I met at the intersection that first night and the guy Caroline and I saw standing outside the convenience store that day. It was Nathan!

He smiled a crooked grin which was just adorable as the first time I saw it. My heart skipped a beat again, I totally melted. I grinned back, turned about eighty shades of red, then looked shyly back down at my phone. I think maybe I sank into my chair almost to floor length. That didn't last for long. I looked back at him again, and it seemed that he had looked away again only to return to looking at me again.

How delightful that feeling was! Of course, as silly me would be, I only resumed looking at my phone again. Was I flirting? Is that even called flirting? I could barely remember. I had to laugh at myself.

I decided to look toward his direction again, but he was gone. My heart sank. Who was this beautiful creature? Who was this beautiful man who looked "familiar"? Then I snapped out of it. I was no longer in that other "space and time."

I decided to leave after being so disappointed in myself. What an idiot! After being alone for almost two years, I had probably missed my chance of meeting Mr. Fine Specimen of a Man. Rats! Oh well, it was a small town. Maybe we would meet again sometime. I thought I would just start coming here in the mornings and maybe I would run into him again. Yeah, that's it! I'm such a genius.

As I walked over to open the door to exit, the door opened to me. It was him! It was that Fine Specimen of a Man. He smiled his crooked smile at first, then he smiled an adorable wide grin. Now I could see his entire face close up and it was gorgeous. It was more than gorgeous. It was beautiful and magnificent. It was strong and masculine. He was the best-looking man I had ever seen in my entire life! *Never has our awesome Creator made such a fine specimen of a man!* I thought. All I can remember is my mouth dropped open as I stared into his beautiful crystal-blue dancing eyes that looked strangely "familiar"? I was such an absolute total hot mess by that time. I couldn't say a word. Neither could I close my mouth!

As he continued to smile, he said ever so seductlvely and ever so suggestively, as I remember, "Well hello there. It's nice to see you again."

Again? Oh yeah, he had seen me, but he remembered? *That is amazing*, I thought. I was able to somehow get my jaw back into position and say, "Well hello yourself." I don't even remember what all he said, because while he was talking, I was just staring. I was staring at those eyes, at that mouth, at that hair, at that gorgeous face. I just continued to stare while maintaining my ever so ridiculous giddy, girlish and embarrassing composure.

Unbelievable, I thought (not at this present time, but later of course). I could not even utter an intelligent word to this Mr. Fine Specimen of a Man. Are you kidding me? Finally, he told me his name, "Nathan. Nathan Rynn."

I thought, *Nathan? That sounds familiar.* Oh yeah, the woman at the convenience store had told Caroline and me his name...duh.

"Oh, ummm, my name is Marisa. I uh, um just moved here, somewhere on the beach nearby. Just down that way [I pointed in a couple of directions before realizing where I was]...nearby, down there." Really, Marisa?

I felt weak in the knees. I thought I was going to die. I had felt this before so very long ago when I was a young girl or young woman. Then again, I began to think of something stranger. I thought about another time and space before this one. Why was that? My womanly arousal made me smile now as I continued to gaze into his eyes.

I finally snapped out of my thoughts somewhat, I guess. All I remembered was Nathan asking something if I were single, available for coffee or a drink tomorrow, ya da ya da da da. I could not for the life of me get past the trance, the spell, whatever you want to call it, enough so that I could speak some intelligent words. I think I finally said something to the effect, "ABSOLUTELY! Are you kidding me? Anytime, anywhere, and any place will work for me."

Of course, Nathan had escorted me to my car, as he was the perfect gentleman. I don't remember exactly how I was able to get to my car, although I believe I was levitating to some degree, so probably because of that and being able to fly as I do in my out-of-body states, I managed somehow.

Exactly how I was able to speak though (if I actually did) and what was said,

I do not have a clue, okay? I think I had given him my number—of course, right? I do remember driving down the paths along the way to that place I called home "just down that way…down there" somewhere. Oh brother! As I said, I was a total hot mess and enamored and giddy about meeting this fine specimen…so much so that I felt foolish about what had ensued. Did he think I was childish, girlish, ridiculous? Why would he, though, if he asked me out for dinner? He must have been attracted to me. Of course he was. I don't mean to brag, but I *am* attractive and appealing to the opposite sex. I knew that. Right?

I was smiling, I was laughing, and I was feeling like a silly sixteen-year-old girl again. Hell, I was sopping intoxicated! I had a crush. Like a teenage crush on a very handsome man, a Mr. Fine Specimen of a Man, that is. Hell, he was gorgeous! Now, where did I come up with calling him "Mr. Fine Specimen of a Man," by the way? What the hell? Oh well, I kinda like that, though.

I had decided to put the convertible top down on the drive home, because I was in love, for heaven's sake. I needed the free wind blowing in and through my hair so the whole world knew.

As I got to the intersection, I raised both arms up and started waving up to the universe, giving praise and thanks in such simple gratitude for finally breaking the eggshell that had been keeping me at bay, keeping me sequestered, keeping me from pursuing any possible human intimacy—with a man, of course.

As I crossed the intersection with arms flying up and waving like a maniac, I looked to my right where a truck had stopped at the designated stop sign, only to recognize the driver was Nathan! I was at the same intersection that I had first seen Nathan the evening I had decided this would be home.

While my arms continued to flair and fly around and, of course, my mouth dropped looking exactly as I had back at the coffee shop! He looked at me with those crystal-blue eyes, smiled, and waved back.

Oh my goodness! Shit! What an idiot! Are you serious, Marisa? Ohhhhh, he must be thinking you are a total nut job by now for sure, just like Caroline does most of the time.

After taking a few long deep breaths and calming down some, I thought, *Oh well, so what? He is either amused and likes a crazy-ass woman or he isn't and doesn't. And by the way, "crazy" can be enticing, seductive and sexy and sort of interesting at times, right? Oh for heaven's sake, that's my explanation and I'm sticking to it.*

Before I arrived back home, Nathan had sent me a text. As I saw the text appear I do believe I nearly ran off the road, but then again, maybe the car had been in flight since I, myself, surely was levitating.

The text said, "Hey Marisa, just saw you sped by looking so amazing and I'm definitely looking forward to seeing you in a couple of days."

"What? He likes me!" I shouted up to the universe and of course, over to MoonGlow's direction, blowing her a multitude of kisses this time.

I replied to Nathan, "You probably thought I was acting silly, but it's your fault. I am looking forward to seeing you again too." I thought I would keep it short so that I did not seem too overly enamored.

As I entered my beautiful and charming abode, Caroline, Charlie and Sugars were in the kitchen puttering about, coffee in Caroline's hand, of course.

"Hello dahhhlings, good morning sweet sweets," I said. Caroline came over to give me a strong hug and kisses on both cheeks. I then knew she was back in reality, in our world, and was okay.

"Guess what dahhling?" I shouted.

"What? What is it?" was Caroline's surprised and zealous reply. By my holler, she knew something extraordinarily eventful had happened in town.

"I just met, found, and claimed for myself the most gorgeous, handsome man I have ever met in my entire life! AND…he happens to be that Mr. Fine Specimen of a Man we saw back at the gas station, dahhhling."

As Caroline stood in shock and for the first time in a very long time, actually an extremely long time, she was speechless.

While holding up my hand giving her the signal to wait on giving a response, if she were thinking of doing so, "And, before you do decide to say anything, he happens to totally and absolutely be interested in me, your best friend. And, he asked me for my number and we are going out in a couple of days. And he's craaaazy over me. Yeah, oh yeah, step aside, aww uhh!"

I had spun around a couple of times by now. I then waved my hand giving her the signal that it was all right now to give me some kind of reply, "Make it a good one, Caroline."

An extremely loud and screeching scream forced itself out of Caroline's mouth as she raised her arms and waved them like a maniac the same as I did in the car. I had to laugh.

"What? Get the fuck out! It's about time and good for you, Marisa!" We both laughed like there was no tomorrow, giggled like we were teenagers again, like we needed to just share a good time long overdue.

We had both been through difficult times, difficult marriages, difficult lives. It was time to just be silly for a while and be like girls again. It was that simple. We hugged, we danced, we laughed until we could hardly breathe. We went full throttle, full speed into simply spending giddy girltime. For a while at least, being sixteen and silly again felt good.

I told Caroline the whole debacle of the encounter I had had with Nathan. She understood how ridiculous and uneasy my initial encounter would be, naturally. "Of course, you did, girl. The moment you said you thought you were in love, I thought, *Oh no, here she goes.*"

Caroline laughed so hard, like I had never seen her do. She laughed until she cried and actually had peed a bit also. It was good to see her that way. It was good for her to be like this and it was good for me too. She was genuinely happy for me, as I knew she would be. Only a best friend who I felt I had known forever and maybe before this lifetime would feel this way. Why was I thinking this? Why did I think "before this lifetime," ummm?

I went up to my room with Sugars. I wanted to just lie in my bed and spend a little time daydreaming of Nathan. Wow, why did I get that feeling of familiarity? What was that all about? I was forty-two as of June 18, but yet I felt as if I were sixteen again and having a schoolgirl crush. Good grief! I couldn't stop thinking of those eyes, that smile, yes that smile of his that could melt my heart and my entire body, making me swoon and faint, and leaving me breathless.

Then he texted me again! "Hey Marisa, hope I'm not being too forward by sending you another text again. Just forgot to tell you that I'm really glad I met you today, beautiful lady."

Are you kidding me?? Not at all, Mr. Fine Specimen. Bring it, baby—whenever you want, however you want and whatever you want, Handsome. Of course, I didn't text that back to him. I was just daydreaming.

I simply replied, "Nathan, not at all. I'm really happy to have met you too. Btw, feel free to text anytime, handsome." What the hell? Was that too much or not enough? Oh well, I'd save it for another time. My mind wandered off as I stared out my window. The curtains flowed and swayed softly through the breeze and seemed to say, "I will carry you off to daydreams of 'familiar' times...times of requited love and passion."

As I was drifting, I broke from my daydream and realized Caroline and I had not even discussed, nor mentioned anything about last night. I felt selfish that I made it all about me and my encounter with Nathan. *I will make it up to her*, I thought, as I drifted and drifted.

Chapter 5

ENDLESS LOVE OF LONG AGO

You have opened the windows to both my heart and soul.

I had fallen asleep until early afternoon. Why was I sleeping so much? *Poor Caroline*, I thought. I did not feel I had been such a good friend since her arrival. I felt as though I had been neglecting her. I ran downstairs only to find no sight of Caroline. I ate a light bite as a late lunch, and decided to text Caroline to see what was up. She had decided to go into town and look around and do a little shopping. She said she was actually just fine spending a little time to herself and explore this "fascinating" place, as she would say. She seemed in good spirits and was on her way home—well, back to my home.

My mind drifted. Caroline and I had gone to college and graduate school together and became certified nurse anesthetists. We worked together for a while, until Caroline and her husband had moved away. We each had a child. Mine was Zach and hers was Samantha. We always stayed friends though, the best of friends, for we were akin.

After Caroline had returned home, Charlie, Sugars, and I gave her such a welcome as if she had just arrived for a long-overdue visit. How had I missed her. My sense of time had changed for some reason and I felt the longing to be with my friend, to spend some girl time and just have fun. I still felt she did not want to talk about last night. I sensed it somehow. I had not told her of my experiences yet so far either. What was wrong with us?

I finally snapped out of my thoughts, "You know what? We are going into town again. Yes again but for some real, nonsensical and crazy girl time. Ok? No arguments! And before you ask, yes, we are going to be back for our next adventure even if it's late. We are going to have some fun, so dress like a slut and mean it girlfriend."

"Now, that's the way I wanna hear you talk." Caroline projected her loud contagious laugh and it was ever so welcoming to me. She gave me a huge hug, the kind we always give each other when we had not seen each for a while. What a great feeling that was. I noticed the tears from her eyes and I the same.

"And by the way, of course, I'm going to dress like a slut just like you, dahh-hhling!" We continued to laugh a bit and went on to our rooms to dress the dress.

Nathan and I had texted a couple of times today. Oh, the butterflies I am feeling. What is wrong with me? I am so totally crushing on this guy. Oh well, we will have to wait for a real date though, and Nathan understood that, right? Caroline will be leaving the day after tomorrow and my time now was to share only with her as should be. Nathan would understand, of course. He is Mr. Fine, you know, and he is perfect. I laughed to myself when thinking that. He was what I had been waiting for and just what I had been needing. Oh boy, I felt like I could not wait to see him though…his eyes, his smile, his body, his everything.

Caroline and I literally ran and jumped into the convertible for our party night on the town. With the top down, red-rimmed sunglasses and red lipstick to match, we were definitely looking hot. With that said, we did have to wear (and I want to emphasize 'skinny' here) our skinny headbands in place just enough to keep our hair from hitting our face and messing up our lipstick.

Yeah, we were for sure two of the hottest, most desirable women this eastern side of the the country along the Atlantic coast. At least for this evening for sure we knew that. Besides, what is the point of being in a convertible if the intention is not to look hot, let our hair fly, swarm, tangle and just get crazy while driving into town.

Am I right? Of course I am. Believe me with my long thick bouncy blonde hair and Caroline's long dark bountiful hair, there was a lot a hair blowing around. If we had not received any attention, something had to be wrong with these people around here, especially the men, right? Guess what? We did get attention! Of course, waving our hands and blowing kisses from our bright red lips helped some too. We had not started drinking yet, but we were certainly acting like it.

We reminisced again about old boyfriend days and laughed hysterically at the antics that once took place when we were kids so to speak. We were having fun as we always do. We were being girls again or pretending we were. So much alike and agreeable we were when it came to being carefree and pretending to be girls again or well, young ladies, I guess. Not that we're old, I must say!

We stopped at the Sea Bay Bar and Grill. Boy, the looks we got! Yikes. I guess I forgot to mention we both decided to wear a pair of those retro one-piece shorts with platform heels. So maybe that caused some attention too. I have to admit I kinda flirted with a couple of guys, but not as much as Caroline. Of course, she was single and available. I thought for a bit that she would ditch me and take on this one guy she seemed smitten with. But she only gave him her number, then looked my way and winked.

As for me, I decided I was single and not-so-available since my mindset was totally on Nathan, my fine specimen of a man. *Holy shit!* I thought. *I barely know him, and I am already infatuated enough to not even give another guy a chance.* Oh well, I did say when I eyed him for the first time, that he seemed familiar. Little did I know what that meant, and what that would come to mean in time.

Surprisingly, I ended up feeling a little more sober than Caroline. Somebody had to drive. Actually, I drank a little coffee for a pick-me-up, along with a glass of water to sober up, and I was fine. It was past twilight now. We still had the convertible top down. The cool, brisk breeze from driving felt good as it blanketed our faces. It woke us up too, and I do believe prepared us for the evening of hopefully unexpected surprises.

As we arrived home, my lovely abode looked dark and the actual MoonGlow, herself, was not in sight. I had forgotten to leave some lights on. I thought Caroline might be too tired to go for our ritual, but she said, "No way am I going to miss this one tonight."

I looked over at her with bewilderment. "Wait a minute. Are you holding out on me? I do believe you have experienced something supernatural these last two nights. Sweet friend, I know you have your right to keep whatever to yourself. I haven't told you anything either about our second evening, but isn't it bizarre that we haven't discussed anything?" We looked at each other with reciprocal stares and agreement. We both paused and nodded our heads in agreement, but strangely we just went about our way preparing for the evening. What the hell?

We prepared for the evening with Caroline's one hand holding a bottle of wine, the other with two glasses, and I with my music. We both started laughing as we approached the boardwalk down to the beach. It was already dark because we had spent time in town. But where was MoonGlow, our sweet Sister Moon? She was hiding, but why? Neither of us could see her. Hysterically, as if we knew what the other was thinking, we shook our heads again and like silly girls—we could not wait to play and dance the dance, meeting our friends again, MoonGlow and High Tide.

Wow, I thought, *"our friends."* Yes, they had become Caroline's friends too. That was all right with me, and made me smile.

We began playing the music. Silly as we were, we didn't care if anyone was watching. I did happen to look up at the house on the hill, which sat to the right of mine. The lights were on and I did wonder if we were being watched.

Swirls of light swarmed the night sky. The psychedelic painting caused a whirling sensation as Caroline and I spun around and flung our arms up towards the starlit dome above us, as if reaching for what was an endless journey, an unattainable end to any means. Were we "reaching for the stars," as the saying goes? I looked to my right and there she was in all her majesty, our MoonGlow again, as she always promised. Never does she disappoint. Never does she stay away—but where, oh where had she been? I am her child, and she my sentinel. Her ever-beautiful but also daunting face at times began to appear on her surface. She smiled and winked me her approval. My head bowed along with my reciprocated smile. With a kiss I gave her my love. What a delight she always is…and always will be.

Suddenly the massive water before us began to roar and thunder as it lifted again on this third night. As the whispers from his abode came forward with him, HighTide let it be known of his own majestic presence, keeping in check with the lover he had always and forever been tied to, MoonGlow.

Caroline and I, this time, gasped as we did the first night as he mightily and with trepidation began to thrust forward His massive liquid projections. His masculine arms again enveloped and held me tightly, as a good lover would.

Not knowing what was happening to Caroline again, as before, I felt his liquid projections taking hold of me as if I were his prey, and as a helpless prey who surrendered and succumbed at some point, he inebriated me with his salty solvent as he thrust his masculine liquid balm down my throat, intoxicating me enough to succumb to whatever he desires, oh so cleverly and oh so seductively. I felt surprised, foolish, and uneasy with these sensations, but yet how could I resist? How could I fight him off? I understood at that moment how my Sister Moon would naturally choose him, take him, the mighty High Tide as her own dream lover, as she sprouted forth on evenings to dance her own dance of allure and enticement. She is such a vixen and she is teaching me well.

Late 1800s - THIRD ENCOUNTER

I felt as if I had woken up from a long and deep sleep. My surroundings were gray and misty for a moment. Then there she was, my Calissa. She was looking the same as the other two encounters. Still in her nightgown with her braided hair pulled and swept back over the front of her right shoulder. Her stare was still those of beautiful dancing crystal-blue eyes. *How I love her*, I thought. My gaze was broken..

I was taken to a room different from where I had first met Calissa. It looked like a small sitting room with Victorian-style furniture and lace-covered windows. I noticed a sewing machine im one corner. My mother was sitting there and only her profile could I see. She was still beautiful, but with a saddened face. Her dress was as pretty as I last saw her. It was not of satin, and had no embroidery or embellishments of any sort.

Sounds of people mumbling and shuffling about outside our room began. It seemed that sound was delayed for a bit after reaching this realm, then suddenly it came, if it came at all, and it was here now. But why did it come only in waves—and partially, it seemed? For no sound could I hear in this room with my mother. I did not know. *It is this "other" realm where I am present*, I thought, *and so it is this way.*

As I looked toward my mother it was relayed to me that sometime after my father had passed away and his children had taken everything away from my mother and me, we had become impoverished. My mother was a beautiful woman, but she could not bring herself to fall in love with another man again, nor could she do so even to have means of support for the both of us. She was saddened and upset with herself, for she loved me so, but she had loved my father so much and so powerfully that she could not bear to be with another man in such a state of true love and romance.

Initially, she had taken a position as a seamstress and laundry servant to support us as well as she could. She even had to succumb to mending, cleaning, and sewing garments for the very women who had been her so-called friends and acquaintances while she had been married to my father.

These women felt some slight amount of pity for her in the beginning, thus enabling her to earn some money by their so-called generosity by allowing her to please them with the very ornate clothes that my mother herself had once been accustomed to wearing. Yet in time, the disdain and contempt from these gossipmongers lacked subtlety. How humiliating it must have been for my mother.

I was yet a child when all of this happened, so I was immune to this humiliation until I was old enough to attend school and had heard this from other children. I had, myself, dealt with the arrows and blows of being taunted and ridiculed.

My mother and I would become ostracized and presumed outcasts in this late 19th-century city of New Orleans. But why, I thought, were we such outcasts? My mother was performing respectable work, right? There was no shame in that, not at all.

I knew I was about to find out, though. I felt it. I wanted to know too. Why had our karma brought this downgrading, this lowering of our class of our livelihood, of our existence? What had happened to us in this lifetime or the previous? Would I even be given the chance to find out, or would I only get bits and pieces? Oh, that karma! She can be a bitch, but she is fair. I hate to admit that, but I do believe she is fair.

My mother began to get up from the chair and walked toward a young girl—or lady, should I say—who was sitting opposite the room. She appeared to be reading and writing. I suddenly knew she was I. I looked pretty just like my mother, I thought. Maybe the beauty we possessed brought jealousy and opposition toward us, even more so along with the past humiliations we had encountered.

My mother came over and caressed the side of my head and kissed my forehead ever so lightly. She loved me and I loved her. Tears began to fall, for I felt how much she loved me, and I felt how sorry and heavy burdened her heart was for ending up with such a lifestyle as this for the both of us. *My poor mother*, I thought.

I looked at myself more in depth now. I was pondering my age. It appeared I was around sixteen, just as Calissa appeared to me as such. It was relayed I had just arrived home from a boarding school. My mother gathered a basket of clothes that had been mended, I assumed, and walked to the door and left. I assumed she was on her way to deliver them to one of the gossipmongers who had become her customer.

I began to fade out of the room. I knew then that the room was at a boarding house in town. My mother and I lived in two rooms.

I was then taken to the streets of New Orleans. I walked along an uneven cobblestoned street, watching people adorned in their late-1800s apparel hurrying on their way. Horses and carriages calmly passed by, unlike the people surrounding them. I was then directed to enter a side street, which seemed more evenly paved, but with dirt.

I came upon a rather lovely-looking dark pink three-story home. I stood there viewing it for quite some time. It was so grand and ornate. "A most beautiful house," I heard myself say.

There seemed to be a busyness of comings and goings. Men were leaving and men were coming. I noticed there were a few women arriving in fine clothing, but a little daring in a way, and some bold in color. It was certainly not the more conservative style of the prominent women walking about like the kind of clothes my mother used to wear. It was getting to be nightfall. I could not tell how much time had passed, but I felt like I needed to observe and needed to spend this time of long observation for some reason or another. What reason I did not know at this time.

Suddenly, I saw my mother walking up. I smiled. I thought maybe she had a delivery and yes, she had with her the basket of clothes. *My poor mother*, I thought again.

I followed her into the home. There was a woman about the same age as my mother standing behind a desklike lectern, greeting a gentleman. She was dressed rather seductively in bright blue with bold jewelry of clear stone earrings and an ornate- sized necklace. Lace was plentiful over her dress. Her upper breasts were high and prominent, which I thought was inappropriate in conjunction with what the "proper" women were wearing. The woman was beautiful though. She had dark raven hair and large dark eyes.

My mother walked up to her and began chatting like old friends with this lady behind the lectern. The words were not audible to me, but I knew there was a pleasant exchange.

Swirls of light swarmed about me and around me. The swirls were moving horizontally in a rightward position, then they began to change direction moving vertically from upward toward downward position with cascades of liquid-filled light projections. The cascading projections began to sprinkle their moistness on me, as I looked at my hand and noticed their tiny beads of illumined liquid. "Hey, is High Tide here?" I asked, almost smiling. I was forced backward as in a cylinder tunnel, quickly moving. I knew I was moving back in time to another age.

The year was 1867. That would have made me five years of age. I was nowhere to be found, but I did see my mother. She was at the dark pink house. She looked different now. She did not look like the finely dressed, prominent-looking woman I had seen when I was three years of age, nor the average woman when I was sixteen.

She was dressed in black. Her shoulders were slightly covered with short puffed up sleeves, and her breasts were set up high and noticeable. She had long pink gloves down to her elbows. Her skirt was full with the length shorter in the front and fell lower toward the back. I noticed an artificial pink rose attached to her waistline. She had those old-timey black shoes on with laces and short heels. Her hair was partially up and her lips were bright red. Still, she looked beautiful, but similar to a lady of the night.

Oh no, here it comes, I thought. Yes, indeed, she was just that, a lady of the night. After the death of my father and after the money my mother had made by selling most of her personal belongings, she had become a seamstress for about two years. Eventually that line of work would not provide for us.

As a seamstress, she had met the lady who stood behind the lectern, and was offered a change of "career," as you might say. It was imparted to me that my mother wanted a better life for me. Since she had lived a grand life for just a short time with my father, she wanted me to attain a good education, acquire society's prescribed etiquette of poise and charm, and marry well to obtain a better status in life.

As I said, I was viewing my life at five years of age, but it was not until I was eight years of age that she had me sent off to a boarding school. By that time, she was making enough and had saved enough to be able to provide better for me. She had even become the madam's assistant as well as being the top lady of the night at the dark pink house. "My poor mother," I said again.

At that time, the lady at the lectern, the madam, was only five years older than my mother, but had inherited the brothel from her own mother who had died the year before. This lady was still what I considered young, at twenty-nine, but was fiery, tough, business-savvy, and fearless, just as her own mother had taught her to be. My mother met her exactly as I thought she had, by washing, mending, and ironing clothes for her.

I began to sob. It was relayed to me how very sad my mother and I were when the time came for me to head off to boarding school. I did not want to go. I cried,

I pleaded, I begged. My heart was so broken, so torn, so shattered. My every bit of my being was in pain. At that time, everyone in town including the children at my school knew what my mother had become and how she made a living. They grew suspicious when we both started to wear better clothes and eventually bought a quaint small home.

Even though the madam, her ladies, and the clientele kept discreet about the goings-on, people became suspicious, nosey, and maybe even jealous. Then the word was out. My mother was not only wanting what was best for me, but she was protecting me from ridicule and shame. I loved my mother in spite of all I had been hearing. I loved her deeply and I always would. Isn't that what you do for someone you love? You love, no matter what.

So off I went to boarding school several hours away, but I was not informed exactly where. I would come home for visits, but as I grew older, most of the time my mother would come to see me and we would stay in a room at the local inn. She did not really want to take the risk of anyone recognizing me or harassing me. She certainly did not want me to end up going to that dark pink house for any visits. I believe that reason took precedence over any other.

It was relayed to me now that after some years had passed, my mother decided she wanted to leave the profession, for I was about to finish my time at the school that I had been attending and head back home. At what time and what age I was when she had made that decision was not relayed. I was telepathically told that my mother had felt so much guilt and shame that she could not continue working.

She had sold our house for extra money. She had repented and gone back to church. She had surrendered to the virtue of humility, willing to face the upstanding ladies of New Orleans as a servant of theirs and succumb again to mending, washing, and serving their needs.

Why, why? I thought. How could she even stay in this town and do such a thing? I began to weep. My thoughts were flooded with why we are here in the first place, why we suffer, why we choose humiliation, why we try to make amends. Of course. This is part of the soul's awakening, of purification, of evolving. We are meant to get past all of these earthly materialistic desires and move on. We are to get the hell out of here—pardon my French. To rise above and go beyond into heavenly realms where only there we can find and experience true love, true peace, true joy is each soul's destiny.

"I know this, I know this, Marisa." I only hope and pray that my mother, at this lifetime I am viewing is in such a place right now. I believe she is, right?

My swirling liquid projectiles returned. I really didn't want to go forward or backward, or whatever. I wanted to stay and see more. I wanted to find out more. Then up the liquid cylinder tunnel I went. Flashes of mystical lights and a menagerie of mystical colors flew past me. I felt at peace. I felt at rest.

And of course, I woke up in my bed What day was this now? I collected my thoughts and then realized it was Sunday. Where was Calissa? I had seen only a glimpse of her since on this last journey, which had been my third journey. I felt sad and disappointed, but I remembered she took me to a period of time before her birth. She told me that she would tell me everything, or at least everything that I needed to know. "All right then, my sweet Calissa. You will tell me more later, but can we make it tonight?"

I smiled and thought how much I was enjoying this journey, yet saddened too. For what journey is not filled with joy and sadness both? Of course, it is so—otherwise, why would we be here in this imperfect world? It is surely not always heavenly here, not a heavenly realm indeed. It can be consumed in sorrow, I was thinking at this point. "Karma's a real bitch!" again I said to myself.

I continued to be groggy for a bit and suddenly blurted out, "What is my freaking name? What is my mother's name? What in the hell is the madam's name? Shit!"

I realized that I didn't even know my name—that is, my name in that lifetime. I must ask Calissa. "Oh God, bring her to me tonight, please, Oh God, please."

I hopped out of bed suddenly and so forcefully that it made Sugars do the very same thing. I chuckled a bit and grabbed Sugars, telling her I was so sorry for having startled her. We quickly went down the stairs and into the kitchen where Caroline and Charlie were.

Caroline was busily making breakfast over the range. "Oh Caroline, you didn't have to start making breakfast for us, sweetness."

Caroline looked quickly at me with that half smile and quirky look. "Who says I'm cooking breakfast for us?"

We both laughed and I knew the tension that I was feeling upon awakening and wondering about Caroline and her experience last night had lessened. While holding my hand over my forehead, I said, "Guess we're not going to mass like the good Catholic girls we are."

"You mean 'were', don't you?" She laughed again. I thought surely Jesus would forgive us this time, since I did believe He had something to do in some way with the mystical messages I was receiving, right?

"Ok, that's it!" I blurted out. Caroline was startled. "What's it? What's happening?" She was looking actually bewildered with her big wide-eyed beautiful stare... (bitch, and just kidding, for looking that great in the morning with absolutely no makeup).

I replied, "Caroline, you are leaving tomorrow. You are leaving me, you are leaving MoonGlow, you are leaving my life, and I need to know that we are still bonded, we are still friends, we are…." I couldn't go on.

I began to weep and sat down at the table. Caroline, as the friend I always knew she was, the constant that I always knew she was, came over quickly and wrapped her arms around me, cradled my head, and spoke her sweetness. She spoke words that I needed to hear.

"Everything is fine sweet friend, sweet perpetual friend of mine. We are sisters, forever perpetual sisters, and I love you."

I started laughing. Yes, I was laughing because we always had called each other "perpetual" friends since childhood. I had not heard that for a while. Neither one of us had mentioned it, but there she was. My longtime perpetual and dependable friend.

"Caroline, these past few nights have been somewhat overwhelming. I don't mean having you here is overwhelming. I mean what I've been experiencing has been overwhelming. I mean every night. What a ride it's been. I can't even begin to tell you. It's been crazy, it's been fascinating, it's been scary, it's been wonderful, amazing…and then meeting Nathan and falling in love with him, and…." The tears came again.

Caroline started laughing. My tears began to turn into laughter again as well. Whatever made us laugh did the trick. Was it my Sister Moon, since she is always sensing me and looking out for me? I didn't quite know, but it was welcome, and we both relished the laughter. I don't remember how long we laughed but it felt so soothing, so comforting, so much like "us."

Caroline began to apologize for keeping a quiet stance about our nightly rendezvous, as she put it. She quieted herself for a bit, then said, "I have experienced similar to what you have, my dear." Now it was my time for my own eyes to express a big wide-eyed and beautiful stare along with my mouth completely open, but with a welcoming plea of "Please tell me, please, please! Then I'll tell you all about mine!"

Caroline held my hand and made me promise not to utter a word until she had completed what she wanted to say. I was thinking, *What did she mean when she said she had experienced similar to what I had?*

She began with a most gentle voice and composure. This was not quite the composure of the Caroline with whom I was familiar. But, hey, I liked it. It was actually refreshing to see this "unfamiliar" side of her. She told me that she too experienced an out-of-body phenomenon and had been transported to another time and space also.

Then she told me something shocking that I suddenly felt light-headed and a pulling force of almost the way High Tide pulled me. Caroline had told me that she had met Calissa herself.

"Ohhhh," I gasped. She said it was during the second night of our mystical state and only briefly. She was told that I was to keep quiet because she, meaning Calissa, wanted to tell the story herself to me. Caroline was being told her own lifetime, but at an accelerated rate. The whole story of her own lifetime, in other words, had already been relayed. I was stunned.

"But why is it going to take longer for me? Why would that be?" I felt awful that I was snapping and seemed as though I was demanding answers from Caroline—maybe a hint of jealousy was there also. I apologized to Caroline. I, of all people, with my spiritual and mystical upbringing, know that everything happens in its own time and each of us has our own time, our own experiences, our own ways of becoming awakened, enlightened. Who was I to mock the Almighty Creator who blesses each and every one of us according to His own plan, His own design, His own purpose?

"It's all about the evolution of the soul," I said to Caroline. I understood. I began to cry again, but not because of sadness. I began to cry because of the joy of this moment and just being in this moment with my friend. How special that was. How blessed we both were.

Of course my Calissa would appear to my friend. Caroline and I are akin, we are "familiar." Then I remembered what Calissa had told me: "In due time, Mother." She would tell me everything that I needed to know in due time.

Unfortunately, Caroline told me that her time for being engulfed by High Tide's liquid (boy, that's an understatement) was over and that she was quite accepting of the news and actually happy for that. She did not really want or need to participate in another mystical ride, I should say, tonight. I said before that we were very much alike, but yet, we are different too. She is not so willing and excited about traveling beyond the veil as I am. Had she experienced more than I thought in other lifetimes? Maybe that was the reason. She is more earthbound and grounded, I must say. She was already shown all what needed to be shown and all what would appease her. She did tell me that knowing what this past life was all about and how she understands the karmic recycling we all must face was enlightening indeed.

So I can most certainly hear Caroline saying to our friends, "Okay, thank you, Sister Moon and High Tide. You both have helped me understand more of what Marisa has been babbling about for years. It's been an amazing ride, I enjoyed it, and what a ride it's been, but it's time to get on with life here in the now and present. See you later dahhhlings." That's my Caroline.

Again, we spent the day talking about our lives, our childhood, past boyfriends, past husbands, and all the antics that females such as we are get caught up in during a lifespan. Some of the stuff was repeats again. Hell, a lot of the stuff was repeats, actually. We laughed, we cried, we listened intently to each other as we reminisced and tried to make sense of some of the silly and unbelievable things we did and the choices we made. For some of those choices caused such chaos. Oh yeah, karmic chaos indeed. But doesn't everybody do that at some point? We would not be here on this earthly plane if we did not. Okay, so we are trying to make sense. What does it all mean anyway? Free will we have and free will we do, but be ready for karma's justice.

In our tiny minds, we are never going to figure that out completely. But I have come to believe that our "higher" consciousness, the soul, already knows some of these mysteries. They are just hidden for a while...until we are ready to be granted the knowledge and understanding we need, so we can leave this karmic world and move on to higher worlds and to higher dimensions of enlightenment. Now that is exciting.

Caroline and I did not feel much like drinking again tonight. Hell, it had been four freakin' nights of alcohol haven here at MoonGlow, and we might just have been about ready for the safe haven of AA. We were too old for this, right? I know we are the "gypsy girls," free-spirited and wild, but we were not in college anymore, nor in our twenties, to say the least.

Okay, let us grow up a little and get back to reality, we thought. Well, that lasted about an hour and a half.

"Oh, what the hell," we both spat out. It was Caroline's last night. Of course, we were going to have a drink...on her. At least one. Well, maybe two...or three. As I said, Caroline and I were "akin." We were the same in so many ways and we were "familiar"...there goes that word again.

And so we gathered the chips, the chocolate, and I really don't have to say the wine...hello?...and went off to the veranda. We played our music and even danced for a while. And ever with a coy passing look, I would glance up at my MoonGlow, knowing that she understood the reason for my being aloof with her tonight, but only for tonight. I would even catch Caroline casting her eyes toward her mystical presence, too. As I said, Sister Moon is Caroline's friend too now. And only friends I say, for you know, Sister is more than just a friend to me...oh, so much more.

I don't remember what time we finally retired for the night. There was a cool breeze and the curtains in my room were flowing and swaying again. The swirls of mystical light could be seen in the far-off starlit sky. Oh, how I was missing them. I guessed I could sneak out and visit my friends, MoonGlow and High Tide, so they could take me to the starlit sky, but I would wait. They knew I was there and would be ready for them tomorrow night. Wait a minute? Tomorrow night? What about my Mr. Fine Specimen, Nathan?

"I want to see him! I gotta see him. Oh Sista, Sista," I heard myself saying aloud. Even Sugars averted her gaze from me and looked toward the mystical lights as she seemed detached from reality. I laughed, gazing up. "Okay, friends, we'll talk later and we'll make some deal."

Chapter 6

LOVE AND MOTHER'S SICKNESS

Love looks like you and I together.

*I*felt myself being pulled back into my body again. I had been somewhere, but where did I go this time? I could not recall, for some strange
reason. I had remembered the other nights, but not last night. I noticed something
bright, shining dead center into my eyes. I squinted for just a moment and noticed
the light came from the top window of the door leading to the veranda. It was
Sister Moon, herself, in all her shining glory. She was peeking at me! I looked at
the clock. It was 4:30 a.m. My own sweet MoonGlow was peeking in on me and
shining her glowlight upon me through this two-foot by nine-inch window. What
a vixen.

She loved me very much and she cared. So much did she care that she wanted
to let me know she would be forever watching out for me. I was so happy to see
her. I needed her. I needed her "familiarity." All I had to do was look out my window, just turn my head ever so slightly her way—for even a slight glimpse given to
her would cause her to press her face upon mine with the sweetest of all kisses. I
would breathe in that kiss of her sisterly love and I would feel loved. Oh, how she
did just that, my sweet, sweet friend.

She communicated to me that this was her way of thanking me for giving her
due reverence. I was so delighted at just thinking about how much she loved me
by personifying herself ever since the time my father had presented me to her. She
had become my very first best friend at that moment in time. MoonGlow was the
name I honored her with at the age of five. I had even named my own home after
her. She was Queen of the Night, overlooking all creatures and creations of this
earth and its galaxy. She provided her undeniable awestriking and mesmerizing
light, and to those who would give her due reverence, she provided her love and

her protection for every reincarnated life karma had us bound.

My MoonGlow knew that Caroline was leaving. She assured me that I would never be alone, though, for I had been alone and felt alone in this earthly realm many times. The strangeness in me, along with knowings of our massive and striking universe, made me such. Others did not always understand who I was, nor did they want to understand. She would make sure that no harm would ever come to me. And now, High Tide was also. He would help keep watch and keep me safe. It couldn't get better than that now…my mighty friends, indeed they were.

It was early Monday morning. I hopped out of bed quickly again, for I wanted to make sure everything was ready for breakfast. I placed fresh flowers in the colorful flowered painted vase that Caroline just adored, and placed them on the breakfast table out on the veranda. I had covered the table with a pale yellow tablecloth, and placed the napkins and silverware. What a nice surprise this would be for Caroline. She would be pleased.

It was a beautiful morning. Master Sun had already made his appearance. Seagulls were singing and getting their own fill. High Tide's liquid was calmly making his way to glisten the shore, and his lovely sounds of ocean waves soothed me gently. Oh, how I loved this life by the ocean. All my life I had imagined that I would one day live like this, in my own beach house, falling asleep every night while my two best friends, MoonGlow and High Tide, kept watch. While waking up every morning to Master Sun's rays and the amazing inhabitants of this life including its liquid and sand meshing and merging, all would cohabitate in peaceful delight the way our Creator intended. How blessed was I.

"Guten morgen, fraulein!" Caroline exclaimed as she pranced into the kitchen holding Charlie in her arms. Caroline spoke several languages, i.e., German, French and Spanish. I never quite learned to speak fluently in any one language other than English, of course, but I have learned some basics along the way from my sweet friend.

"Ich spreche kein Deutsch!" I replied. We laughed, but then the cloud of sadness fell over me, for Caroline would be leaving me today. Oh well, then again, this is life, but then again, there would be Nathan in my life now (or so I was hoping). At least I had something amazing to look forward to later this evening.

The four of us enjoyed the morning with the lightly flowing breeze and our seagull friends singing their songs. Caroline was delightedly surprised and thanked me abundantly for the prepared breakfast, food, and gracious table setting. We had a most pleasant time. All was well.

I helped Caroline get her bags together. Charlie and Sugars somehow knew she was leaving us. They continued to walk the cat walk around and around her, rubbing their cheeks and sides against her. I smiled and told her that maybe they would miss her more than I would. She looked at me. We both began our teary-eyed stare. "I promise I will be back soon, sweetie, my perpetual friend."

I laughed and said, "I know you will…or I'll come kill you." I think we both then decided we would remain cheerful and be grateful for the few days we spent and the amazing journeys we both took with our beach friends.

As I walked Caroline to her car and exchanged our hugs and kisses, she said, "Marisa, you know, you're going to be given a lot of revelation concerning that past life in a very short time. I have been told this. You will have your answers in due time, my sister."

"In due time." I remembered those word from Calissa.

As she backed away in the car, one more thing she said to me. "And when you know everything you are to know, I will be here for you. Everything will be okay. No problem, don't fret. And most of all, remember you've got that Mr. Fine Specimen of a Man to get a hold of. You better tell me everything when you do!"

I smiled and blew her a kiss. "I love you." Caroline mimicked the kiss and said, "I love you too," waving as she backed out.

After my friend had faded out of site and out of the site of my MoonGlow's sanctuary, I quickly returned to the house. It was about noon now. I immediately took my phone and sent a text to Nathan. I wanted to see him. I wanted to look into his crystal-blue eyes. Hell, I wanted a lot more than that! I sent a text letting him know that Caroline had left and that I was free now to get together.

Well, it didn't take long for a reply. He responded, "Hi Marisa. Well hell yeah, I wanna see you!! Will call in about an hour and make plans to meet."

I laughed and giggled just like a schoolgirl again. "You're unbelievable, Marisa!" But why not? He wants to see me, yay! I'm smiling again and just right after Caroline leaves. Shame on me, but she'll understand. I'm excited and I deserve to be," I said to myself.

It was almost two hours until Nathan called. Of course, it was Monday and he was working. Nathan had told me in one of our few conversations that he was a commercial real estate developer and owner of several of the developments throughout the coast of both North and South Carolina. He had done very well, but I didn't stay on the topic too long for fear of him thinking I might be prying into his worth, if you know what I mean. That did not matter to me, for I had my own money and did just fine. That was certainly not the reason I was attracted to him. As I said before, there was something "familiar"…something that drew me to him, and that something was quite fascinating. It was as though I knew him already.

I did find out that he had been married and had a daughter, but was reluctant and hesitant about discussing it. He said he wanted to keep it light and just "think about you," as he flashed me that adorable crooked grin to a wide flashing smile that had me feeling faint and—well, a couple of other things.

We met for a late lunch at the grill. I must say I had to have a glass of wine beforehand and then during the lunch. I was so nervous, yet so at ease too. Our conversation was light, was cheerful. I remember I smiled a lot and Nathan did too. Ohhhh, how I loved his smile, his hair, his hands, his arms, his chest, his eyes…yeah, his eyes.

Nathan walked me to my car. Unfortunately and unexpectedly he was going to have a long evening today because of the drive to a site out of town. We would meet up tomorrow for a "real date," as he said. I thought, *If this Fine Specimen of a Man wants a real date with me tomorrow night, a Tuesday night, having to drive back here, then he is interested.*

He placed his hand on the small of my back and pulled me toward him. I don't know why, but I thought of how High Tide had pulled me toward him on my first encounter and I had gone limp "as if he had suddenly become my lover… the thoughts of a man I had known…not in this lifetime, but somewhere in time and space had come to me."

I felt lightheaded as my eyes closed. I was suddenly consumed with this man before me. He had me. I was his. I knew that and I wanted that. He kissed me long and hard. His strong muscular arms had me wrapped helplessly in total surrender to this man. That was all I remembered.

I drove home somehow. I remember the flowing breeze against my face and through my hair. I loved him. I loved Nathan. That's crazy, is it not? *I am such a mess*, I thought. *A hot mess, though, I must add.* Somehow I knew he felt the same. I laughed again my schoolgirl laugh. *He likes me.* I don't remember much of the rest of the afternoon and early evening either. I just continued in my daze, my daydream about that beautiful man. I wanted to stay in that state. I felt good. I felt alive.

I sat on the veranda all alone this time, for my Caroline had gone. She called me just a few minutes earlier letting me know she made it home. We had a nice conversation—and yes, she had asked if I had talked with Nathan. "Of course, you did, girlfriend! You better have talked with him. He's a cutie pie! Oh, I mean, a Fine Specimen of a Man, dahhling." Yes, he was.

It was time. Since I would not be with Nathan tonight, I would meet up with my MoonGlow and High Tide. I collected my wrap, my phone, and began the music which began the dance, the dance of ever ancient and ever new.

"Marisa." I looked up and to the right. There she was, my MoonGlow, my sentinel. Her being was effervescent in her glorious phase, illumined and clear as she appeared to me now. She pursed her lips and blew me a kiss. I kissed her back.

The mighty sound of High Tide's liquid pierced my ears this time, while his spiraling wind almost elevated me above the sand. The voices of those in his recesses were louder this time, but still I could not comprehend the words.

He was oh so powerful this time. *I am alone this time*, I thought. Just as I thought this, I looked quickly at MoonGlow and was comforted by her smile. I remembered how she had told me early this morning that I would never be alone and that High Tide was my friend too.

High Tide's liquid mounted up to the heavens, it seemed, with his majestic commands. I felt his magnetic pull. I surrendered as he thrust forward his massive fluid arms and pulled me toward his chest as I felt the downward journey into the recesses of his bowels, where all along I had known…there lay hidden secrets of lifetimes past and forgotten. Forgotten is seemed until the time was ripe for those secrets to emerge and be made known to a soul who needed to know. The soul who needed to right the wrongs, to make reparations of karmic sentences incurred through centuries old would eventually become cleansed, awakened, and enlightened. It is only then that the soul can soar, can fly, can elevate to greater awareness. It is only then that a soul can experience true love, true peace, true joy. This is what God had intended for us because He loves us. He wants us and He wants us to be with Him.

FALLING MYSTICAL VEILS…

I soared through the crystal liquid projections, through eons of time and light into worlds of the Falling Mystical Veils. For as I entered each one, another veil would fall, taking me into another world, another time, another space. I felt my being illumined with those crystal liquids, pure for just a short time like a blink of an eye.

1800s – FOURTH ENCOUNTER

"Return to me…it is written." I had heard these words again. *Return to whom?* I thought again. I still did not know.

And there she was, my Calissa. She was smiling at me. I smiled back and thought, *My baby girl.* I thought of my son, Zach. *He is still my child too.*

Calissa continued to smile and relayed, "You know, Mother, as I said, in due time you will know everything. You will know everything you need to know." It was as if she already knew my thoughts of how I wanted to know names, dates, etc. So Calissa began relaying such to me.

My name was Collette Marie Duprey, born June 2, 1862, in New Orleans. I was French, I thought, just like I am in my present life—well, half French in the present. My mother's name was Nadia Duprey who was married to my father,

Markus Duprey. I had already been told my daughter's name, Calissa, but she would not tell me about her father as of yet. Of course, he would have been my husband. I needed to have more relayed to me about what came about and what led to my marrying her father.

I was sent back to the room that my mother and I were living in from the last encounter. I heard my mother coughing. I looked over as she was lying in bed and shivering. I saw myself walking over and knelt down to touch and hold her hand. She was sick but she would recover some, but not completely. *My poor mother,* I thought. *My poor, poor mother—how I love you so much more than you will ever know.*

I realized I had started helping my mother in her work of mending, laundering, etc. I would come back after my work and take care of her. "That is what you do when you love someone," I remembered saying.

I had started to go to the pink house myself and had met the lady behind the lectern. I had become acquainted and somewhat friendly with her. Her name was Madame Mabelle Lefevre. Everyone called her Madame Mae. Of course, she was French, just like my mother and I were. This was New Orleans!

The pink house was grand, I must say. Its three-story structure stood almost foreboding. The shutters were trimmed with a cream-colored paint. The front of the house had an inviting porch with several chairs and small tables scattered about. Why, I did not understand, because I would think the customers would not want to be parading about in the front of the house allowing anyone to know they were there. Oh well, that was just what I thought. There were two great southern oak trees on either side of the path leading to the porch. Dispersed alongside the path were varying flowers. A wrought-iron fence stood proudly surrounding the front and either side of the house. The double door gate stood taller than the gate itself. It was heavy and somewhat difficult to open and close. I do believe they wanted it that way.

What a beautiful, lovely place it seemed. I laughed just thinking of what this house had become. I would soon find out though how it came to be. For the name of this lovely place was called the Jolie Maison Rose and translated in English, The Pretty Pink House. *Naturally*, I thought, *and how fitting.*

"Bonjour, Mademoiselle Collette," I heard her say with a half grin to me as I saw myself entering through the front door (as usual my travel in this past life is like I am watching a movie and I am one of the characters in the movie).

Madame Mae was fluent in English as well as in French, since she was a businesswoman and dealt with many diverse customers who came to New Orleans for business and such. Well, it was a brothel! It was relayed that most of the time the French language was spoken in the house, but not so when her clients were there. It was then that English dominated the spoken word. During all these encounters that I was viewing and having relayed to me, English would be spoken as it was presented to me.

Madame Mae was a stunning lady. She was a couple of inches taller than I, with raven hair swept up and back by a beautiful jeweled comb, with a few ringlets about the face. Her dark eyes were wide, glaring, and beautiful. She was regal-looking, I thought, and rather elegant. She seemed to be dressed like the fine ladies in the town here. If I did not know better, I would never have guessed she was a madam. She stood poised and spoke well and with charm. There was a kindness in her eyes when she looked at me. Actually, "stared at me" would be more accurate. Anyway, I could not help but like her instantly.

I looked about the place for a bit while I, Collette, was actually having a conversation with Madame. I was in the foyer, I guess. It was rather large and as I said, Madame was standing behind a lectern. A desk with stacks of paperwork was behind the lectern, with two kerosene lamps sitting but not lit up at this time. Above the desk was a picture of the city of New Orleans, lined with busy people and rain-soaked streets.

A beautiful young lady walked up to the lectern and gave Madame a kiss on the cheek. She was stunning, with dark hair in ringlets, about my height it seemed, big breasts, and an ordinary dress at this time. *Maybe it was late morning or early afternoon,* I thought.

She politely said, "Bonjour, Collette," and came over to give me a kiss too. We had become acquainted too, it seemed. Maybe even friends? It was relayed to me her name was Annabella Lefevre. She was Madame's daughter. *Wow,* I thought.

It was also relayed to me that Annabella and I had indeed become dear friends and that we even spent time together. I would go on errands with her and just spend time at the brothel talking with her in her room. We ended up sharing each other's "secrets," so to speak, of our mothers' choices and how we ended up the way we did. Well, who else was I going to be able to discuss such taboo subjects with anyway?

I realized Annabella and her mother had asked me to work at the brothel and I don't mean as a maid, housekeeper, or some other reputable occupation. I was stunned for a moment that this kind of information had been relayed to me, but then I relaxed and thought, *No, I am ready to know what I need to know when it is to be given to me.* This is what Calissa had been trying to tell me.

Calissa appeared and gave a half smile. She wanted me to know that "all is well" no matter what our lives had been throughout the centuries. We are here to learn and grow and ascend to better heights. We have all experienced the inevitable karmic recycling of many births. We humans need many births to make our atonements and become awakened so we can move on and ascend to the higher realms. I knew that, but I needed to have Calissa tell me anyway.

Because of my mother's illness and increased weakening condition, I would succumb to Madame's and Annabella's offer. I know that they were just concerned about my welfare and my mother's health. For I learned that Madame Mae and my mother were good friends.

My mother had never judged anyone for who they were, whether it pertained to being respectable or not. She was friendly and polite to everyone. Madame knew this about my mother, for I knew somehow that she was just the same. So the two of them were friends for many years. Madame had come to her aide when the prideful and prominent women of New Orleans had shunned my mother after my father's death. It was shortly after that my mother decided to work for Madame. As I said, she needed the money and she wanted a better life for me. It seemed the tables would turn and it would be my turn to be the one to do what I must to take care of my mother.

I felt uneasy being presented to the next phase of this lifetime gone and done for over a century. I needed to know, though—and so it would be done. I would find and would have the strength to get through it. I knew Calissa would help me. I knew Sister Moon and High Tide would also.

I was fading out again. I was pulled back into the galaxies of the Falling Mystical Veils. The crystal liquid projections were now a menagerie of pure pale mystical colors. Their hues would change from brilliantly glowing to a fading of almost absent color. They would taunt me, it seemed. But nevertheless, it was captivating and utterly fascinating. I could bask in this flight of time and light forever. "Please don't take me back. Please let me stay here and bask in this delight, at least for a little while longer," I said.

---❁---

Then I roused and woke up in my bed. Again, the curtains were swaying and flowing gently through the breeze. The sky was lit up as always by its constellations and by MoonGlow, herself, as she always does every night. I thought I had woken up again the same way as always, but now Charlie was back with myself and Sugars this time. *My sweet babies*, I thought. They were both perched up in the bed looking out the window. Did they see what I had seen? Did they go, too, where I had gone? They both lept up to the window ledge and just continued to gaze into the horizon. Oh, that beautiful horizon. "Yes, babies, I want to go back too," I told them.

It was Tuesday morning now. Nathan had called me after he sent a text asking if I were up and about. I swooned at the sound of his voice. Oh, that masculine voice of his. What kind of hold did this man have on me? What kind of spell was this? I was enamored, I was helpless. And I was loving it! Yes, I thought, I needed to focus on the here and now.

I put on some music and danced with the cats for a bit. Yeah, I was on cloud nine again. Thoughts of Nathan took precedence over everything else, it seemed.

I quickly showered, dressed, and decided to call my mother, Diane. I was missing her now that Caroline had left. I needed my mother and a talk with her. I had not seen her since four weeks ago when she had come over for a visit. I missed her.

She was delighted and cheerful. We had a lovely talk about Zach and about Caroline's visit. Of course, I did not mention our "evening travels," as I might call them, but she kept asking, "Is that all? Anything else the two of you did? Hmmm?" I suddenly felt that she knew something. Maybe in time, I would know. I did not tell her about Nathan yet, either. I wanted him to just be mine to daydream about and take delight in for right now.

"Do you miss him, Mom?"

"Yes, dear, you know I still do."

"Me too. A lot, it seems, since Matthew died. I think of Dad a lot more now than ever since I moved into this grand old house. He's here, you know? I can feel him."

"I have felt him too, Marisa, in your grand old house, as you call it."

I was surprised to hear my mother say this. She was a spiritual woman, but she clung only to what the Catholic church had believed, and would not say much about what my father and I believed beyond our Catholic upbringing. I always felt as though my father and I knew so much more than what we had been told and taught.

Zach gave me a call shortly after chatting with my mother. I had so much enjoyed my visit with him on the phone. He talked about how well he was doing with his studies, his involvement in extracurricular activities, and about a girl named Ashly with whom he had become smitten. How happy I was to hear that. I did not mention anything of Nathan to him though. For goodness' sake, it was way too early. I caught up with telling Zach how lovely MoonGlow and her surroundings looked and had progressed since he was just here a few weeks ago before heading back to school. I had been missing my son so much—*my baby son*, I thought. *No, no, he's a young man now. I know that and I'm a proud mother to have raised such an amazing man.*

Chapter 7

WHO AM I REALLY?

For all those who think you have no voice, then write it.

I grew up believing I did not have much of a voice, nor would people want to hear what I had to say. Part of the reason was because of my knowledge of the 'elsewhere' that my father had imparted to me. Along the way, things changed. I began to believe that I had much to say. We all have something to say, no matter who we are and no matter from where we come.

The written word is more powerful than anything verbal from the human mouth. The written word enables you to ponder deeply, to escape and fantasize, to hope and dare to dream beyond your wildest imagination. It's an escape, yes, but an escape that you want. It is an escape that will incite, elicit, and conjure up feelings, thoughts, and desires you never knew you had or even dreamed of until you put pen to paper and let your thoughts and imagination flow.

The written word is given to read over and over and to ponder and ponder again and again innumerable times. It is there, right there for you to do so. Yes, the written word tells you as it is whether it is truth or whether it is falsehood.

I had wondered in this lifetime who I am besides what I do. What makes me myself are all my faults, my shortcomings, my goodness, my charity, my selfishness. I had come to realize it is the ancient that makes me who I am. The ancientness of my soul, the wonderment and mystery of my soul, the experiences of all those soulful lives, of all those people I had been and am yet to be, of all those choices I had made and am yet to experience. Every life, every thought, every decision, every choice and every experience is a component of the beautiful tapestry of the making of a beautiful soul which we can eventually become. I am who I am, and also I am who I am to be. I am an enigma. How beautiful is that? Yet, every other soul is exactly that too.

Travel came to mind. How much have I really traveled? I have traveled much in this lifetime, but to imagine how much in other earthbound lives is unfathomable, I thought; and not to mention the dimensions, galaxies, and worlds beyond this merely lowly plane are beyond comprehensible in this human mind state of mine. Where all have I actually been? Who all have I met?

Present and past lives of travel and meeting people of different cultures, faiths, and values can weigh heavily when pondered upon. Even traveling in the present broadens one's mind and allows it to contemplate a bit and eventually say, "Hmmm? I guess maybe we're really all the same?" Every soul has its own journey, but every soul wants the same. We want to find our way…our way back home whence we came. Is that it?

And so I write, because it allows an escape, an adventure, a satiation of a desire inculcated in the deepest depths of my soul. I smile…and I feel both peace and excitement. I am at bliss.

I was a bit tired, so I decided to nap a while after lunch. The cats had agreed to join me, of course. As I drifted, I felt the vibrations of my soul's departure. I was taken to a garden of delight. It was consumed with mosaics of colorful flowers unseen in any garden in the earthly realm. Fields and fields of innumerable gardens could be seen. A man approached me with a kind smile. It was my father, Robert. We did not embrace. We did not need to. All what was needed was his kind smile, and in return, a smile from me.

He relayed to me, "We are different, my daughter. We are of a different kind. We belong elsewhere. I am at that place now. And when it is time for you to leave, you will be here too. You will never need to return again unless you wish. Your karmic births will be complete. You will understand this some day, my daughter."

"I'll be going home then after this, right Dad?"

I thought of the voice I had heard a couple of times now, "Return to me…it is written." Something told me that it was not from my father, though. I still needed to know.

My cell phone rang again. It was mid-afternoon now and I was back where I was supposed to be. It was Nathan who brought me back.

Excitedly, I answered and blurted out, "Hi handsome!" I felt foolish at first but he immediately replied, "Hi beautiful!" That eased me and made me feel—well, actually, beautiful! We discussed the time he would pick me up and take me to the end of summer festival in town. I was so much looking forward to our first official evening date.

As soon as we wound down our conversation, I quicky went back upstairs to look through my wardrobe, wondering, *What should a girl wear when she's got a date with Mr. Fine Specimen of a Man?*

Though I considered myself to be fashion-savvy, I was so nervous this time. I was a wreck. I wanted to look beautiful for Nathan. I wanted to look sexy, desirable, and irresistible, actually. Then the phone rang again. It was Caroline, my life saver.

"Oh boy, let me tell you, girlie, you need to sex it up!"

Caroline always knew what to say to calm me down. Or did she? "Sex it up" meant nervous work to me. It meant I needed a drink first to get relaxed. And so I did.

"Oh, thank you, dahhling. But remember, this is a festival where a lot of other people are going to be around. I can't be too sexed-up, as you say."

"Oh really? So you and Nathan do not plan to be together all alone and all by yourselves after this boring festival is over? You and Nathan are not going to be dancing under the sheets and having….'"

"Stop!" I started laughing. "Well, yeah, I guess. Oh, hell yes, Caroline, I want that so much, but you know I have to be somewhat presentable. It's our first date, dahhling!"

Caroline proceeded to instruct me, since she knew I needed her help. She would be the one to calm me down first by instructing me to have a drink. I would listen as she would suggest what to wear, how to have my makeup, and what to do with my hair. I allowed her to go on and on since I was indeed a nervous wreck. She was my godsend right now.

I do believe Caroline had ending up having me looking as though I had "sexed it up" to some degree. I had chosen a sundress with a white bodice top held up with skinny spaghetti straps. The skirt was just slightly full and above my knees, painted with black flowers and splotches of red and white. I had chose black flat sandals since we would be doing quite a bit of walking. Yes, Caroline most certainly did not approve of my choice in shoes, so I promised her the next time I dressed up I would wear the kind of heels that just might kill the man. Anyway, it is a festival and wearing heels would look ridiculous, right?

My makeup was flawless and I wore a not-so-bold lipstick called "the perfect pink." I took part of my top hair and pulled it back and up with a barrette, leaving a few strands on either side of my face. I wanted to leave my hair down for my fine specimen of a man.

I had taken a few pics and videos on the phone to show Caroline. Naturally I wanted my friend to see how well she had instructed me.

"Ohhh la la! You most certainly have sexed it up, missy, even though you have those frightful sandals on. Just kidding. They're cute…I guess." Caroline was proud and boasting, of course. I do have to give her some credit. She had done a fine job preparing me for the evening. I must say, yeah, I looked pretty hot.

Nathan drove up and naturally I watched him get out of the car. He looked like the natural perfect specimen that he was. He was wearing perfectly fitted dark blue pullover shirt and jeans. His hair was nicely combed back and he had the scruffy day- old beard that I had told him I really liked. Actually, I should have told him that I thought it was undeniably sexy as hell, but that would be later.

As he walked up the steps, I opened the door and noticed he had the most beautiful long-stemmed yellow flower in one hand.

"Hi, beautiful Marisa...wow." He shook his head as his eyes moved up and down, lusting at my body. I knew it was lust. I still remembered how it goes.

As he walked up to me, his other hand had been placed around my waist as he gave me a gentlemanly kiss. I think I told him hello too, but I was as always in my trance. That spell he would somehow put me under immediately was ever so present.

"You smell so good. Just as good as you look." Really, Marisa?

Nathan did not mind anything I said. I knew he enjoyed whatever came out of my mouth, even if I had had a couple of drinks already. I am definitely sticking to that.

"You know, you look really hot, if I can say that." I saw an unexpected shyness in his face and smile.

"You can tell me that anytime, mister. I know I do, cuz I sexed it up just for you."

"You have indeed, miss." He raised his eyebrows.

I felt a sudden blush coming on. Did I really say that to him?

"I mean, ah...well, it is our first date, so I just...well...." I stopped the gibberish enough so we could continue revealing physically rather than verbally how attracted we were to each other.

After giving my makeup and hair a checkup, we finally left my house. I had not had the time to show Nathan my lovely home, but that would come later.

We spent the later afternoon and early evening at the town festival. Fortunately, Nathan knew quite a number of people there. Since he was a real estate developer, he had come to know the people who owned businesses and held positions in the town.

We also ran into Stan and Paula. They seemed happily surprised to see me with Nathan. Stan had even pulled me aside at one point and stated, "You look happy, Marisa, and so does Nathan. By the way, have you been drinking a bit? I can tell, but you just keep up the happy side."

What? He said that to me? I only had a couple of drinks before Nathan had come over. Anyway, so what?

The evening went quickly. We had fun browsing, playing and teasing with each other, and taking a few bites and samples of the festival's displays. I loved the fact that I was with this amazing man. How did I ever get so lucky? Who would have known that I would end up here and meet someone like Nathan?

Crazy me, I thought. Of course, I would end up meeting Nathan. It was not luck. It was destiny. My MoonGlow led me here because it was indeed destined. I do believe the smile on my face never left me the entire time I was with Nathan this evening.

Nathan walked me to the door. I can't remember if he actually lifted me up while his arms wrapped tightly around my body, but I do remember a feeling of being afloat, of just hovering, of just being in suspension. I was just caught up in that moment…that moment of just "being." I was soaked, I was drenched, I was submerged in liquid love. *Liquid love? What is that?* I thought. All I considered for a moment was High Tide's liquid. I laughed.

"What's so funny?" Nathan asked.

"Oh I'm just silly. Silly in whatever it is I'm feeling with you, and I love it." *Wow*, I thought. *I actually said that.*

Nathan smiled. "I know what you mean. I feel the same. We're funny like that, you know?"

And what did he mean by that? That word came to mind again—"familiar." I do believe we both felt "familiar" at that moment.

After entering, or shall I say floating into the house, Nathan and I continued the embrace and the exchanging of a thousands kisses, it seemed. Though I knew the both of us wanted more to happen tonight, it seemed right that we were to wait. *Please no*, I thought. *Yet, that is destiny.*

"I…I want you so bad." He placed his hand on his forehead and wiped his face. "But I think I should go for now…just this time. Strange, isn't it?" He smiled his crooked smile.

"I know. I know it's strange, but yes, next time is all ours."

As he turned around to begin his descent down my front steps, he turned halfway around for a moment and looked at me, "Marisa, my dream has come true. Been waiting for a woman like you." With a pause, "Well, been waiting for you, woman."

No other words were exchanged. Just a mutual exchange of a smile was all that was needed right now. Little did he know, he had taken me aback and I gasped a soft sigh while the tears welled up in my eyes as he walked away and into his car. Somehow I knew this man. Somehow I knew that he knew me also.

I continued to watch through my window while his truck drove away until no more I could see of its existence. I spent some time just standing at my door thinking of what he had just said to me. Did I hear him right? Over and over, I would repeat what he had said: "Dream has come true…been waiting for you, woman." Finally, I succumbed, "Yes, he did say that."

Needless to say, I was on cloud nine. Actually, I was way so totally above that freakin' cloud nine. I was way up there dancing with the stars and having their stardust glisten me with their kisses.

Where were the cats? They didn't even show up to greet Nathan this time. They are certainly not shy. Maybe they knew. Maybe they knew something magical was happening. Something magical and mystical was being exchanged in the living room—so much so that even the cats knew they were not to share in this experience. Amazing, I thought.

Both Charlie and Sugars were perched together just sitting quietly and staring at me when I approached them in the bedroom. Yes, I knew then, they did know. "Let's get ready for bed, sweetie pies!" They broke their frozen stance and followed me into the bedroom. As I got ready for bed, I looked toward my open window with the softly flowing curtains swaying again, as they do every night and every morning.

Nathan sent me a text to say he was back at his condo. "Marisa, I meant what I said as I was leaving. You're the special woman I've been waiting for. Can't wait to see you again."

"Oh boy, I am so craaaaazy about you, my fine specimen…oh my, my." Of course I did not text that response, but I did let him know I felt that he was special too. I felt so blessed that Nathan had come into my life. Oh, how I wished now that he had spent the night with me.

I quickly gave Caroline a call. I had promised her that I would tell her everything just as a good girlfriend would do after a real first date. She was surprised that I was calling her tonight rather than in the morning. She was ecstatic to hear how everything went well, but she could not for the life of her understand why that all that "sex it up" did not lead to the two of us hopping into bed. That's my Caroline.

I looked back out the window and started my ritual of gazing and meditating. As I looked outside waiting to catch a glimpse of MoonGlow, I felt she had been trying to get my attention. I did want to apologize again for not partaking in our nightly ritual. I knew she understood though. I had needed this time with Nathan.

My Sister Moon understood because she, herself, is one who sought her lover, her companion. Now, my sister comes out and finds him every night. Every night, he is there for her to drench her with his "liquid love." Yes, High Tide has kept her company every night throughout the centuries. As she illumines the night for all, he guards her, keeps her, and provides for her the sweetest abode in his liquid love. For this, I thank you, High Tide.

There she was. My MoonGlow, my sister, was radiant as always. Her face was looking toward her High Tide, but she changed her position, and brightened her moonlight upon my face. She smiled and as always, she blew me a kiss. Yes, she understood that tonight I would not walk down to greet her and dance the dance which belonged to her…the ancient dance of wild, free-spirited gypsies and untamed lovers. She has taught me well.

I felt myself leaving again. Walking along the moonlit shore, the sand glistened from the wetness of the Great Liquid. Celestial songs of angelic beings filled the heavens above as I gazed and was mesmerized by what seemed to be falling stars. They began to disappear as they fell, but others would appear just as quickly. They were endless. They were innumerable. They were awe-striking.

PEBBLE WALK...

I was taken to another place. I was on a narrow path, a pebbled path. There were large mossy rocks on either side of the path. To the left and right were trees and flowers of various kinds and colors. Swirling in the wind was a menagerie of colors strewn about. They would appear and then disappear. There was a soft warm breeze and childlike laughter that could be heard now. I was around eight years of age. To the right of me was a young boy around the same age. We were laughing and frolicking along the path together, side by side. We were holding hands and glancing every now and then at the bright light we saw ahead of the path. The more we moved forward, the light would step back as if we were never going to get to it. At the same time, I thought we were pure, we were innocent. We were untainted and unknowing of any fetter, any sin. We were children, I thought. Why was that?

Suddenly it was relayed to me that the boy was Nathan. We stopped and Nathan turned to his right. He stepped out of the path and started to leave. He walked on toward some trees. I was quiet and still. I said nothing. I knew he needed to go. He had to go. There was something he needed to do.

And there she was. There was Calissa. "You are correct, Mother. You are correct about your duty to write. It is to be."

"Oh, my Calissa. How I love you and how I love seeing you." I couldn't take my eyes off her. I then realized I was not eight years old anymore. I was myself again.

Calissa smiled and continued on. "People do not know that each life is actually not separate from the next one, nor the past one. We also sometimes live several lives in a particular body. Our lives change all the time, but they are all connected. It is like picking up and moving on as you did after your husband transgressed onward." I thought I was puzzled for a moment about the word "transgressed" instead of saying "died," but then I understood.

Calissa continued, "Life is continuous in this universe. Every experience of each soul is just another phase and another change of evolving and becoming awakened. It is all about growing as a soul, maturing from infancy to maturity to pure love. Everything in this universe is all about love. Nothing more. But each soul chooses whether to love or not to love, but in order to advance upward, it must be completely consumed and drenched in love." Here I go again. I thought of Hi Tide when she mentioned "consumed and drenched." I had to laugh at myself for a moment.

She continued, "A soul may take many centuries and lifetimes until it is mature enough to choose only love. It is then a soul gains entrance into a heavenly realm where it was created to be with its Creator, the Universal Creator…Who is consumed and drenched in love, for He is Love Himself."

I thought, *Yes, you are right. A soul is to be so evolved as to know nothing but Love, nothing but Love. I am to become this way too. We are all to become pure love, eventually. That is why we are here.*

I slowly came to be again in my room and in my body, but as I was doing so, I heard the words again, "Return to me…it is written." I now knew. It was Nathan's voice. "We are familiar indeed," I said to myself. I am to return to him, as he is to return to me.

I sat up in bed and as usual, Charlie and Sugars were looking out the window, and I as usual, I too, replicated the scene of the pebble story I had just viewed. Oh my goodness, was I ever going to get it right? *It is so hard to love at times, is it not?* I thought. *Oh God, let me get this right.*

What the hell was that all about? I wondered, thinking of the pebble walk with Nathan. I then thought, "Oh yeah, maybe it was about the 'love' thing that Calissa was talking about. Innocence, maturity, then pure love. Yet, I knew those words of 'return to me," were real and came from Nathan. I dozed again for a while. I needed to rest after all this drama.

Chapter 8

MADAME AND THE PRETTY PINK HOUSE

"Smile pretty, my pretty baby"....Madame Mabelle

*I*t began as a strange morning for me, Charlie and Sugars. It was Wednesday now. I felt the cats felt the same as I did, since they continued to follow me around and wanted to rub up against me every chance that I would let them. Do they see what I see? Do they just sit perched and watch everything? Hmmm?

I pondered over the visit I had last night with Calissa. Everything made sense though. She would of course know more than I, for she was not of this world anymore, right? I was still here, stuck in this earthly realm because I was not all love yet. Oh well.

Then there's the pebble walk which was strange. I do believe that will be figured out eventually, maybe?

I received a call from Nathan, then somehow absolutely nothing else mattered anymore. There was absolutely nothing to ponder but Nathan, himself. My man….my fine specimen of a man, oh yeah, the one I am to return to because 'it is written'.

He was on the road on business today, so we would not be seeing each other tonight. Tonight I would spend time with my Sister, MoonGlow, and her lover, High Tide. I missed them and I missed the dance. I will miss Nathan, too, though.

"For heavens sake, Marisa, you hardly know him!," I was smiling to myself. But after last night are you kidding me? Of course, I'm crazy madly in love with him already. There was that 'familiarity' though and that feeling of love already, so soon, but loving it anyway. I was ready. I was ready for love again.

Nathan and I discussed the evening we had shared. Our discussions had been meaningful and we both felt we got to know each other quite a bit in just one evening. But more than anything else, the intimacy of just holding and touching each other that we shared was beyond the best. The rest can wait, "but not for too long." What a state of ectasy this fine specimen of a man had consumed me with. Yes, next time we meet, he will stay with me even if I have to tie him up. Hmm? That's a tempting idea.

I cleaned up a bit today and worked on the flowers in the garden and picked a few to put into Carolines favorite vase again. My phone rang. "Caroline?" Yes, it was she.

"Oh how I miss you, my perpetual friend! I miss you, I miss you…," I rambled like ninety miles an hour. She laughed and laughed and I loved it. I had always loved her loud, bellowing beautiful laugh.

"For goodness sake, we just spoke yesterday, but hey, I get it. I am definitely one whom people just love to talk to every day."

She was working an evening in the O.R. today, so we talked for almost an hour and caught up on everything. "Do you miss work? I mean real work like I do?" she said and laughed.

"Hell no! I got a man, remember? And a very fine specimen of one, might I add. Do you hate me?"

"Yes, of course I do!" Caroline continued to laugh, but she was genuinely happy for me. She was happy about my date with Nathan yesterday and more of those to come.

"You have got to be kidding though, Marisa! That man is gorgeous and you two haven't done the deed yet. What is wrong with you? He's Mr. Fine, right?"

She laughed as she kept teasing me about the fact Nathan and I had not slept together yet. "But, I have to say it's about time you've got yourself a man, though. You needed one!" she continued on.

I concurred with her. I did need a man, and it happened to be Nathan that I needed, and now he was here. Now he was mine. I knew he was mine, and I was his. Really, Marisa? "No, no," I said to myself, "I have known him forever. I know I have."

"Don't worry about me, Caroline. I'm actually ready for more now, especially with my fine specimen of a man."

We continued to chat for quite a while. Oh, how I missed her—I made her promise to come see me again soon.

The evening came quickly. I was quite the busy lady today. I was also quite the happy lady today, too. Love will do that, you know.

I grabbed my phone and my wine, kissed my babies, and walked down along the boardwalk excited about meeting up with my buddies. I was elated and high-spirited tonight. Hell, I was ready to dance, and to dance without ceasing. I missed my Caroline, but my Sister Moon would be there, naturally, in all her glory keeping watch over me, protecting me, and cheering for me too. Yes, she was always cheering for me, always wanting what was best and what was meant for me.

There she was. MoonGlow was shining her glowlight upon me once more. She was looking at me with eyes wide open, for usually she came looking downward toward her High Tide—but this time, it was I at whom she was looking. It seemed she was doing her best, more than usual, to comfort me. Why was his attention so much on me? She smiled and blew me a kiss. I reciprocated and blew her a kiss too.

I danced her gypsy dance and blew her several kisses more, flailing my arms and catching my hair as it blew in the ocean's wind, turning and twirling like a ballerina ready to take flight. Yes, I loved my MoonGlow and she loved me. I somehow knew she had come to me in every lifetime, in every age, for she loved me and she had always been my friend and my sentinel. There is something to be said for the ancient dance which she has taught me. For when one surrenders to her ancient dance, there comes an awakening, a knowing of the secrets of the universe and the secrets of past lives.

The mighty roars could be heard. I wondered for a moment if anyone else, whether on land or in water, could hear High Tide's highly clamorous and thunderous roars. His liquid projectiles flew and sprayed in various directions like sheets of brilliant crystals. His torrential rain continued for the longest time, it seemed. I stood drenched and spellbound for quite some time, just waiting for him to take me. What was keeping him?

My thoughts wandered. I looked up at the starlit sky and longed and hungered relentlessly, it seemed, to take flight into that space. Oh, that space I longed to go again for another delight of starlit tangled hair! Why was I thinking this? It seemed familiar, but yet maybe a flight that I did not quite remember, for I knew an earthbound soul would not always remember every flight, and certainly not in detail.

"Come summon your lover, my sis," I heard myself say to my Sister Moon. "Come summon him so he can take me into his recessed bowels and reveal the secrets and even sins of long ago that are keeping me bound in this karmic doom." I was somewhat taken aback at what I just said, and just as quickly, I continued. "My unrelenting longing beckons me to dance this ancient dance of wild winds and wild dreams of long-ago gypsies."

MoonGlow suddenly came forward and downward as if ready to touch this earthly plane. Her glowlight was magnificent and beguiling. Her flirtatiousness was reciprocated this time by High Tide. His liquid poured forth against me, drenching me again with his delight, pulling me forward again, holding me again as a lover and taking me into his deepest crevices. It was then I knew this would be a turning point in my travels with High Tide. I would learn of my secrets and my sins. I had asked for it, right? It was time. Somehow I knew it would be a long visit this time in timelessness.

1881 – FIFTH ENCOUNTER

I was back in the room with my mother. She was in bed again. She needed to take to bed more often now because of her weakness. As always, I thought *Poor Mother.* She was able to perform some of the work here in the room, but I was the one who had do the errands, deliveries, and such.

"My Collette, dear, come sit with me." I watched myself go sit beside her on the bed, and hold her hand. I do do know what words were exchanged, but I know we had a lovely conversation for a while, and then the expressions and ambiance became saddened. Our finances were dwindling and we were becoming near destitute.

I had just turned nineteen years old. Why did I not have a man in my life? The thought was strange, but it was relayed that I had seen and been with a young man for a few months. The time was unknown. I had become intimate with him, but of course my mother did not know just how involved I was. This young man disappeared in an accident, it was relayed to me. I guess I had been heartbroken. Nothing more was relayed. All I knew was that I dearly loved my mother more than anyone. I would do anything to help her and to take care of her. I guess I did just that.

Calissa appeared. I sighed deeply and smiled. I was so elated to see my precious daughter. She came over and kissed me on my left cheek, and gave me a long, loving hug, it seemed. I needed that. I needed to see my daughter.

"Mother, we dwell in time upon this earthly plane. Everything is timed, everything is planned, and everything has its place. This is how it is and comes to be. When you finally get to take flight out of this sphere, you will have no more worries of time. Someday, we will have our time together, but not now."

How beautiful those words were for me to hear. I felt myself crying and longing. I felt a longing for that "someday." Yes, it would come, but "not now." Oh, but the torment of just waiting, of just being, of just existing in this plane at times until we can finally let go, and go to the place where all is well!

Annabella and I had just finished doing some shopping, it seemed, as we walked back to the Pretty Pink House. Madame Mae was nowhere to be found when entering. It was mid-day, it seemed. The curtains were open and the parlor seemed cozy and inviting although rather huge and bold-looking at the same time. Old Victorian furniture filled the room. Colors of pink, red, and brown were vibrantly scattered. I saw two oversized portraits of women dressed rather seductively. They had rouged cheeks, bright red lipstick, and updo hairstyles with small dark blue hats topping their heads. Their dresses were quite low-cut, laced up and with breasts plumped high. *Yes, quite fitting*, I thought. *It is a brothel, you know.* It appeared that one of the portraits was Madame Mae and the other was her mother, but I did not know her name.

Annabella had gone to get some tea for us. We sat together on one of the ornate sofas and began to chat. I began crying. It was relayed to me that I had begun discussing my mother's poor health and our financial situation. Annabella was a dear as she wrapped her arm around me and handed me a handkerchief. She told me she understood and said with a strong southern accent, "I know my mother and I have already told you, but you are still welcome to come work for us. I know you said you have nothing against us or what we ladies are doing for a living, but I know you don't wish this life for yourself. You are a fine lady, Collette, and I know…." I looked at her with tears still flowing.

"Annabella, I think I do want to work here. I need to. I don't have a choice. It's for the money. I need the money for my mother and myself. I can do this. I do not condemn you and your mother, the other ladies, the…."

Annabella stopped me. "I know dear. I know. I also know that you and I are really not that different. We are akin somehow. I feel that."

"Akin?" I said. I knew, though, what she meant. She seemed "familiar" too. I wondered and pondered what all of this meant.

Everything seemed so different this time. I mean to say that the experience of knowing about this lifetime is somewhat different now. I feel like I will be experiencing more of myself in an almost reality-type world rather than messages being relayed to me as I am used to. It is strange, it is different, but it is inviting.

Madame Mae came dancing through the front door, it seemed. She was dressed as one of those fine ladies of New Orleans. This time, she was looking all prim and proper. She was all smiles and had bags of clothes that she was about to happily display. When she saw that I had been crying and saw both of our faces saddened, she immediately dropped the bags and came over to the sofa.

We happily scooted ourselves so she sat at the other end next to me. I told her the reason for my grief and that I was ready to come to work for her. Well, I guess I was ready. She quickly leaned over and wrapped both of her arms around me as if I were her child, her daughter. I thought she probably did that for all the ladies here, though. I was not for sure what all I said, for in this state of consciousness, words were relayed at times wholly and sometimes only in parts.

Madame Mae told me to tell my mother that I would be working more for her now. To keep from telling an outright lie, I would be helping her with some paperwork and "numbers," as she said, and that would require evenings since she and the ladies got most of their sleep in mornings. Anyway, that was the gist of it. The explanation would work out at least for a while, unless my mother actually knew better but remained silent, saying nothing. If so, I cringed at the thought that my mother suffered silently about her daughter's choice.

I needed to head on home after my talk with Annabella. I knew did not want to tell Mother what I had decided to do. I would in time, I thought, but not now or right away. My mother was going to be so disappointed in me when that time came, though, if she did not figure it out on her own. It would break her heart, but I was doing it for her. I was doing it to make sure she was cared for and for that, I would do what I must.

I had prepared dinner for my mother in the large kitchen downstairs where the residents of this boarding house were permitted to cook. My mother was up and about now, yet still weak.

I was at one end of the room, looking at the both of us sitting at the table. We were actually smiling and laughing at times. It was relayed that I had told my mother that Madame Mae had some extra work for me to do and that it would take up some evenings. I would be working separate from the goings-on downstairs and the rooms where the ladies took their own business. *Good grief!* I thought. All I knew was that I must have been working many hours, since my mending and laundry duties continued to go on.

I came to the Pretty Pink House early the next evening. The evening was only for Annabella to orient me and "instruct" me, as Madame would say. I was shown around the house. I must say it was clean and well-kept, and rather pretty and feminine. With all the various shades of pink and nicely kept tablecloths, doilies and such, the house was quite welcoming.

The back of the house had an atrium-type enclosure with various plants and flowers, and chairs. This area was enclosed by a ten-foot stone wall all around the back of the house. The customers were able to come out and smoke their cigars, chat, and well...whatever they did. I felt uncomfortable at the thought, but I must say, the house looked rather inviting and very classy, unexpectedly cheerful. I already knew that because of the elegant ambience, the clientele were men who were wealthy or at least above average financial worth. There were many who traveled and came from throughout Louisiana and out of state. They would come here for business dealings, and of course for the services of this pretty pink house.

Annabella would do no work tonight. She was my mentor at this time. I believe we talked and discussed for hours the "art of pleasing pretty," as she and her mother would say. I saw us laughing and giggling. She told me that she was relieved I was not a virgin. "My mother would never have permitted you to start here, my dear."

So it came to be that I learned the "art of pleasing pretty" until there were no questions left. I laughed to myself, for I knew some of this "pleasing" already.

I went on to learn the "art of smiling pretty," "art of looking pretty," and the "art of teasing pretty." I learned how to flirt, how to tease, and I must never forget how she taught me to make a man feel as if he were the only man there and the ONLY man who mattered.

I learned the "art of dressing pretty" like a "pretty pink lady" should. Yes, Madame Mae never used the term "lady of the night."

"We are the pretty pink ladies. We are distinguished from what some call a 'lady of the night.' We are classy, we are poised, we are polite, and we are the best at what we do."

Madame had walked in and asked if everything had been discussed. Annabella had gone over everything she would normally discuss, but her mother would continue after that. Everything seemed so cavalier in Madame's talk, so at ease and natural, and so exact, as if there were simply nothing wrong with what these ladies did and who they were. *Besides, this kind of work is old as the universe*, I thought. I smiled for thinking that. Madame had a way of putting me as ease and after a bit, I was actually smiling and asking questions. Ohhhh, the questions, of course. Yes, I had been with a man before, but not in this way. At that moment, I felt a delight I did not quite understand—but I would find out soon what would become of me in this house, The Pretty Pink House.

Madame then started the discussion on the "art of pretty manners." Because I had been to boarding school and had learned all about manners, dress, and poise, along with conversing and being presentable at socials, there was not much to teach in those areas. I did feel as though I needed to learn a thing or two more about the "art of pleasing pretty," though. I knew Madame Mae had the experience and maybe she could add something that Annabella had not shared.

I was also instructed that in order to work for Madame, I must promise by verbal contract that I would devote myself to complete discretion. I was not to leave this house with any talk of her business. The particulars of that were discussed in much detail.

Annabella pulled out a dress of dark-blue satin. The dress was held by thick spaghetti-type straps which were, of course, a "pretty pink." All the ladies were required to wear pink in their dress. The bodice was naturally tight fitting and a little smaller than a woman's natural size, to accentuate her waistline and push up the breasts. The skirt was a little full with scattered lace and ruffles. *Very sexy*, I thought. She wanted me to try it on and give it a try.

Afterward, she curled my long hair and started pinning up some strands to the top of my head. Ringlets dangled along and beneath my jawline, and long bouncy curls hung over the back of my shoulders. As she helped me don the hosiery and lace up my black shoes, I knew I could hardly wait to take a look at myself. But before she would let me go to the mirror, she explained a few things about the makeup. She applied a very pale facial powder and dabbed some rouge over my cheeks.

She said the lights in the parlor were different at night. Madame uses sheer material draped lightly hanging over the lanterns to dim the room and give it a most sensual and inviting color of pink and rouge. "You will see. It's quite nice and the men love it." She winked and smiled. "At times, we use some drops that Doc Charles gives us to make the pupils looks bigger. It accentuates the eyes, the sensuality, you know what I am talking about, right? The men love large eyes and pupils. Mother and I do not think you need to do so. You have big beautiful blue eyes and with those long eyelashes, you don't need much of anything else." I was relieved.

Annabella took my hand and up I stood. She walked me over to the mirror. I was startled. "Is that me?"

Annabella giggled. "It surely is, sweetie, and you are a beauty! Madame will be proud."

I noticed she called her mother "Madame" when not talking to her directly. I have to say I was very pleased too. Yes, I looked like a lady of the night. I mean a "pretty pink lady," but it made me feel very sensual, very womanly, very seductive. *I got this*, I thought. A part of me did feel some shame, but yet a part of me felt powerful. Why was that?

I had said a prayer to myself and it was relayed to me. "Forgive me, Lord, Your mercy is bigger than I am. How do you see me? I am a sinner, indeed. I promise to one day get better, leave this life for another, and make my atonements. For now, I am doing this for my mother and myself too. Amen."

Madame Mae walked in. She took a step back and gasped, "My, my—you are a pretty one. You are going to make us a lot of money!"

I felt ashamed for a moment, and I do believe Madame knew this. She quickly came over and took both of my hands and led me to a chair. "Look sweetie, I know the reason you are choosing to do this, but then again, it is a business. Believe me when I say this. You are stunning. You are going to attract the attractive ones and not the homely ones. Yes, all my clientele have money because that's the way we roll here. I have built up a classy and elegant business here. That's why I call my ladies the 'dames jolie rose' (aka pretty pink ladies), because they are pretty, and they are the best at what they do here.

"Listen, you do not need to feel ashamed or embarrassed with me or anyone else here, and certainly not with the clientele. Remember, you are doing this for your mother and for yourself to survive. Let me tell you something—I bet that in no more than a year, you will be leaving because you will find a nice reputable man who is going to want to take you away and marry you. The very pretty ones don't stay here long. You just watch and remember what Madame Mae told you. In the meantime, let's make some money so you can take care of your mother, shall we?"

I looked over at Annabella to see her expression. She was quite stunning herself. I hoped she did not feel any jealousy or resentment toward me. She was beautiful, even more so than the others. She was still young, though, at nineteen, like myself. Her time would come too of finding a man to marry. I noticed her smiling at me. It was a loving smile, a sisterly smile.

Madame Mae asked if everything had been covered, and if I felt tomorrow would be a good time to start. I said that it would. She then proceeded to give me more of her own instructions, going over some of what Annabella had discussed and some inclusions of her own.

Back in the beginning when Madame had asked me if I would consider working for her, I had told her I had been only with one man, and that it had been a real relationship, so she knew I had been with a man in a good way. She would never have hired me if I had been a virgin. I believe Madame would never have felt good about doing so. She was very kind, as I knew she would be. She said I would be treated with utmost concern and kept under her watchful eye for as long as I needed her to do so. She would not let any harm come to me. She wanted to make certain that all matters that I felt uneasy with or unsure of would be brought up with her without any hesitation. Madame was like that. She was good to her ladies. She had her expectations for us and would not hesitate to tell us what they were, but she was fair, she was kind, and she was motherly. Every one of her pretty pink ladies loved her.

After I got undressed and wiped the makeup off, Madame walked me to the door. "Remember, Collette, it is very important and necessary that we do not discuss our occupation with anyone. We dress like all the other fine ladies when we leave this pink house. We conduct ourselves like ladies of the day." She rolled her eyes as she said this.

We both giggled a bit. "Stay loyal to me and I will stay loyal to you. You already know that I know your mother and she is a good woman. Stay honest, trustworthy, and loyal to me and I will take care of you and your mother for as long as you want."

I started to get teary-eyed. She kissed me on the cheek and sent me on my way.

What a beautiful, kind woman, I thought. As it turned out, she was exactly that.

I had gone home for the night. Mother was already in bed. She had been reading when I entered the room. "So what happened this evening?" she was eager to know.

I did not hear what all was said between the two of us, but I guess I lied about some stuff. I know I could not have discussed the instructions I was given, and certainly not about the dressing up part. *My goodness gracious! I am a real mess*, I thought. Anxiety and sadness fell over me. How in the world did I get this way and decide to do what I did? This was another lifetime. This was my past. This was all a part of me, of my soul, of my karma.

I woke up the next morning with a slight bit of anxiousness I could gather while viewing myself. I went about my usual business, preparing breakfast for my mother and myself. I then spent time helping my mother with the mending and such before leaving in mid-afternoon with the deliveries. I had told my mother that I would not be back until late because I was going to start my business work at the house. She smiled rather reluctantly and suspiciously, I thought. We kissed each other on the cheek and I then went on my way.

I was thinking about how much I had been presented with in this encounter so far. How true it was that it did not matter what all was presented, for there was no time, no matter or concern for time in this realm...this realm of the past and of the ancient.

Just as I walked out the door of my mother's room, I was suddenly standing across the street from Madame's. It was midday when I arrived at The Pretty Pink House. It was relayed to me that the year was 1881. It was mid-July and it was a hot, sultry day in New Orleans. I gazed at the dark pink house and thought how grand it looked.

How beautiful it looks from the outside indeed was my sentiment. Although the décor inside was quite nice, knowing of what occurred inside this house when twilight began ran rancid in my mind for a moment. The sins of sinners, the lusts of those who lusted, the labors of those who labored in this beguiling and deceiving form of labor and pleasure were worth pondering. How peculiar, I thought at this moment, that such a life was unbeknownst and unthinkable to those who did not partake and indulge in this world of sensual gratification. Little did those people know the reasoning of what led anyone to succumb to this. "Oh how blessed they are," I could hear myself say. If they only knew of our desperation, our sadness and our needs.

This would be my first day, my very first day of being a "pretty pink lady." I would never be able to turn back the time now in this karmic web I had chosen and that I had entered. *I will seal my fate*, I thought, *for whatever may lie ahead.* Not only was it my fate in this lifetime that I was viewing, but all the others ahead of this time and at the present time that I was a part of now.

I struggled to open the 8-foot wrought-iron gate, and then struggled to close it. I saw myself laughing a bit I do believe that I was thinking it felt like I was entering a convent! I had to laugh at that. Well, at least it eased the anxiety for now.

I walked up the pretty path to the front door. I still thought, *What a beautiful house! Keep thinking that, Collette.* I opened the door and found Madame Mae sitting at the desk doing some paperwork. She was fanning herself due to the July heat. I felt a warmth of love at that moment. Why? Because I knew Madame Mae was a good woman. She was a good woman inside, but sometimes life leads you to appear that you are not good.

She looked over at me and smiled, "Well, my pretty pink lady, Amelia, are you ready for more instructions?" I was puzzled. Amelia? Had she forgotten my name? I placed the basket of clothes on a small sofa next to the desk.

Madame walked over to me, kissed my cheek, gave me a quick embrace and proceeded to explain, "My pretty pink ladies are given names other than their birthnames. You are to be presented as Mademoiselle Amelia. I do not in any way want my pretty pink darlings to be known to anyone by their real names. It it for their own good and for their safety. My clientele are prominent, respectable, and wealthy men, but we do not want them to cavalierly, I should say, discussing their escapades concerning any one of my pretty pink ladies."

She continued, "My ladies come from various places, some even from France. They are beautiful, well-mannered, and polished, and that is because I see to it that they are. I have a friend in town who instructs them and polishes if they need to be polished.

"Because my ladies are the best at what we provide, these men will definitely want to discuss such matters with their peers. They are rather braggarts because of their wealth and position. Also, the reason why my business does so very well is because they do brag about their rendezvous with such beautiful ladies as I have here. So it's not all so bad that they are the way they are. Men will be men. You understand me, my dear sweet Mademoiselle Amelia, am I right?"

I quickly answered, "Yes Madame, of course, I completely understand. It makes perfect sense." Smiles and nodding of heads were exchanged. She also told me that because my mother had raised me so well and had sent me off to a fine school, I did not need any "polishing." That made me feel somewhat special. I considered it was amazing how well Madame Mae had done for herself even if it was… well, unacceptable to those living in the other world with their haughty grandeurs of snobbishness and misconceived respectability. *Oh, those fine upstanding ladies of New Orleans. Bitches,* I thought.

Madame continued to tell me that contracts were signed by every gentleman who was a patron of The Pink House. Even those who are guests were to sign an affidavit stating a declaration of discretion.

"A contract?" I was somewhat surprised but impressed just the same. Madame stated, "This is how I am and how I do my business." As she had said, she definitely took care of her pretty pink ladies. She also said in the contract she demanded that all patrons were to respect the ladies, be polite, never harm, and never to display outright lewd gestures, especially on or toward the ladies while visiting in the parlor, but what they did behind closed doors and on trips, well, that was their business as long as it was agreeable to the pretty pink lady and the client.

I was impressed. Who ever knew? She continued to list all the other expectations and I continued to be amazed. *I can do this,* I thought. Well, she made it seem like a piece of cake—for now, anyway.

Madame proceeded to show me the rest of the house in its entirety. Because it was July, the windows were open. From the foyer was the parlor to the left, which had been shown to me. To the right of the foyer was the dining area, which Madame made into a room for those men with appointments and those who had been invited by the others, and at times by Madame herself. The room had tables against two of the walls where the spread of food was displayed, which included various meats, bouchee, and hors d'oeuvres, not to mention all the drinks readily available for her patrons. Multiple chairs and small sofas filled the rest of the room. Large paintings of fine artwork, composed of landscapes and townships, smothered the walls, though they did not prevent the room from looking large and grand. It was very masculine in décor and a sharp contrast to the parlor.

"I prefer the parlor," I unexpectedly said to Madame.

She looked at me with a smile, "So do I, my dear. That is why this room is only for the men, only for the men."

After leaving the dining room, we walked through the foyer, past through the large parlor, and proceeded to head down a long hall which contained the staircase. I thought the reason for these spacious rooms with their large windows and high ceilings, and then having a center large hallway was to help with the ventilation during these many long months of summer weather.

Before going upstairs, Madame pointed to two rooms which were past the front parlor, and stated that these particular rooms were parlors also. "The second and third parlors are to congregate when things get a little busier and the merriment of our patrons get a little overwhelming in the front. They are a bit smaller than the front parlor. It gives our other customers who are a little more subdued and shy a chance to think a little more, if you know what I mean."

I had no idea what she meant, but I was sure I would at a later time. While walking up the staircase, what I was shown upstairs was very vague, like in a mist, a gray mist throughout, so I do not remember much. I know there was a large sitting area at the top of the stairs where there were several ladies sitting and chatting. Some were in their bedrooms, resting or sleeping, I assumed. They were just bedrooms, naturally, many of them.

Madame did not work this house 24/7. She had her ladies work as much or little as they wanted, but she did set the hours from five o'clock p.m. through 1 o'clock a.m. as far as having the place open downstairs for her clientele. I sensed that some of the ladies actually lived here, while others lived elsewhere nearby.

There were "other rooms upstairs for my clientele who desire to entertain any of my pretty pink ladies a little longer. Of course, they pay more for that and for that reason, the ladies and I both are well obliged, if you know what I mean." Madame bent her head and slightly raised her eyebrows with a little half grin. "It's a business, you know, and a business demands money."

My, my, this was such a huge house, I thought, *and so many things going on.* I actually laughed to myself. I believed it was relayed to me that I was not to be shown too much or know too much about the upstairs at this time. Madame and my MoonGlow were such sweet ladies.

After walking back downstairs, we walked into the kitchen, located to the right after passing through the front dining area. It was quite large, as were the rest of the rooms downstairs. I was introduced to Miss Nellie, a middle-aged black woman who had a large welcoming smile and a greeting anyone would be delighted to accept.

She politely nodded her head and said, "Welcome, Mademoiselle Amelia," after Madame had introduced me. She was such a pleasant lady. Alongside her was another black lady helping out with the cooking and getting things ready for the evening. Her name was Miss Ella. She did not speak, but looked shyly with a slight smile.

Madame and I sat in the parlor on one of the small sofas as she proceeded to tell me a few other notable instructions. The most notable was one she explicitly suggested, "Never, ever look any of them in the eye." Really?

She explained by saying, "At least if you see or consider a man good-looking or desirable, that is. You, my dear, will probably have the good-looking ones. Let me tell you, it will mess you up, I promise. If you find one of these men attractive and think you have a chance that he will fall in love with you, or that he will want to marry and have babies with you, the chances of that happening are next to nothing if they are already married. A few of my pink ladies along the way have been whisked away off to happily ever after, or they thought so."

I think because I had looked at her with my bewildered wide blue eyes, she sighed and continued, "Well, I do have to tell you a few of my pink ladies get their little hearts so broken by looking at these good-looking successful men in the eyes. I would hate myself if that happened to you, but on the other hand…." She hesitated. "You are very beautiful, Collette. Because of your beauty and potential prospects for yourself and, well, for me and my establishment, of course, I know someone will want to whisk you away. I already told you that it will be just a matter of time, probably less than a year. I just hope you choose someone who is available, meaning not married, and someone who is very kind and will end up treating you well. Actually, I hope it is for love. Just think about that please, if you will, my sweetie."

I thought for a moment and asked, "How do I avoid looking someone in the eyes?" Madame laughed and then we both had a good laugh together. She proceeded to teach me how to do just that. It actually came easy. I did know for sure that I would be definitely using this trick (no pun intended) tonight.

My first night! I was getting anxious. Was I really going to be able to do this? Of course, I have already done this. I was standing here watching this past life of mine as it unfolded before me.

I went up to see Annabella. I was so happy to see her. I could feel that she had become like a sister to me, as I had to her. We embraced for the longest time. I was nervous and she knew it.

"I know it is cliché, but the first time is always the hardest. We will get dressed after supper. Then I am going tell you a secret!" She called it "supper." I smiled. Sounded so southern.

We both laughed and scurried on downstairs into the kitchen along with some of the other ladies. I remembered I took delight in being with these ladies. They seemed natural. They were smiling and chatting with their sweet southern drawls ever so politely. How I loved them already. If I had not known, I would have never thought of the services they were providing when evening fell. Well, my feelings for Madame Mae grew even more. At least she hired the best "crème de la crème," she would say. Maybe everything was going to be okay, at least for a while.

Annabella went back to her room after we had our supper. We chatted for a bit and when I mentioned how friendly and polite the ladies were, she laughed. "Yes, I agree surely they are quite friendly. We're like sisters here, but we do have quarrels and such every now and then. But when Madame knows about it—it's not pretty, if you know what I mean." She sounded like her mother now. "As for the ladies being polite, well, Collette, I mean Mademoiselle Amelia, you will soon be part of our conversations which are not so ladylike. I mean concerning the men and kind of helping each other out in certain ways by discussing certain things and such. Do you know what I'm talking about?"

I blushed a little, I believe, and said, "Yes, I believe I do" and smiled along with her.

It was beginning to become evening. I remember Madame said our work started at 5 o'clock. We proceeded to get dressed. Our makeup was applied first and our hair was skillfully arranged around our faces. We helped each other with our corsets and bustiers. I could not imagine how these women wore these in that time. Even in my present time, I know women wore such things, but only to dress up for an intimate rendezvous with a man, and then only to be taken off quite quickly of course. Men are like that, I was thinking. A woman spends all this time dressing up the part that they want you to, but just as soon as they look at you and start drooling, they are ready to quickly have you take it off. Oh well.

The hosiery went on and was held by garters. We slipped into our lace-up shoes and one after the other looked into the faded narrow mirror which lay against the wall. I knew I had thought at that time how beautiful Annabella was with her long dark hair, huge dark eyes, and very large breasts. Then it was my turn.

I looked at myself in the mirror and realized just how beautiful I was also. I realized just how sensual and accentuated my looks were after just a few minutes of dousing our faces, fitting, pulling, pushing, and tugging our garments and body parts. Then voilà, what a metamorphosis! Yes, we may be dressed to go to work pleasing men in a most taboo way, but somehow I felt strong, confident, and empowered.

Annabella exclaimed, "Oh my, oh my, you are a beauty, Mademoiselle Amelia!"

I smiled. She smiled. Suddenly, I felt faint. I stepped back and was looking at a chair nearby. "Here here, sit down," Annabella told me. "Okay, let me tell you the secret. Well, it's really not a secret, sweetie. We all know about it, even Madame Mae. It's whiskey!" I had to laugh as soon as she said that. Her big beautiful dark eyes had widened even bigger and her smile could have had any man clamoring for her attention. And she thought I was a beauty? I wondered if she even knew of her own beauty and how she could turn the heads of many men. Then I wondered why I had thought that. Did I already know this?

"What do you ever mean, Annabella? I mean, Mademoiselle Camila?" I knew this was her "pretty pink lady name" as Madame Mae would say.

"I mean that the ladies are permitted to have a drink of some whiskey before we start the proceedings for the night if you wish. It helps you to relax and focus. It makes you feel good. It especially helps the new ladies or the ones who are really new like you, my sweetie. You will see. I promise you will do fine and do well. Madame will guide you too along your proceedings tonight. She will fill you in some more on how to proceed." She held my hand while she explained about the whiskey and "proceedings." I thought that was a somewhat strange word to use, but—well, okay.

We scurried down to the parlor along with the other pretty pink ladies. My, my, how beautiful everyone looked. There were about fourteen of us at the time. Madame had said before that the number of ladies per night varies…some more on 'busy' nights, and I am guessing on weekends?

Yes, indeed, Madame's ladies were quite beautiful and yes, indeed, they must be "the best," as she said. There were brunettes, blondes, and redheads; those with light pale skin, those with olive complexions, those with colors of mixed race such as the Creoles; those who very petite and those of stature; those who were very buxom and those of normal size. All were well poised, smiling, and polite, yet very seductive and sensual in their appearance. Why did women get a bad reputation from being this way again? Oh yeah, they gave their bodies for money. That's right. And I was about to become one of those women. Oh well.

Madame Mae suddenly appeared as she waved her hand. "Bonjour, my pretty pink ladies. My, you all look very beautiful and just the way I like you to be. The men are going to love you, indeed." She started walking over to all the ladies to pin a pink paper flower to either a side of their bustier, shoulder strap, or waistline. Whatever was fitting or maybe more appealing did she do in this manner.

Mademoiselle Camilla (Annabella) whispered to me, "This is what she says to us every evening upon arriving. Although, if she sees a pink lady who is not looking her best, she will ever so politely say something different but as she pulls her aside." She smiled and winked.

Lastly, Madame Mae walked over to me with a loving smile, pinned a pink paper flower on my right pink shoulder strap, and lightly put her arm around my mine. She led me to the second parlor and sat down with me on the sofa.

I was nervous. My stomach began to flutter and again I started to feel faint. "I trust Mademoiselle Camila told you about the whiskey?" I nodded yes. "Well, it will do you much good." She had already poured a glass to share with me. I struggled to swallow the first sip and then as I gave a cough, she lightly chuckled, "You'll get used to it. Just one more sip and that will be enough. This medicinal dose is always good in the beginning, my dear." She then started talking softly, but the words were not comprehensible to me at this time. All I felt was that she was behaving in a motherly way toward me. How consoling that was to me. I was comforted by knowing that Madame had been a good motherly figure to me and to all the girls, ever kind and caring. She took good care of us like a true mother would.

"Now, I must tell you about the smiling again. You must always have a smile on your face. It is ever quite pleasing to our clientele, and if you must know, they get nervous too, sweetie. Yes, they actually do."

Well, I guess maybe they do, I was thinking. I am sure even if most of them are well-to-do with fine educations and lucrative businesses, they must have insecurities, of course.

Madame, proudly relayed these words to me. "You see, my dear Mademoiselle Amelia, you are most beautiful, and so are the others of my flock. Men can be somewhat insecure in the presence of such beauty." She lightly pressed over her updo and ringlets as she said this, for she, too, was quite the beauty herself. I would learn later how she still had her own "encounters," and with a grin that I could feel for a moment on my face, I took a little delight in knowing this.

She took hold of my hand gently and led me to the front parlor. The lanterns were dimly lit now and covered with light see-through wraps that gave the room such pretty shades of various pink hues. I felt the ambiance of the room which projected a most romantic and inviting milieu for what was yet to come.

Madame Mae smiled at me. I looked at some of the other ladies. Some were quite at ease, smiling, laughing softly, and operating as skillful experts of the trade. Ever so lofty in their style and manners, they seemed secure and even proud of their womanly charms and the magical effects that they were soon to cast upon their prey. *Who really has the power?* I was thinking. *Somehow, I feel it is the woman. The woman really has the power. I shall dwell on all I am viewing and seeing at a later time,* I thought. *What an amazing scenario I am about to view, what a ride!*

Now for just a few of us there, we ladies were a bit coy and stood around in our awkward stance attempting to be seductive, skilled, and carefree like the others. Of course, we had our smiles on. Yes, we did learn this was something that Madame made perfectly clear that we should always do. "And the rest will come naturally, my sweeties," she would say while holding up her delicate hands and having her fingers flow ever so gently and lightly up above her. In time, I would realize that I always loved seeing her do this, and I would come to do this quite frequently too with the clientele. For as I learned my way to discuss matters in a coquettish fashion to these highly sophisticated men, I would learn just how Madame's Pretty Pink House earned the reputation of having the most beautiful and delightful ladies all across the southern states.

The whiskey had served its purpose. I was becoming a little more at ease. There were several clients in the front parlor now, parading around their worth. It seemed surprisingly odd that they were vying for us, as if we were the prize, and they wanted us most eagerly. This made me feel more at ease even more.

I noticed Madame stayed in the front parlor for a while this evening since I and another lady there were "new," and she felt accountable and wanted to hover over us as a good mother would. I smiled over at her and she politely excused herself from a conversation and walked over to softly say, "Remember, Mademoiselle Amelia, continue to smile pretty, my pretty baby, and win a prize for Madame tonight."

I remember I felt startled, but the whiskey continued to ease and keep me at ease. On the other hand, it gave me the prodding that I needed to start that coquettish fashion that was expected of me. I felt beautiful tonight. I felt as if I wanted to conquer and that I was capable of doing just that. Like a lion sees his prey, I was a lioness seeking my prey now. I thought of my sickly mother. I thought of fine ladies of New Orleans. I thought of how people would look down on us, shun us, ostracize us.

Then I glanced at a mirror hanging by the wall before entering the foyer and saw a most beautiful, voluptuous, and seductive lady. It was me! I was she! I proudly lifted my head further up and with a slight push I touched my breasts and gave them a slight upward push too.

As I turned around, a rather nice-looking gentleman of about forty years of age stood smiling and politely said while slightly bowing, "Good evening, most pretty lady. May I have the pleasure of speaking with you?"

I shyly continued my smile and said, "My, of course, sir, you may indeed."

Our conversation went on with smiles and flirtatious gestures that I could see. He would place his arm around my waist and bring me closer to his body. I saw that I was reciprocating. He was rather nice-looking, as I said. I felt my womanly body getting aroused. He stared at my breasts, but yet in a shy and respectful way, I thought. He seemed so sweet, I thought. He was pleased with me. He wanted me and that made me feel good. It made me feel good that I was wanted. The only problem was that I looked him in the eyes! *Damn*, I thought. *Oh well, I will learn.*

The conversations in the room became mumbled and no other information would be relayed to me. All I knew was that I made it through the evening. It was late when I saw myself in the foyer with Madame and a few of the other ladies. We were chatting and winding down for the night. I and the other ladies had finished our business for the night. I somehow knew there were other ladies who would stay the night with their clientele. We were all safe, though. I knew it was safe here.

A large black man came walking from the dining area. "Miz Mad' Mae, I wil hep the ladez hom." His name was Big Sam. He had a wide smile as Miss Nellie did, but with a speech impediment and probably limited education. Big Sam was about 6 feet 4 inches tall. His stature was big and solid. Madame had hired him several years back as her helping man around the house, as well as for the protection of the ladies here. He stayed at the house in a room off the kitchen. This was his home.

He would take me and another lady, Isabel, home for the night. He would do this for Madame every night for the ladies who did not either stay here for an overnight with a client or did not live here.

I saw Big Sam come around the front of the Pink House with his carriage, and off we went. I was the first one to be dropped off at the boarding house. I politely thanked him and he replied, "Yez, Miz Colla." He never could pronounce my name correctly, but none of that mattered. He was a kind and good man. He knew of course what kind of business Madame was in, but I do not think a man such as Big Sam would even judge or think wrongly of any one of us ladies. All I knew was that he was protective of us and that he treated us kindly, as the ladies treated him the same.

As I was about to enter my mother's bedroom, the goings-on of this night went through my mind. It was relayed to me that I was saying, "All it takes is a beautiful fake smile to hide an injured soul, and they will never notice how broken you really are." How sad. Was this quote in reference to my mother or about the business in the Pretty Pink House? Either one could apply.

My present self said, "Saltwater cures all wounds. Am I right, High Tide?" I felt saddened. "Oh where are you High Tide? I need you now to soak in your healing waters. The Great Liquid that you are, I need to be cleansed and cured." The waters ever ancient, used for us to heal our wounds, were sleeping now.

But I am afraid of his ocean waters, I remembered. *Why is that again?* I still did not know at this time, nor in my present time. *Why am so afraid? Why can I not bathe and swim in the depths of his delights? Someday I will know, but not at this time.*

I felt myself being pulled further and further. I knew it was time to go. It was time to go back to that place of my present lifetime's sentence. That place of one of those karmic realms called Earth, where I was to reside once more in its everyday life of time, as we call it. I was going back to the ticks and tocks of minutes, of hours, of days and years. Time flits by so quickly in one lifetime. Time holds no captives indefinitely. It releases us eventually, each and every one us at some moment whenever it chooses to do so. Yet, what does it do again? It takes us back, all the way back here again in this earthly realm only to have each of us doomed to watch this selfish beast called Time hold us captive once more.

All unknowing of exactly what will be came racing through my measly human consciousness, as I went back to that place of measures and methods, of planned and unplanned sequences of durations and events. I heard myself say, "What will become of you now, Marisa? Who shall you be from this moment on? What will your life possess now, and what will your gypsy soul conjure you to become? For you know, your spirit is wild and untamed…as it should be."

Chapter 9

NATHAN, IS THAT YOU?

I have loved you past many many moons.

I woke up in bed and with slight blurred vision looked over at the clock. It was seven o'clock, and it was Thursday morning. I looked over at Charlie and Sugars who had woken up too and were lying there staring out the window.

As always, the curtains were swaying, the ocean waves were lightly swishing as the seagulls were starting their breakfast. The window that was nearly open all the way began to show a moist mist, and various colors like a rainbow hurled across its entirety.

I sat there staring and thought of the rainbow of promises that never sprouted or were never kept in my lifetime, or maybe even in the past lifetime that I was having the honor of experiencing. Yes, I considered it an honor, indeed. How many souls can experience such? Maybe it was not what I wanted to see and wanted to know of myself, but I did ask for it to be revealed to me. Yes, I wanted this and so it shall be.

The three of us scurried downstairs all together as I thought how Caroline would enjoy this moment. I wondered for a moment if Charlie missed her. He always seemed so attached to her.

I received a call from my mother. She wanted to talk again. After our talk on Tuesday, she said she had been thinking and reminiscing about my father even more. It had been ten years since my father had passed away. She was still living in her house. She never complained much about being alone, though. She was very involved in her church and volunteer work, and she also had a sister and her family living in town.

"Mom, I want you to know that while I took a nap on Tuesday afternoon, the day when we talked, I dreamed of Dad." I proceeded to explain further. I do believe it made her feel better.

"I do believe in that stuff, you know. I always have. It's just the church's teachings...." She stopped.

"I know, Mom. Thank you for telling me this." She knew that Dad and I were of the same kind.

I had decided to tell her about Nathan. She sounded sincerely ecstatic for me. I knew she had felt uneasy about my living alone. She seemed relieved that I had a guy around now. Well, he was not really around a lot at the moment because of his business and needed to travel. Oh well, I told her that Nathan would be calling today and that we would be getting together. I almost did not want to end our call. I was truly missing her and promised her that I would come to see her soon.

The cats and I spent time having our breakfast together. I noticed for a moment that there was a slight temperature change when the wind blew in through the kitchen. It felt good, and then I thought of the autumn. It would soon be coming—and oh, how I loved that colorful season. Autumn was my favorite time of year.

My cell phone rang and caused me to come back to reality. I quickly ran over to see who it was, and yes, indeed, it was my Mr. Fine Specimen! I quickly answered and there it was, the most manly voice on the planet. It was voice that made me swoon and melt in sweet delights.

"Hey, Beautiful—wow, have I missed you! I wanna see you so bad today. Are you up for it?" He laughed, as if he knew my answer already.

I thought for a moment before I answered, but I said it anyway. "The question is, mister, are YOU up for it?" I felt myself blush while giving a quick girlish laugh back at him.

"Well, missy, my beautiful Marisa. Yes, I am definitely UP for you anytime." I could feel myself blush even more and could feel his body close to mine. It was as though I was having a conscious out-of-body and that he was also along with me. Oh how "familiar" it seemed. Oh, how enticing that fine specimen of a man was! He told me he was going to stay in town all weekend and that he wanted to see me "more than once" if he could. Are you kidding me? Well, hell yeah!

"Helllooo, handsome. You can see me a whole lot more than once. You can see me as much as you want. And get as much as you want." Did I really say that, Marisa?

"Well, pretty lady, that sounds really good. I'll take that as a definite yes."

I wanted him to come over to my house, to my beautiful MoonGlow. Hell, he had not even been past my living room. This time I wanted him to see the house in its entirety and be a part of it. I wanted to cook for him and have dinner on my veranda. I wanted him to stay with me, to merge with me and bask in each other's delights. So I ended up asking him to come stay with me the entire time that he was planning to be in town.

With absolutely no hesitation, he said, "You better believe I will be there!"

I did what needed to be done for the day. After I took a shower and began to dress, I was feeling a little nervous again about what to wear.

"You can do this, Marisa."

This time I had put on a slightly low-cut black dress with wide shoulder straps. The dress fit snug to my lower waist with a slightly flared skirt down to a couple of inches above my knee. I had part of my hair pulled back loosely and up again but in a more dramatic look, along with a pretty jeweled barrette. The rest of my hair fell down below my shoulders. I had put on a more dramatic look for my eyes this time also, and painted my lips a dark maroon. My black open-toed high-heeled shoes showed off beautifully painted nails.

I stood back from the mirror and stared at myself in front, sideways, and backwards. "I must say, Marisa, you do look rather hot again! Or should I say, sexed- up? I know this man of yours will most certainly think the same. Damn, am I ready for Nathan or what?"

It was 6:30 p.m. when Nathan arrived. I watched him drive up and get out of the car with a dozen roses this time. This time they were a pale peach color, and quite beautiful.

Nathan was wearing a light-blue dress shirt this time, and jeans. His shirt fit him well, so that his broad shoulders and chest were noticeable. I bit my lower lip and smiled. "Damn, he looks really hot."

My breathing began to deepen and my womanly desires began to mount. I wanted him to spend the night with me this time, and he would, of course. I wanted so many sensual things and so much from him tonight.

As he approached the porch and started walking up the stairs, I opened the door and put my hand on one hip, slightly turned to the left while accentuating my womanly figure. He grinned his adorable crooked grin.

"Wow! Damn. I mean, forgive me, I am just…you are stunning, Marisa! You are just beautiful."

His compliment made me blush for only a bit, this time. I guess just knowing I did look rather hot made me feel more confident.

He bowed like the gentleman that he was. "These are for you, my sweetest Marisa, even though there is nothing I can give you that could even come close to how beautiful and fair you are tonight, my lovely lady."

My heart skipped a beat and maybe a couple more, as I felt this "familiar" man before me. I then shyly grinned back and gave a slight curtsey (*How lame*, I thought for a second). He loved it though and showed it with a wide grin this time. I finally got a couple of words out, "Thank you, handsome."

He walked in and noticed that Charlie and Sugars had come along to greet him too. He quickly gave them pats and seemed to be quite as ease with them.

They seemed to enjoy greeting him, but I knew they would never greet him the way that I would greet him and would always intend to greet him. I placed the flowers in a vase.

Without any more hesitation, he came forward as I turned around away from the vase. He grabbed and wrapped his right arm around my waist and lower back and pulled me into him. It was forceful and it was strong. I welcomed it. I loved it. I wanted him more than anything or anyone at this moment.

After what seemed endless passionate kisses, I broke our embrace, as he looked about the room. "Your home is absolutely beautiful, by the way. Wow, there's something about it…something inviting, it seems. There seems to be an invitation relayed as one walks into this amazing place." I knew what he meant without even trying to question this somewhat bizarre comment. This place, my home, was just as Nathan said.

"I'd love to see the rest of it, Marisa, but before we do…."

We embraced again and kissed each other for a time which seemed timeless to me. We each agreed that since I had spent this time preparing dinner for him, that he wanted to show his appreciation and spend some time just talking for a bit with me in the kitchen as he helped me finish.

I poured Nathan a glass of merlot, and as the gentleman that he was, as I must say again, he made a toast to me and to us. "To you, my lovely Marisa. You are a precious jewel, and somehow I knew and felt that you would come along at this present time. May this evening bring us both to a place of 'familiarity' that we are meant to be, as if written in the stars."

I suddenly froze and was puzzled for a moment, but of course my soul had already decided that I knew what his soul meant by that. He, too, was just as stunned as I was with a bewildered look. Yet it seemed we both agreed without saying that what he said was true and had been definitely written in the stars, indeed. I most certainly knew what the words that I had been given—"Return to me…it is written"—meant. It meant that Nathan and I belonged together…again.

We seemed to come out of the trance by some force. Nathan began to help me as we took our food and plates out to the veranda. There was a nice slightly cool breeze. I had a wrap around the back of my chair. Without asking or suggesting, he grabbed it and gently covered my shoulders. We both smiled as he winked and kissed me. I simply melted. I wanted him so badly.

How in the world did I get this far in life to have such a gallant man as Nathan suddenly appear? I then looked toward the horizon over the ocean's waters and there she was! My beautiful MoonGlow. She winked and blew me a kiss, which I thought was reassuring. Now I knew for sure that my fine specimen of a man was here to stay.

We took a walk along the shore. I noticed how MoonGlow would keep her gaze on us. I felt somewhat uncomfortable, but yet knew that she was portraying a somewhat motherly role at the moment, as well as the sentinel that she was. She and I both knew that tonight would not be a night of dancing the dance of gypsies. Tonight would not be the night to be summoned by High Tide to take flight and drown in his great liquid. No, no—for tonight I would be with my Nathan, my man. It was time now for Nathan and me.

Nathan stopped our walk as he pulled at me and thrust my body up against his. We kissed. Then as quickly as we kissed, he backed away and took my arm and started to twirl me around as we both laughed and felt the feeling of being young lovers again. I felt that "familiarity" again. It was déjà vu, likened to a space and time long ago. I felt we were long-ago lovers at this moment. We were on the beach and it was romantic as I knew it would be.

The waters were racing in now. I knew High Tide was about to be summoned soon by his own lover, but somehow I also knew it would not be until Nathan and I had gone back to the house.

We continued the dance. He would twirl me and then bring me close to him. We would kiss and it would start all over again. I glanced up at MoonGlow and saw her winking at me as she brought forth her beautiful face each time. I thanked God silently for the magnificent creation that he brought to me as my friend and sentinel. *Friendship comes in all forms*, I thought.

Our lovers' eyes met again. We kissed a long and passionate kiss. *It is time now*, I thought. Nathan replied, as if he had heard my thoughts, "Yeah, let's go back to the house, my beautiful Marisa." He took a part of my hair and ran it through his fingers. He took a strand and smelled it. Oh how I loved that. I turned my head toward his hand and kissed it.

"Yes, Nathan, let's go," I said with a panting that told him how much I wanted him.

Nathan and I headed for my bedroom, as he closed the door behind. The window was open and a welcome cool breeze could be felt. The curtains were swaying as they do. I had put on some soft smooth music of Sade and I started to dance for him. He unzipped my dress and kissed my neck. I could feel the wetness and heat of his mouth and breath.

Again he took my hair. He removed my barrette and ever so gently while breathing into my hair and lifted it over and over in sections. He began to take steps back toward the bed as I had already pulled down the covers. And he stepped back, his stare never left me. He watched me take off my dress as I continued to dance the dance. Yes, it was the dance that MoonGlow had taught me. My hands fingered through my hair, lifting it up and making my body spin around in front of him. I slowly took off my black bustier and portrayed my breasts to him, proud and flirty. I turned around and while having my back toward him, I slowly took off my panties.

I knew he watched my every move without ever taking his eyes off of me, and as I stopped to look at him he stood up and walked toward me. He took me with a strong force again as he did before and wrapped both arms around me. He looked down at my breasts and began to cup one and then the other. His wet mouth upon them felt warm, and excited every womanly sensation in me now.

We were both panting as our breaths met. His breath was warm as it forced my mouth to devour his. He lifted up one of my legs and wrapped it around his hip. I knew he wanted me just as much as I wanted him. Our eyes met while his hand touched my wetness. He smiled and gave me a look of knowing, of "familiarity," as I did the same.

We both began to move with synchrony as I invited his manhood. We were connected. We were the same. We were one. His panting became deeper as my head fell back while our bodies continued our synchronized moves. I looked up at the ceiling and saw the words, "Write your name across my heart."

We were together for the rest of the night. We made love and we became the lovers we had always been. Why did I feel this way? Why did I feel as though I already knew him and that he knew me?

Finally, we would talk about his wife and daughter. I had been wanting to know who they were, where they lived, and how old his daughter was. Sadly and reluctantly, he told me that he had been divorced and his daughter, Alexis, had been killed in a car accident six years earlier. Alexis had been eleven at the time.

I could not believe what I was hearing. I felt sorrow for him and what he had lost. The thought of losing my own son, Zach, came to mind. How would I ever get through the death of my child? I did think it was strange that my own husband, Matthew, had died also in a car accident.

I would hold him and console him for what it seemed like forever. As I did, I felt that "familiar" feeling again. I felt that Nathan and I were connected in a very familiar way that was of old, that was of long ago. Why was that?

CARPET RIDE...

We fell asleep in each other's arms. The cool breeze continued to bless our faces. I had awakened at some period in the night and felt myself going toward the window. I started to fly upward and toward the world above. I had a companion to my right. We suddenly were placed on a carpet and it began to take flight throughout the illumined night sky.

The constellations were plentiful and showers of brilliant kaleidoscopes continuously shifted their diversity of patterns, shapes, and figures. My companion and I were mesmerized with silent and fixed gazes. As the spectacular colors and movements began to fade, we looked at each other. It was Nathan looking back at me. I felt a love that I had felt before. It was "familiar" indeed. The love was of long ago and far away. The love was ancient, but yet ever new. We both knew at this moment we were to be…to be as one.

I woke in the early morn. It was Friday now. Nathan was facing me. I watched his breathing. I gazed at his face. Oh, that beautiful face of his. Even the hairs of his morning beard were tantalizing. I stood up and walked over to the curtains, which were swaying as they always do. The soft sounds of High Tide's waves were soothing. Oh, how the breeze possesses sweet aromas and intoxicating passions that can literally lift the soul right out of its body, sending it to places of rest…or even unrest.

I heard Nathan moving in the sheets. As I looked over his way, he looked at me. "Good morning, my beautiful woman."

"I love that. I love what you say to me and how you say it. It makes me swoon." I slightly turned and fell back a little.

He laughed and stretched his arms toward me. "Come here, woman! Do you like that?"

"Yes, I do, Mr. Fine Specimen, sir. I most surely do." Nathan laughed and I thought how much I loved his laugh, too. I did not believe there was anything I did not love about him. He was handsome and manly. He made me feel safe. He made me feel that I was everything he wanted, especially after last night. Little did he know that he actually did make me swoon and sent me to flight, as he did last night on our kaleidoscope carpet ride.

We spent some time together for another hour or so making love and just holding each other. We talked about last night, and about now at this present moment. I knew I already loved him and I was sure that he already loved me, though no such words were exchanged yet.

Somehow we managed to get up, shower, get dressed, and have breakfast before he had to leave for work. Nathan had a condo a few miles from here. That was not his primary home, though. He actually had a home about two hours away in the city. He kept this condo to stay in as he traveled up and down the coastal areas. Wondering how lonely he got kept creeping up in my mind. Since he lost his daughter six years ago and it was quite recently that we had met, I was hesitant to ask and inquire about such feelings. I felt sorrow for him, though. I know the right time would come for more intimate discussions.

Before Nathan had to leave, we kissed on the front porch and then we kept kissing. He would pick me up and spin me around playfully and lovingly. Thoughts of having this handsome man in my life made me swoon, and I could not imagine him ever not a part of my life now. I yearned for him in a way that seemed so familiar and ever so right, ever so like home.

As I went back into the house I had already started missing Nathan. "For goodness' sake, Marisa. Well, that only took a second to miss him. What are you going to do?"

Nathan would be back this evening, though. He would spend the rest of the weekend with me. Just the two of us…the thought made me start playing some music, and filling the house with music and dance was just what I needed. The cats seemed happy for me as they scurried around playfully.

I began to think about how I would miss traveling back to my past life for the next couple of days since Nathan would be here. Oh, how I missed Calissa. I missed her so much. I even missed the Pretty Pink House. What? Well, I guess I missed Madame and the girls, and just everyone. Plus, I wanted to continue my journey. I wanted to go back to my story. Yes, it was a story and I was loving it. What an adventure it was. I was enchanted indeed with this adventure—my adventure—with this unveiling of a past life that had belonged to me.

Suddenly, I snapped out of it. Caroline had left me a text message. We continued to text for a while. She was working today and she never called me when she had to work, so texting sufficed. I told her that Nathan and I had "done it." She went crazy, naturally. She texted me a few words, then was silent for a while before resuming. I do believe she may have passed out for a bit.

Nathan came back to my home in early evening. He had called me earlier to say that he wanted to take me out for a nice dinner at a local restaurant along the beach. He wanted us to watch the sun set together. He also said he wanted us to spend the weekend as a "couple." How that delighted me beyond anything! I knew in my heart why he said that word "couple." I felt it too. I already loved him, so naturally we would.

The hours seemed to fly by. We were together. We seemed as one. Everything we did seemed natural. Whenever we made love it was as if for the very first time, even though we knew it was familiar. Nathan told me in the early morning hours that he loved me. I told him how much I loved him too. Yeah, it was early, but yet again, I believed we both knew that our love was real—ever ancient and ever new.

On Sunday morning, Nathan told me that he wanted to stop by his condo to pick up a few things and that he would return shortly. I told him, "Don't take too long, mister— you'll make me start missing you. You're not supposed to be leaving me until Monday morning, you know." I gave a long wet kiss and pulled his lower lip. My hands caressed his chest, and somehow one landed on his crotch.

"Yes ma'am, beautiful! I promise you I will."

What a magnet pull he was to me. We must have been together in another lifetime, or two, or three, or more. We were connected like magnet and steel.

After about thirty minutes, he called me, "Hi, my beautiful lady. I just wanted to hear your voice. I've been gone way too long."

After a quick laugh, my eyes teared up for some reason, for he had just been gone for thirty minutes. I pulled myself together and broke my silence. "Yes, you have been gone way too long, my fine specimen of a man. Yes, you have, so get yourself back here—pronto."

"I can see your smile, Marisa, and it overspills my heart. I can even feel it and it seems to blanket me with those sweet kisses of yours. I don't know what it is, but one smile of yours can fill up an ocean full of Marisa in me. I'll be back soon."

Whew. Yeah, that was my man who just said that.

The hours flew by again. It was early Monday morning. I did not want him to leave, nor did he want to leave. We said our goodbyes, which took longer than it should have.

I stood on the porch watching Nathan leave. Waves and kisses were exchanged. I waited until his truck was facing away and pulling out. Then the tears came. Why my heart felt such melancholy, I did not know. He would be coming back in a couple of days. "You have him, Marisa. He is yours." Still a sense of melancholy blanketed me.

Who was this man that I was so enamored with? Who was this Nathan Gregory Rynn, that I felt such love for and such a familiarity toward? Yes, I did love him, and you know, I knew that he loved me too. That made me happy. That made me content and that made me feel safe.

I spent the rest of the day keeping busy. I had lots of errands to run and cleaning to do. The cats seemed to love my way of keeping busy. They kept looking and following me around. Their company was always a pleasure for me, and so were their antics. What a playful twosome they were.

I would call Caroline and discuss the weekend I had spent with Nathan. Oh, how the tables had turned. I, now, would be the one to have something to share about my rendezvous with a man.

I would talk with my son, Zach, and my mother afterwards. It seemed I wanted to speak with family. I felt lonely for some reason after Nathan had left. I was missing him so much, as if I had lost him. Why? I continued to ponder this for several hours.

As the evening got closer, I was so looking forward to traveling again. Fortunately, Nathan called me again. That reassured me that I had not actually lost him. How silly of me to feel earlier as if I had. I still did not understand why I did, though.

Although I missed Nathan, I had missed my encounters with MoonGlow and High Tide, and I knew they had missed me too. I also missed everyone who was in my life back then…back in 1881. Can you believe that? Anyone who heard me would be thinking, *Girl, you are indeed one crazy lady!*

I did my usual routine. My music, my wine, my flowing sarong that would lead me to the dance of dances. I felt gypsy wild tonight. I had missed it. I was longing for it again.

I think this time, I almost ran down the boardwalk to the sands to begin my gypsy dance and wait for MoonGlow to come to me. It seemed it was taking too long.

There she was. She came suddenly in splendid intensity. Her face appeared with a smile this time, instead of her lips being pursed. She lowered both her eyelids, then began to purse her lips and blew me that familiar unadulterated kiss of hers. As she opened her eyes again to see me, I smiled, curtsied, and reciprocated the kiss. I flew my arms up and swayed them as I turned my body around.

I said to her, "MoonGlow, are you begging for that wet kiss from your lover, High Tide, tonight? Are you going to make him rise to the occasion tonight?"

I felt very sensual tonight. I thought of Nathan and how we had finally made love this past weekend. I was missing him. I bit my lower lip.

A strong force of cavernous winds came my way. I looked out in the horizon and saw High Tide rising up in full force. His great liquid was mounting up quickly and deliberately. I now stood frozen and felt him pulling my being unto him.

The mighty force did not dare to hold me captive to this world any longer. His masculine arms took me and forced me into his lower recesses, deeper and deeper than ever before did I go. So mighty and swift were his liquid projections spiraling as I descended, that not a drop touched me this time.

Moon Forest - I continued the journey. I could see others along the way Who were they? I did not know.

I was placed in a forest, it seemed. The trees were massive and plentiful. They seemed to reach endlessly toward the skies, or was it toward the top level of High Tide's existence of this world we called Earth? I knew it was nightfall in this forest. There was some amount of light, though, and the light came from the moons.

I started to count the moons. There were seven of them, of various sizes. I remembered the past encounter I had with the seven moons when I was walking along the beach…along the earthly plane in The Place of Tears.

It was relayed to me that I was in the Moon Forest. This forest was for souls to spend time contemplating. This was a place to remember what your previous life had been, as if a life review were to be presented. It was a place to dream, too. It was a place to think about what you should have done and become.

As I looked beyond the trees, I could see dark figures of beings. Maybe they were human, or maybe some other alien being? I could not tell, for they were darkened, like silhouettes. I was not afraid. There was no fear here. There was only a sense of being alone and of the need to contemplate.

A feeling of certainty came over me that this place was where dreams of longings were kept. The dreams of remediation and redemption resided here. It was a purgatorial realm.

Suddenly, I was pulling back. High Tide was pulling me back from the deepest recesses of his bowels to a another level of inbetween.

1881- SIXTH ENCOUNTER

I was back at the boarding house. I had returned to my lifetime in 1881. I was in my mother's room and I was sitting on her bed. We were talking.

I looked over to my right and there she was. My Calissa was back. She smiled a tender smile and we embraced. "Oh how have I missed you, my lovely daughter."

Calissa, my guide, my watchman, my daughter of long ago had come back to spend some time with me. She looked lovingly at me and said, "Mother, I have always loved you, and forever I will. We all have to spend time in reviewing our lives and our choices. We all have our karma to settle. It is only for the best. In the end, there will always be love. There has to be. It is the only way to proceed." Calissa faded and left.

I watched myself at my mother's side. A young black lady walked in.

"Morning, Miss Collette." She was quite pleasant. I knew she was there to help my mother. She had been taking care of her in her illness. Her name was Isabel.

It was relayed to me that Madame Mae had her assigned to be my mother's caretaker. Madame had insisted for she and my mother, Nadia, had been longtime friends. Plus, she did not want me to fret about my mother's care since I was working for her now.

After Miss Isabel had helped with my mother's care, she left the room so that we could have some time to ourselves.

"My Collette, I want to speak about things, my dear daughter. You can not fool me. When I look in your eyes, I can see the truth."

My mother's eyes, as well as my own, teared up and neither one of us could speak for a while. She looked deeply into my eyes and began to speak.

"I feel as though my heart is drenched with wine and I almost can not feel a thing anymore. I have cried throughout the night and I have prayed that this was not the truth, my dear daughter. I know you are working at Madame's. The work is not entirely what you said. It is the work that I, your mother, had done years ago in that pink house."

"Mother, I am so sorry." The tears and gaspy breaths prevented me from speaking for a bit. We just held each other and cried for a while.

"I must do this just for a little while. I need to do this. You are sick and I want you to get better. Look at what Madame has done! She has brought Miss Isabel to take care of you. You are better off because of what I have chosen to do. We are both better off. It is only for a little while, my dear Mother. You know I love you."

She allowed me to speak and ramble on with one apology and explanation after another. Though she was crying along with me, she settled down after my almost never ending justifications for the sinful life I had chosen.

"You know, Collette, we have an ever-merciful God and I do believe He, and He alone, understands all the difficulties we lowly humans endure. He understands also why and for whom we make such choices along the way."

"Mother, please tell me more about Madame and who she is, where she came from, and what happened in her life. I want to know." I sat down next to her and positioned myself comfortably for a long chat with my dear mother.

It was relayed to me that Madame Mabelle was a Creole of color. Her father was of French descent and her mother was Spanish/black. Her features were more Spanish, it seemed, and she was stunning. Her hair was raven, full-bodied and wavy. Her eyes were dark and had a sparkle.

My mother had met Madame's mother, Angelique, after she had married my father. She would deliver clothes and household goods to The Pink House for Angelique's charities.

Yes, I thought. *I knew there was such goodness in these women.*

Some months after meeting Angelique, my mother would be introduced to Mabelle, who was Angelique's daughter. Mabelle was five years older than my mother. Madame Angelique would come down with consumption and die shortly. It was then that her fiery, business-like, no-nonsense daughter, Mabelle, would become the madam of the Pretty Pink House, aka, Jolie Maison Rose.

My mother and Madame Mae would become good friends. Madame loved my mother because she was not like the other fine, upstanding, prominent ladies of New Orleans. My mother was kind and took to being friends with everyone, even the madam of a brothel. She would see the goodness of people and of Madame Mae.

Now I understood why Madame was so kind to my mother. Because of my mother's nonjudgmental demeanor and genuine friendship, Madame gave her work when she needed it, and now she gave her Miss Isabel to take care of her during her illness.

My mother went on to tell me how Madame's mother had acquired the home and then how Madame Mae, herself, had ended up making the home a grand mansion. Madame's mother, Angelique, had a married client, George Latham, who had been very smitten and had taken her as his mistress. He was the most wealthy and prominent attorney turned banker in New Orleans. He also owned several businesses throughout the lower South. He would fund Angelique's business to make it the most lucrative and aesthetically pleasing brothel of old New Orleans.

As time went by, Angelique's daughter, Mabelle, would find that she herself would be the favorite of George Latham's son. His name was William who had studied law, as his father did. William would eventually come to provide Mabelle

(Madame Mae) with the resources to expand and make this lovely home an even more lucrative, inviting and charming place to come and play. Well…it was a brothel, you know.

Unfortunately, William, was married, too, as his father had been, but he loved Madame Mabelle. Because she had become his mistress, William would eventually help Madame invest her money along with his own. He would do so enough so that eventually Madame would own the brothel outright, along with some farmland and a restaurant/bar in town. Yes, Madame was doing well, and this is why she was so generous with her pretty pink ladies, too.

My mother and I continued to chat for a while. All was somewhat well, I thought. We were smiling now. I knew my mother still loved me. I was grown now.

I was brought back to the Pretty Pink House. I could see myself in the foyer talking with Madame and Annabella. We were laughing at something. We were happy and all was well with us.

I peered over to my right into the dining room and past the kitchen. Miss Nellie and a few other ladies were cleaning and cooking while humming their tunes. Big Sam would come in and out the back screen door carrying various boxes and whistling his own tunes. What a normal-looking house. What a normal-looking family. This was part of my home and family now. I could feel the tears welling up, and thought of my mother.

Madame Mae had gathered some things around the house which seemed like household items. Big Sam was helping by packing and placing them near the front door. I knew Madame was at it again. She was being charitable. Maybe it was her own way, too, of making atonement to right her wrongs.

Madame cheerfully took me by the arm and led me to the second parlor where she had recently become accustomed to taking me when she wanted a talk. We sat down and smiling a bit, she said, "Collette, I want you to know again that I am pleased with how you have acclimated to our business and how well you are doing, my child. I knew you were going to be one of those special ladies, the kind that knows just how to bring in the business. You have indeed been bringing in the dollars, have you not?"

We both raised our eyebrows and nodded agreeably. "I mean, your clients are paying such top dollars now and asking for you incessantly, it seems. What I am trying to say, dear, is would you consider spending more time here? I know you want to spend as much time with your mother as you can, and it is your choice, of course, but I…I…need to ask."

I looked away for a bit and considered my mother's condition. I thanked her for bringing Miss Isabel to my mother to tend to her while I was not there. I told her I would consider it even though in my heart I did not feel I would.

I was making money, all right. As a matter of fact, I was given the knowledge that after a few more months I would have enough money that we could actually move out of the boarding house and buy a small home, so that my mother and I could have a place of our own. That was how much money I was bringing into Madame's house, and to myself as well. I actually felt a sense of pride. I know, I know—it was not a respectable choice of income, but I must have been doing something right to be paid "top dollar," as Madame Mae would say.

Madame would say of me, "Collette, you are making my business some top dollar, my sweetie. It is because of your beauty and sweet sophistication, I hear them say. My very wealthy clientele most certainly do enjoy their time spent with you. My, my — maybe you need to share some of your secrets with me, hmmm?"

I was indeed her best pretty pink lady as far as being chosen the one to arrange appointments with the most wealthy of clients who frequented the services of The Pretty Pink House. I would only blush and politely tell her that I really did not know of any secrets except for the ones she had taught me herself. She would proudly nod her head and respond that she appreciated my saying so.

It was then relayed to me that I was very learned in putting on the airs, as they say. I knew how to flirt and how to please, yet be a lady at the same time. I do believe that having been to boarding school and learning my alluring manners, I would be able to entice and charm the best of the best clientele that Madame had in her brothel this side of the Mississippi.

As I was given this knowledge of of my success, if you even want to call it that, I, Marisa, would experience an aching feeling in the depths of my heart and definitely my soul. I would wonder if this lifetime was even real and if it even ever existed. I would feel a shame from time to time, even in my present earthly life. I would tell myself, "Surely other souls experience unacceptable and demeaning lives too, don't they? It's not just me, most certainly."

I felt for sure at that moment that I knew every soul's progression and enlightenment comes from making the wrong choices. Otherwise, nothing makes sense in existing in this dark, fallen world of ours. Why would we even be here if we were already perfected?

After discussing with Madame my desire to buy a small home for my mother and myself in the near future, she looked surprised and said, "Collette, I understand how you would love to move and have your own place for yourself and your mother, but if you are still wanting to remain discreet and have people not entirely know how you get such good income, my dear, moving out and buying your own home would get everyone in this town asking questions. The truth would definitely come out. That's inevitable."

She was right about that, of course. I would always walk or either catch a ride with Big Sam to the house, but I would always be careful of who would be watching. I knew some of those fine, upstanding prominent women would be wondering and even speculating what I was actually doing, but moving out would probably confirm their suspicions. Besides, I knew at that point I had decreased the amount of time and work spent on the mending and cleaning of other people's fancy stuff. I did not need to do that anymore, I thought. However, I did tend to only a few, so that it would not make them suspicious about how I was making ends meet for myself and my mother.

We would stay at the boarding house. It had been our home for quite some time. It was small quarters, but it had sufficed. Besides, this grand beautiful mansion here at Madame's had become a home to me also. Madame and Annabella had definitely made this lovely house a second home for me.

So I would continue to make the fine upstanding women in New Orleans believe that I was still mending and cleaning for just a few. Little did they know how much money I was actually making. Or did anyone know? In time, I would find out.

Madame and I stood up. She place her hands on my upper shoulders and gave me a sweet kiss on the cheek. I loved her, I thought. She was like a second mother to me. Yes, of course, I was making money for her. I was an employee indeed, but I knew she loved me too. Hell, her own daughter was working for her too. I laughed and everything seemed fine again.

That afternoon an older distinguished man of around fifty years of age walked through the front door. Smiling he asked, "Is Madame here, please?"

Annabella politely said, "Good afternoon, Doc Charles. Yes, she is. I will go find her for you."

It was relayed that Doc Charles was the doctor of the house, so to speak. He would come over and check on Madame's ladies. He would make sure they were "clean and safe," as Annabella would tell me.

I also noticed when Madame Mae appeared, she and Doc Charles seemed to have a special connection. It was more than friendly, if you know what I mean. I do believe the doc took extremely good care of all the pretty pink ladies here for our sweet, polite, and beautiful Madame Mae.

As Doc Charles was about to leave, two of the ladies packed a small travel bag of some sort and walked out with him. I wondered why. I saw the the three climbed onto the carriage and left.

It was relayed to me that they were being escorted back to Doc Charles' office. But why was that. I began to feel the sensation of nausea and lightheadedness. There was more to it than being examined. Were they pregnant? Was the doctor about to perform some horrific, abhorrent procedure of abortion? Those were my thoughts.

In my present lifetime, I was adamantly opposed to abortion. I was living in the days when the advancement of knowledge concerning fetal development was well- documented and known. I did not know for certain, but then again, the sickening feeling I had been immersed in gave me that interpretation.

How very sad. Such must have been the life of many women in this profession during this period of time? Did I ever partake in such an oppressed state? No knowledge of this was given. I only prayed that I had not.

As early afternoon came, Annabella and I were preparing to go out for the evening. It was then I realized that the two of us had become close friends. She was like a sister to me. This evening, we would enjoy going out on the town and just being the young women that we were. We were nineteen, but of course, in my present life it just did not seem right, for some reason.

It was relayed to me that Madame did want her ladies to take time off and just be who we were. She was pleased that her daughter had taken such a liking to me and that we were best of friends. Today was Tuesday, and Annabella and I would enjoy the evening off.

As Annabella and I approached the front parlor, a young pretty woman of mixed race, probably a Creole, said, "Well, I see you two are going out for some fun. I wish I could go with you, but it is my night to work. It is all right, though. You all have fun."

I saw that we chatted with her for a just a short time. She was a inch or so taller than Annabella. She was striking, I thought. I could see that her skin was smooth as velvet. I thought of how her clients must enjoy her.

Shame on me for thinking such things, I could hear my thoughts saying. Oh well, what is a girl to think when in a place of pleasuring our clients?

Her name was Estella. My thoughts of her were that of being a broken girl. There was a very sad side of her, I was thinking to myself, but why? At that moment, it seemed to me that she was known to be very elusive—she kept to herself, and never seemed to reveal much of her past to anyone there. Surely, Madame must know more. Yet, it was relayed to me that Estella and I had become friends in spite of it all.

I began to wonder where Estella had come from. What kind of life had she lived, and what brought her to this house? Never was that information relayed to me. I would see her several times in my travels here, though.

Annabella and I were dressed down, it seemed. Our appearance was not provocative, nor was it fine and upstanding as those ladies who boasted their worth in dollars by their dress, as they would frequently glance around to see if others were looking and admiring their class and style.

We were dropped off by Big Sam at the end down of the French Quarter. I was given the knowledge that this was not actually the appropriate way of having single women walking about on their own in this area, but we did anyway.

There were a diverse number of people going about their business as Annabella and I were happily going about ours. We seemed to be rather elated. Maybe we were happy just to be normal for a while.

I could hear the unfamiliar music of old New Orleans. It was inviting in a strange way. It made me want to dance. I thought of how I loved to dance back home in my present life. Had I always been this way? Had I always enjoyed the dance and the music? I do believe I had.

I noticed Annabella enjoyed every moment. She had come alive and so did I. We were just beings girls right now…not women. We were being what we should have been—and what we should not have been were pretty pink ladies at the Pretty Pink House.

Should I have not thought of it that way? Somehow, I felt I had betrayed Madame Mae for thinking such a thought. I know if my friend and I had lived another kind of life, a better life, we both would not be, nor go back to the people that we truly were or should I say, had become.

I quickly forgot my sad and negative thoughts, and set myself back in what was before me. And what I saw before me were two young ladies enjoying the night. We had entered a busy food/drink and dance hall establishment. It was actually owned by Madame, herself. Yes, Madame and Annabella were doing well.

As we were having fun, I would notice glimpses from young men looking our way, smiling and flirting with us. Little did they know who we were or whom we had become.

Even so, we played with them. I watched from a distance our exchanges of words, of laughter and flirtatious gestures with the young men. I felt somewhat appeased during this viewing. I knew it was not all bad. Life had not been all bad. Then suddenly I felt a pulling.

I was back at the Pretty Pink House and it was Friday now. It was relayed to me that it had been over three months since I had entered the Pretty Pink House. The month was November.

Annabella and I were in her room getting dressed for the evening. We were helping each other with our hair and with our bustiers and stockings. I could see that I was no longer anxious or apprehensive. The two of us were happily going about our business…we were getting ready for work.

I looked into the mirror and as I moved about from left to right and back again, I thought how beautiful I actually was. Oh well, at least I was making the money that I needed for my mother and I to survive, right? I said to myself, "Life is not always pretty. You have to do what you think you need to do to survive. At least if I have to resign to a business such as this, I can look pretty while I'm at it." I thought, *What an odd thing for me to say.*

We quickly went downstairs and joined the other pretty pink ladies in the front parlor. As soon as we noticed Madame Mae making her way in, she smiled and slightly bowed her head. We had all stood up with our backs straight so enhancing our perky breasts and smiling our always sustainable smiles.

Again she was pleased. "My, my. My sweet pretty pink ladies look so lovely and poised. You are most certainly mine indeed, if I must say please."

I somehow felt a need to curtsey before Madame, as if she was the Queen Bee that she was. So I did just that. She looked at me with such a surprise, relaying that she was pleased as my gesture. I could see a couple of the other ladies looked puzzled and maybe displeased by my giving such a gesture to our Madame. Oh well.

As the evening began, the house was expectedly lively. It was a Friday night. Many of our clients tonight were from out of town and even some out of state. They had arrived for a business gathering of some sort in the city for the weekend.

I knew I had an appointment with an upscale client this particular night. I was waiting for him. I saw myself walking toward the foyer to see what Madame was doing, and with whom she was speaking.

I caught a glimpse of a young man who was dressed very nicely in a suit and top hat. Madame was ever so smiling and seemed to be a bit flirtatious in her gestures. The young man, on the other hand, seemed rather reserved and maybe a bit shy. He seemed to be a little uneasy to be exposed in a place such as this.

He turned my way. Our eyes met. No, I was not doing as Madame had taught me, and that was to never look directly into the eyes of any client, especially the younger ones.

We both seemed to be somewhat spellbound for a moment. Did I know him? Did he know me? He exposed a slight smile…a crooked smile…and politely dipped his hat and gave me a nod.

I quickly removed myself from the spell, which seemed to be indubitably the case. I took a step back and heard myself expel a deep, regretful sigh. I knew I had committed the grave and wrongful deed, and that was I had looked him in the eyes. But oh, what beautiful eyes they were. Madame then looked over with a somewhat stern yet discerning posture, acknowledging that I had caught myself doing the unspeakable.

But what's so wrong with looking at this handsome young man? Is it not normal to do so? I, Marisa, was contemplating.

Of course, it was wrong because I might fall in love, or get too involved, or end up getting hurt, or not be able to keep it all "businesslike" and nothing more. The list went on in my head. Or maybe, I thought, just maybe he may fall in love with me and want to take me away…away from Madame.

Madame had excused herself with this fine gentleman. She walked up to me and, as always, slipped her arm underneath mine and escorted me to an empty room down the hall. She sat me down. It was her time now to expel a deep, regretful sigh.

"Mademoiselle Amelia, I want you to know that I am not upset with you. You are a beautiful young lady. I know you were not expecting to see such a handsome and very young man at such a place as this. I understand that you would find him agreeable and he would feel similarly about you."

She again would give an even deeper, more regretful sigh. Though she said she understood what just happened, it didn't seem that way to me. I deduced she seemed rather perturbed that I had broken the cardinal rule of the house.

I wanted to know—why did younger men not go there? There were younger men who were wealthy too, right? Or maybe not? I knew it was all about the money, though. The older men had the money, and they trusted Madame Mae with their indiscretions. Yes, Madame had built a lucrative business and a very pleasurable business, so she would keep their secrets, and she would demand her pretty pink ladies to do the same.

I was not relayed the entire conversation, but I knew she did not tell me who this young man was, nor did she keep me any longer dwelling on my mishap.

I went back to the parlor and proceeded to mingle again. I was smiling now and wanted nothing more than to enjoy the evening. I knew I was looking forward to meeting with the man I had been scheduled to meet. I had become quite well-acquainted with him and he was always polite and pleasant. One thing I knew for sure was that Madame Mae had the best of the best clientele. It was safe here. Or was it really?

I was back with my mother as she was sitting up in bed and having breakfast. I wondered for a moment how and why all of this past life was being presented to me in such a way. Certain moments of time, of conversations and events, would be presented in sequences, but not given fully and not explained entirely. Oh well—at least I was feeling blessed by what I had been given. I was very thankful to the heavenly beings for this gift.

Miss Isabel had helped my mother with a bath, while I gathered some clean and mended clothing to take to the few customers I had left. I understood that I needed to keep up the appearance of being respectable, and so I did.

I had taken an afternoon nap the same time as my mother. After I awakened, I spent time just talking with my mother about the past. She wanted to talk about when I was a little girl and we would spend all of our time together. She talked of how she had dreams of my being finely educated, marrying a fine, upstanding man and having my own family. She had made me start crying and she, herself, would do the same.

"Mother, I promise, it will happen. I promise you that I will not work like this much longer. You have always told me that I'm a beautiful girl. I will marry a fine, upstanding man some day. Even though some would consider me tainted, I know such a man would have me, Mother. Do you know what I mean, when I say that with my beauty and my knowing how to please a man very well now, I will very soon marry a wonderful man?"

"Of course, I understand everything that you said. Promise me that you will marry for love, too. I want you to love someone, Collette, and I hope and pray that when you do marry, you and your husband will leave here. You will leave and forget the past here. I won't be around much longer, my daughter."

I stopped my mother from continuing. We held each other and we cried a thousand tears. Somehow I just knew that as I watched this strong, beautiful, and kind Collette who loved her mother dearly and would do anything for her, she would indeed be all right.

I left early evening to the Pretty Pink House. As I wrestled with the huge wrought-iron gate, I stood for a couple of minutes looking at the house. Yes, it was a beautiful sight. I thought how this house could have been different. It could have been a real home for a family instead of being a brothel. I imagined children running around the front yard and up the stairs to the grand porch. I imagined a couple, along with elderly grandparents, enjoying the little ones who would run happily to them sharing warm hugs and kisses.

As I imagined, I would ask myself, "Why didn't I have this kind of life back then?" I thought for sure reincarnation existed, for nothing seemed fair or made sense if certain people seemed to have it all while others did not.

Again, I snapped out of my daydreaming, as it was now. I quickly went up the stairs and opened the door to the place I belonged at this given time in a past life of long ago.

Madame was at the lectern checking the schedule. I quicky gave her a smile, which was indeed a sincere smile. I felt at that moment how elated I was to see her, my surrogate mother in a way. I was back at my "other" home, and it was all right.

I noticed some of the other ladies were chatting and getting ready for the evening. Then I noticed Estella—the "broken girl," I had called her. She was the tall, beautiful, and stunning Creole who always seemed quite mysterious and elusive. She had not been here last night, for she had taken a few days off "to see her family."

It was relayed to me that whenever any of the pretty pink ladies would say she was taking time off to be with "family," it meant they were going off with one of Madame's clients on another business trip for a few days. If a clientele took a fancy to any particular lady, Madame would allow her to take a few days of travel. Not all of us would be permitted to do so, especially those who had not been at The Pretty Pink House for long. Estella had been here for more than a couple of years. It would be permitted for a lady to travel with a client also—and most definitely if the price was right. Madame's demands for taking one of her ladies temporarily would indeed include top dollar. Yes, Madame was raking in the money, as one would say.

I then thought how naturally Estella would fit the mold of someone to take away on some luxurious travel. She was beautiful, elegant, and very learned.

Estella walked up to me and asked, "Soooo, how did everything go with you and Annabella the other night?" She spoke like an educated woman, just in the tone of her voice and the way she carried herself. I wondered at that time where she had come from.

"Oh, we had fun. It was nice just to be out and being, well, just us," I heard myself say.

"Yes, there is another world out there, as you already know." She gave me a wink. Estella's eyes looked down for an instant, and it seemed as though she was saddened for just one moment in time.

She then just as quickly broadened her smile and twinkled her eyes and resumed her usual happy stance and sophisticated composure. I knew she was not always like this. I had caught her at times with her sad eyes exposed when she would no longer be able to contain what her broken heart had hidden. The surrogate name, "the broken girl," was what I had given her, for surely her eyes told me so.

It would be relayed to me in time that Estella and I would talk frequently as if we were the best of friends. We would laugh and share our experiences. Annabella and I would even have her join us in our room at times.

On one evening, we would discuss our feelings about being a pretty pink lady. We would tell our stories of being with our clients and what they were like, and even discuss the forbidden subject of how we used our "pretty skills" to please. We would giggle and laugh and for moments we would become young girls. We would act silly and carefree, as it should be, right? Yet, the three of us ended up here at The Pretty Pink House in a life shunned and ridiculed by the very fine, upstanding prominent ones.

Estella would never tell me how she ended up here at this grand house. She would keep secret from where she came. Yes, it must have not been a fine childhood. She was undoubtedly a "broken girl."

"We are all whores in some way or another, my dear," she said—meaning all women, including the fine upstanding ones. That was what she had come to believe. "Especially women who are broken-hearted with unrequited love. Women who have never found the answers. Women who have never allowed themselves permission to feel, to cry, to ponder, and to find their deep, wounded selves. Women who never are allowed to heighten and better themselves. Women who have never given themselves permission to become who they were meant to become...to have their dreams come true."

These words from Estella would be spoken only to me—and oh, how powerful her words sounded. These words would haunt me and cause me to contemplate from time to time the enigma of this beautiful, intelligent, gentle, but sad woman. She had seemed "familiar" to me too. She was akin. There was without any hesitation of a thought that I had loved her. I knew she had loved me too.

I ran upstairs to Annabella's room. She was delighted to see me, and I was so delighted to see her. We hugged and gave each other a kiss. Annabella was first and foremost my number one sister of the pretty pink ladies. I loved her so much that I do believe we had lived many lifetimes together.

We enjoyed our time as usual while we continued our familiar ritual of primping and getting ourselves dressed and beautiful for the evening. She shared a jasmine perfume with me. We both stood and looked at ourselves and at each other in the mirror as we predicated undeniably our positions here at the house. Yes, we frivolously concurred we were the best of the best of all the pretty pink ladies. We giggled as young girls do, and then made our way downstairs.

Madame seemed to dance into the parlor as she collected all of us to perform her usual inspection of the perfection she expected from us, her pretty pink ladies. She paraded herself throughout the room, giving her nods and smiles of approval or unfortunately, her frowns and head-shaking of her disapproval. Those disapprovals of her prized possessions would surely be corrected instantaneously. Each one of us ladies knew by even the end of our first night on the job that Madame was a strict disciplinarian and her expectations and demands would be taken seriously, or we would be escorted out the door. She was kind, as I previously described her, but she was a businesswoman first and foremost, and the business she and her mother had created would not be undone. "Or would it?"…were the words I heard myself say aloud.

Fortunately, or maybe unfortunately for one of the ladies, only one pretty pink lady had her hair not so perfectly done according to Madame's decrees. Even so, she resumed her smile after her abrupt correction. "Now, you all are my perfect pretty pink ladies. Remember, smile pretty and make me proud." She seemed to once again dance as she left to enter the foyer.

It was relayed to me that I had an appointment as I usually did with one of Madame's clients who would occasionally come into New Orleans on business. I saw myself taking delight in conversing with several of the ladies, and catching myself peering into the foyer to see who entered.

Big Sam would make an appearance on occasion to make sure everything was in order and that the ladies were doing well. I smiled thinking how lovely it was to have Big Sam here. It felt safe.

Some of the gentlemen would seem to want to go and mingle with the ladies, and some would have already have scheduled an appointment. Yet, some would continue on into the dining area to converse with the other clientele and business associates.

Amazing, I thought. Most of these men were probably married with children.

Did any of their wives know?

They come into Madame's house and it is another world for them. It is a world of secrets and sins, I thought. *It is a forbidden domain of fantastical imaginations, undeniable pleasure, yet a fool's paradise. Yet, it can be delusive and destructive to one's soul. It is a world of constant craving which in the end requires one to seek even more of the insatiable forbidden fruit. It is quite amazing, baffling, yet comprehensible. It is the desires of the flesh and all the fantasies that it consists of, and all of which have been around since the beginning of our bodily forms.*

Then there he was. He had come back again. He walked up toward the lectern where Madame Mae was speaking with a client. He looked toward the parlor and immediately at me. I was taken aback again and took in a deep sigh. I quickly looked away and tried to regain my composure. I tried to remember what I was doing. I felt as if a trance was coming on. The young man had cast his spell on me again.

It seemed as though Madame and this young man had been prolonging their discussion beyond the usual time. I was wondering what in the world the discussion could have been.

Madame walked up to me, placed her arm around mine, and pulled me to the third parlor, which was empty at this time. "Mademoiselle Amelia, I know you have been glancing over my way and noticing my talking with the young man whom we talked about the other day. I again want to reiterate that I am discreet about my clientele, such as their last names, their work, and so on. I also have them sign contracts stating that they will not divulge this information to my ladies, either. Everything is confidential here, as you know."

I nodded that I understood exactly the rules of Madame and her Pretty Pink House. "I most certainly do, Madame."

"However," she continued, "the young gentleman and I have made quite a deal. He is very interested in seeing you on a regular basis. He says he is enamored by your youth and beauty. He promised me he understood that in no way is he to divulge who he is and so on. This is strictly business and it will remain such."

My heart started beating innumerable beats a minute. "Really? Me? He wants to spend time with me?" was what I wanted to say, but of course, I did not.

She was adamant and actually forceful in her words and the way she presented them. It was relayed to me that the "deal" was quite a deal indeed, meaning money, and lots of it. Madame and I would both be paid very well. I understood that Madame could not have let a business deal such as this slip by. It was all about the money, right? Or was it?

I asked Madame what I should do about the client whom I had an appointment with at a later time that evening. She immediately said not to worry. "I will take care of that. He will understand. In the meantime, I need to have you spend some time in the parlor with this young gentleman. His name is Daniel. Do not look him in the eyes, my dear. Remember that!"

She escorted me with her arm around mine to the front parlor. I had started to feel butterflies. I was actually looking forward to meeting this man. If I had not known better, I would probably have floated my way to the parlor. I was definitely on cloud nine. The spell had already been cast, as I said.

I began to feel weak at the knees. I would have loved to have had a drink right about this time, I thought.

As Madame and I looked around, we noticed the gentleman was not in the parlor. Had he left? I felt began to feel sick to my stomach. Madame then led me through the foyer and motioned the young man to come out of dining area.

No, he had not left. He was still here. Yes, he wanted to see me…to be with me. As I nervously looked toward him, I tried my best to not look him directly in the eyes. I seemed to keep looking up at his forehead. "Oh brother," I said to my present self.

He smiled, took off his hat, and nodded a polite exchange with me. I thought, *Madame did not make the right choice this time for her business. I am definitely going to fall for this one. Most definitely will I probably have my heart broken for the first time.*

He reached over and took my hand slowly up to his mouth and gave it a gentle kiss. I returned with a slight curtsey and half smile. Really, Collette? I had thought the curtseys were only for Madame. I was so obviously nervous. So explicitly apparent was my nervousness, that I began to feel sorry for myself.

As I, Marisa, watched myself from afar now, I was at ease seeing myself at nineteen take fancy to this handsome young man. Hell, I even got butterflies, myself.

I looked over at Madame and sensed a displeasure. She definitely must have not felt favorable about the kiss on my hand, maybe? Or maybe it was a feeling that she was having a premonition of some sort, as if "What have I done now? You, mister, are not going to take my pretty pink lady away from me."

He escorted me to the parlor and after asking me if I would like a drink, I watched him as he poured me one. I felt that "familiar" feeling again, as I did when I first saw him in the foyer last evening. His face was at a profile angle now and he looked so handsome. His jawline was strong and he was smiling. His hands were masculine and I began imagining him taking those hands and pulling me toward him as he poured our drinks. I knew I was in trouble, but in a good way.

"You know my name is Daniel? Madame Mae told you already?"

I nodded, "Yes, yes she did. It is a very nice name. I like the name Daniel. My name is Mademoiselle Amelia. Of course, you know that." I finished with a slight giggle, then took the drink and swallowed it in a very unladylike fashion, I must say.

"You're very beautiful, Mademoiselle Amelia, even when you have a drink." I felt myself blushing several shades of red. My heart was racing and I continued to feel weak at the knees.

I felt myself, Marisa, being pulled back a little away from their presence. I began watching the young man continue to chat with me as he continued his smiles as well. He was pleased with me, it seemed. He was enjoying my company. I knew I was beginning to feel more at ease with him. I am sure the drink had something to do with that, as well as just being in Daniel's "familiar" presence.

I then saw myself in a room with Daniel. He had sat down beside me for a talk. I began to feel he had broken the contract between himself and Madame. I began to know that he had told me about himself such as his name, where he was from and what brought him here. I was waiting to find out most of all why he had chosen me.

He told me his name was Daniel Anthony Ryan, Jr. of Irish descent. He was twenty-three years old and had not yet married. He lived in Charleston, South Carolina. He and his father had a trade and transportation business along the lower South. It consisted of buying, selling and delivery of commodities of grain, cotton, foods, etc. to merchants. As his father was getting older and the business was doing so well, he would take on more of the traveling that it entailed. That would lead him this way to New Orleans.

He was breaking all the rules now. He was breaking the rules that he promised not to divulge in the contract he had signed.

I was fascinated by this man. It was not because of who he was and as far as his wealth, but for the kind of man that I felt he was. I felt a genuine kindness and politeness about him. He sat there just talking with me. He sat there breaking all the rules of Madame's. *Wow*, I thought. *Why is that?*

I heard myself suddenly say, "My name is not Mademoiselle Amelia. My name is Mademoiselle...I mean Collette. My name is Collette Marie Duprey."

I began to cry. I was sobbing. I felt so embarrassed for the first time here at The Pretty Pink House. "I am so sorry. I'm not supposed to tell you my real name. I'm not supposed to be breaking the rules, like you just did. I...I mean, I'm not supposed to be crying and acting like this. I am so sorry. Please don't tell Madame. I will make it up to you. I promise."

Daniel, like the man I knew he would be, took both my hands and held them up to his face, "Shhhhh, it's all right. It's all right, Collette. Collette, what a beautiful name you have. Just as beautiful as you are to me right now."

He began wiping my eyes with a handkerchief. He brought closer to me and began touching my face. "I saw you the other night. I saw you and the other girl at the dance hall. I watched you."

My mouth dropped. I was stunned.

"I thought you were the most beautiful lady in the world. I saw you and your friend leave and get into the carriage with the large black man. I was told by a patron there that he knew your friend worked here at this house, so that is why I came over last evening. I wanted to see if you were here too. I found you."

I thought for a moment how he had called me a "lady". Really?

"But why? Why would you want to see me when you knew…or if you thought I was…well…one of these girls?" I felt myself being ashamed more than I had before.

"Because, Collette, I know you." He took a deep breath in and repeated, "I know you. And you know me too. Don't you? I am hoping that you do."

I nodded and could not say anything more. I was baffled. Yet, at the same time, I understood too. Deep down I understood what Daniel was saying and what he meant. "We are familiar, aren't we?"

"Yes." He laughed and nodded. "We are familiar. I don't know exactly how, but I feel it and so do you. Nothing else really matters, though. I know this is sudden and so unexpected. I am staying here in New Orleans for about eleven more days. I want to see you every night. I want to get to know you. Well—" he looked up, "I want to get to know who you are right now in this present time. I think you know what I mean."

"Even though I'm a lady of the night, and I've done things a true fine lady should not have done, nor ever do. I'm tainted, Daniel."

"No you're not. Not at all. Not to me. I understand and know more than you think." He continued to stare at me. I saw his eyes looking intensely at my face, my hair, my neck, and then back to my eyes. There was something about his intricate probing of every bodily particle of matter while he delicately fingered through my hair and lightly touched my face. I felt his love for me, which was yet quite surprising and unexpected, but inherently inviting as he caused my breasts to rise and fall.

He placed both of his hands on my face and moved closer to me. Then I looked into his eyes. I saw his eyes. There they were. In his blue eyes were those crystal-clear dancing lights and then I knew. They looked "familiar".

"Yes, you do. You do understand. I have looked into your eyes, and now I see that you do know me. I see you now, and I know you too."

Immediately, I, Marisa, thought of Nathan. I thought of his eyes, which were the same as Daniel's. *Are you Nathan?*

My soul was taken away for a bit. I looked over to my right and there she was. My Calissa had come back and I began to cry. "You are back with me again. I have missed you so much. I know you are not to be with me so frequently, but I do miss you so, my sweet daughter…my sweet baby girl."

Calissa smiled her smile and came closer so I could see her beautiful blue, crystal-clear eyes with those dancing lights that I saw in Daniel and that I also saw in Nathan.

"Mother, my sweet mother, people come and go and some are never to be seen or heard from again. Just for a moment in time are these people to be with us. Lightworkers come and go too from elsewhere, just to sprinkle and douse their wisdom and blessings upon us. Then just as quickly as they do, they vanish and are gone. 'Take it or leave it,' they seem to say. They deposit their gifts and then they are gone."

I looked at her rather perplexed and she immediately gave a half smile with an understanding nod. "Then there are those people, those souls, who are meant to stay forever with you. There are those souls who are akin to you, a part of your soul, and will always be with you. I am one of those, Mother. I will never leave you. I will always love you."

She was gone. She went elsewhere. I cried, but I was elated that she came and imparted her wisdom once more. I was elated that she confirmed with me that she would always be with me and would never, ever leave me. I began to think of Daniel and how I was almost sure now he was also Nathan in my present life, 2010. Was he? Is he? How could he not be?

Daniel and I spent most of the night together. I told him my story. I told him my story in depth. I told him everything that I could get out. He knew all about my mother and how she had been treated badly after my father's death. He knew how she had worked here at the Pretty Pink House too, so that she could give provide for me and give me a good education. He knew how she had become sick and why I resorted to this life as she had done. He knew everything and he understood everything. There were no questions, no judgement, no condemnation. He still was here with me.

Daniel and I lay together on top of the bed covers. It felt like home, just holding each other. He did not receive the services for which he had paid Madame. That was not why he came here, though. He came because he knew me.

It was then that I, Marisa, would understand that he and I had been together before in another place and time. Maybe even centuries before now, we had shared a life together. After all, this period I was viewing was more than a century ago itself.

Somehow I knew also that Daniel was ahead of me. He knew more about ourselves, about us so to speak. Maybe he already knew about our past lives together. I began to believe that Daniel knew so much more than I did, and that he was more awakened and enlightened about such things as these…these carnal lives we live and have lived, along with the karma that we carry along our ways and that keep us bound on this regrettable yet sometimes delightful plane.

Tears would fill my eyes again as I thought how the heavens had blessed me in spite of all my bad decisions and all my wrongs. Most of all, the tears would fall because I had met a man of such chivalry, such decency, and of such love and kindness. I felt I had been unworthy of such a blessing. Who was I, anyway, to deserve this man?

The morning came. We had spent the night talking and holding each other. No sexual favors were given. How odd, I thought, for I had wanted him badly and I knew he wanted me too. Somehow, we both felt we needed to wait.

Daniel needed to go. He told me he would be back tonight. It was Sunday now. It was relayed to me that we would be together for several days more before he would need to leave New Orleans to another area on business.

After we said our goodbyes for the day, I saw myself quickly getting washed and dressed for the day. As I entered the front parlor and greeted a couple of the ladies, I could see Madame in the foyer. *Oh my goodness*, I thought. *Did she know what happened last night? Did she know I was with Daniel all night?*

"Good morning, Collette." She coyly tilted her head and blinked her eyes. *She knows what happened last night*, I thought.

"Good morning, Madame."

"Let's go into the second parlor and talk a spell, my dear."

I nervously walked with Madame as she had her arm around mine. As I said before, she always walked with us in this style of hers whenever she expected to have a chat with us.

"So did you have a pleasant encounter last night?" so politely and softly did she ask me. Yes, she was smiling too.

"Yes, Madame. Daniel was very nice and a true gentleman. Everything went well."

"Well, obviously, since you umm," as she tended to her hair with one hand and looking away, "spent all night together. But I already knew the two of you would. You see, Collette, this gentleman, as you say, has taken such a fancy to you. He wants to spend several nights with you. He has paid top dollar, as I told you. You don't mind that, do you now? Now, if you do, and it bothers you to be with him for that period of time, you can tell me and I can arrange a change or different plan of some sort. You know, I try my best to keep my pretty pink ladies happy, and they do the same for me. Am I right, Collette?" Her wide smile made me smile too.

Actually, my smile was because of how delighted I was just thinking of spending several nights with Daniel. Actually, my smile was due to the idea of seeing him naked and having us spend time in carnal lust…eventually.

"Yes, Madame, it is fine with me. I am willing to spend several nights with the gentleman, especially since he is paying top dollar, as you said. I am always here to do my work and have your business prosper, Madame." Really, Collette?

"Well there you go. I am so happy to hear that, Collette. Now, you are not falling for this gentleman, are you? Not looking him in the eyes, are you? I would be very displeased and disappointed if so."

"No, Madame. Of course not so," I lied ever so blatantly.

It was relayed to me that Daniel and I would consummate our union the next night that we were together. "Consummate our union?" Why was I thinking this choice of words? Especially after thinking of carnal lust, it seemed so formal, but I smiled and knew naturally we would.

Chapter 10

AND SO WE CAME TO BE

You came to me and you saw the
beauty in my soul before we ever met.

*I*t was Tuesday morning when I awoke. I had to look at the calendar on
my phone to be certain of the day. Are you kidding me? It seemed as
though I had been gone forever. It had only been one night and Nathan had just
left yesterday.

I began to reminisce about my visit back in time. I thought of all the changes
and how I had adapted to that way of life. I thought about the ladies who had
become my friends. I was saddened for a moment when I remembered how my
mother and I had cried together for the life I had chosen. I realized I had two lives
and two families. I was pleased to know from my mother that Madame Mae was
a generous woman, a kind woman. She took care of us too. Not only my mother
by having Miss Isabel as her caretaker, but she took very good care of her pretty
pink ladies.

I began contemplating of who and what I was in 1881. I was nineteen, young
and pretty. I was working in a brothel to take care of my mother and myself. Yes,
I was a pretty pink lady at the Jolie Maison Rose…The Pretty Pink House. I am
not actually proud of who I was in that lifetime, but I am not ashamed either now.
I was who I was. Shit happens, as they say. No one is ever perfect. Every soul that
lives in this lifetime right now is here because of their karma. If not, they really do
not belong here.

Yet I guess maybe there are those here only as lightworkers, who are here to
sprinkle and douse us with their wisdom and deposit their gifts, as Calissa said.

Those people who look down their noses and portray themselves as better than
others once lived a not-so-prominent or charmed life. I know this now. *Never will*

I judge again, I thought.

But Daniel! I met Daniel. I had met a young, handsome and successful man at a brothel. Can you believe that? And the best of all, he was my "familiar" one. Yes, I did indeed believe that Daniel was Nathan now. Calissa was right. Daniel had been one of those people who would always be with me, as I remembered Calissa's imparted wisdom.

I snapped out of my thoughts. I jumped out of bed and began to dance the dance that my MoonGlow taught me many years ago. Charlie and Sugars watched me with their peculiar looks while talking to me as if they were saying, "There she goes again with that dancing shit she does."

I hurried back to the window to look for her. "Oh, how have I missed you, my dear sweet forever friend." My eyes filled with my salty tears. They were tears of joy and of sorrow. I had missed my very best friend, though I had seen her just last night. It seemed as if it had been forever without her closeness and without her presence.

It was early morn, and there she was. My MoonGlow was still there. I do believe she was there on purpose just to see me. Her face was present as she smiled. I waited and she blew me her intoxicating kiss. How I loved her kisses. How I loved her love for me. With tear-soaked eyes, I said to her, "How blessed I am, dear friend, to have you in my life and to have you love me so." Our God had blessed me indeed.

I waved goodbye, just for today. This evening we would meet again. I ran over and grabbed Charlie and Sugars. I do not believe I was able to give them enough of my hugs and kisses. I had missed them too.

I laughed as we all scurried downstairs. I laughed for thinking that I had been gone for such a long time when in reality, I had not been gone at all. "I am living an amazing life here, my sweetie pies. I have the best of two worlds and it's actually true that I'm living in two worlds!" I calmed down for a moment—and just for a moment— thinking of what was yet to be in my past life and in this present life. "Nothing is perfect forever here, though. Everything comes and goes. Only after we leave for good will it be perfect."

My phone rang. "That must be my man!" I proclaimed crazily to Charlie and Sugars. I must have scared them a bit, for both took off in flight in opposite directions as I ran like a schoolgirl crushing over a cute guy who was new in her life.

I had left my phone upstairs and so I was running as I had never run before. If I did not know better, I would swear I leapt over two to three steps to make it in time.

"Well, hello, handsome," I said breathlessly.

"Well, hello, beautiful. You sound just like you did the last night I was there." He laughed that ever manly and seductive laugh of his. "Guess you had to run some to get to the phone, huh? Guess you miss me, then."

I blushed, wondering why I was blushing over the phone. "I forgot that I left my phone upstairs. I do believe I could make it to the Olympics, though, even now at this age. You should have seen me gallop up these stairs. I knew it would be you calling. Well, I hoped it would be. Oh, and I do for sure miss you, you know?"

"Not to be presumptuous, but I know, cuz I miss you so much too. Had a dream of you last night."

"Oh yeah, well you are a dream to me, mister. Every moment is like a dream since I've met you." Really, Marisa? I was somewhat surprised at my boldness, but then again, why not be bold and just let him know everything I was feeling?

"Lady, I love you. I love you, Marisa."

After my travel to 1881 last night, I knew certainly now why we had fallen so quickly in love after knowing each other for only a couple of weeks. I knew everything now…well, a lot more than I had before. I could feel in the depths of my soul that he was Daniel. He and I had shared a lifetime together. I wondered for just one moment if it was possible that we had shared other lifetimes. I resumed my being in the present, and quickly responded.

"I love you, too, you know. I love you, Nathan." And of course, I started to cry.

"What's wrong? Why are you crying?" Nathan's voice had softened

"Oh, nothing. Absolutely nothing at all! I guess…I…I guess I am just overwhelmed, overjoyed, and over the top elated that you even exist. You actually exist and you love me. And I love you back. You are in this life of mine. I don't understand how it happened and how it happened so quickly, but it happened, and I'm just elated."

"Yeah, so am I. It's only Tuesday and next weekend can't get here quick enough. I wanna hold you, kiss you, and love on you."

I thought for a moment what I had said to Nathan about not understanding how our relationship had happened so quickly. Of course, I knew. Of course I knew because he was Daniel and we had shared a life together over a century ago. On the other hand, it came to mind to wonder why had I not met him earlier in this lifetime. That I did not understand.

We continued to talked for a few more minutes since Nathan had to meet with clients. He was making me swoon so much that I had to sit on the side of my bed to keep from fainting. I felt that feeling again of being a schoolgirl with a compelling crush— and you know what? I loved this feeling. It was time for me, and it was time for Nathan.

Of course, most assuredly he was making me swoon. I remembered the valiant, very charming and kind man that Daniel was. Chivalry was most definitely not dead as some would believe, for my Nathan had never lost it.

As we closed the conversation, he said, "Marisa, my beautiful lady, I look forward to tasting you again."

"Tasting, huh? I love that. I love the way you talk to me and the things you say to me. I wanna taste you, too. I wanna hold you. Come to my bed soon, Nathan."

He paused for a moment and said, "Not only the sweetness of your body, my lady, but once I tasted the sweetness of your soul…any other would just be the ordinary."

I do not remember what I had said to him after his words. I only knew that I had entered through a doorway, it seemed, as in a trance. Yes, he had tasted the sweetness of my soul in 1881. So now, he has again tasted my soul's sweetness for him.

I was literally on cloud nine now as I sat on the side of my bed peering out the window with no signs of MoonGlow and High Tide. It was morning and it was a glorious morning. It was a morning for singing and dancing. It was a morning of daydreaming and having dreams come true. My dreams had come true, I thought. The Creator of all the universe and those beyond had blessed me. He brought my Daniel back to me. How odd that I was thinking this. Yet again, "Daniel came first and now he is back as my Nathan," as I giggled. He was back again.

My daydreaming ended abruptly when my phone rang again. It was Caroline.

"Oh my goodness. You are calling me on a Tuesday morning? I miss you, dahhhling! There is so much I need to tell you about my weekend with Nathan."

"Why do you think I'm calling on a Tuesday morning, sweetie? Not just to talk with you, pardon me, but I wanna hear all the scoop…the juicy part that is with that fine specimen of a man! Wanna hear everything about how great he is in bed…tell me everything!" Caroline bellowed her bold, loud laugh that I truly loved and truly had missed.

I probably ended up telling her more than I should, but oh well. I trusted Caroline in every way. She was one of the few that would accept me for myself, never judging or criticizing. Though we had our differences in many ways regarding our spiritual beliefs, she always listened and just accepted me. Or were there really that many differences in the spiritual sense? In some way, I am not so sure. When it came to the spiritual, she never would discuss much, until she told me of her experience here at MoonGlow. Maybe some day she would open up and tell me more?

"I hope you come back to visit us soon. Charlie, your lover boy, really misses you. I want you to get to know Nathan a bit, too. Just a bit, you know what I mean?" Caroline and I knew each other's teasing and we could always have fun with it. Never would either one of us ever cross lines, especially when it came to our men.

As I loved on my cats, the doorbell rang. I had not even heard the arrival of a vehicle, which I would normally do.

"Marisa Bordeaux?" As the man asked, I wondered why he left the hyphen off my last name.

As I confirmed myself as the inhabitant of this intriguing residence, I stood stunned and amazed as I watched another employee start taking out vases of flowers from a florist van. Multiple vases were being removed and carried carefully into my house. Flowers of various kinds and colors filled each vase, and each so different from the other.

I stood there speechless. The two men clearly recognized my expression and shock of the spectacle before us.

One of the men handed me a card. I quickly opened it and slowly read it to myself. "Your beauty is new and with no comparision, yet your beauty seems ever familiar and ever ancient. How long have I loved you? I have loved you forever, Marisa, and forever it will be….You will always possess every bit of my love… Nathan."

I was speechless again and stood frozen. How did such a man as he even exist? How is that even possible? How could I be the woman that this man would choose to love and to have? At that moment I felt undeserving, but why so? Why was I unexpectedly questioning my worthiness?

I quickly attempted to give the gentlemen a tip, but they both told me everything had been taken care of. As they left, I slowly closed the door behind me and stood as if in a trance, shifting from admiring one vase of flowers to the next. Never in my life had a man surprised me such as this. But this was not just a man. He was my man. He was my Daniel of long ago. He was the man who had tasted the sweetness of my soul, as I had tasted the sweetness of his soul. How long had we really known each other? How many times had we shared our lives together? Would I ever know the answers? Would MoonGlow and High Tide ever be so kind to reveal everything to me, or was it written in the stars to reveal what had been decided, and then nothing more?

Another ring at the door presented before I could get to the phone to call Nathan. There were not only two, but several men standing near a couple of trucks that had parked outside the fence.

"Ma'am, are you Marisa Bordeaux?" As I nodded and said yes, "We're from Mr. Nathan's crew. We're here to do…uh, to actually set up the stone fixture for the entrance. The name of your home is MoonGlow?"

I was speechless. I remembered I had told Nathan how I wanted to put up a five-foot stone fixture with MoonGlow's name along with a quote of mine, so that everyone who came would feel the enchantment. I had hope they would feel it anyway.

I finally spoke up. "Yes, I am Marisa. You have to forgive me, for this is quite a surprise. I had no idea that Nathan was going to do this."

I stood on the porch as I watched the men get ready to plant the stone fixture. They had asked me beforehand to confirm the exact placement. I still remained stunned and in awe. "Wow, Nathan has done all of this for me. And the flowers! Unbelievable."

I finally walked back into the house. The cats were being a little naughty now. I found a few of the leaves and greenery spread around in various areas. It was all right, though. At least they had not knocked over even one of the vases…as of yet, that is.

I ended up placing a few of the vases on the veranda. I shook my head as I looked out toward the Great Liquid. How I loved hearing its sounds. How I loved watching in awe and being mesmerized of the rise and fall of its massive liquid. How beautiful it was. How fearful it was.

As I continued to observe the movements, I remembered I had learned that this mysterious liquid hides what is hidden. It hides in its deepest recesses of its bowels our secrets, our desires, our longings of ages old and deep. This liquid hides from our physical eyes with its solvent veil, and chooses to reveal that what is hidden only when we are ready. Or did it reveal when the Great Liquid itself was ready?

I called Nathan. I was elated. I was giddy. I was a hot mess. I do believe if he had been here, there would be nothing he could do but totally surrender to every command I asked, that I needed, and that I wanted. Those commands would Nathan not be averse to, may I say. Those commands would have been welcomed by many a man.

I could not thank Nathan enough for all the flowers and the incredible stone display. Yes, I cried. Of course I did. They were tears of joy and gratitude. They were tears of love. That love was the strongest I had ever felt for anyone. It was powerful. It was fixed in stone.

"MoonGlow is complete now, my sweet man. I totally love it. Her name and my quote fit beautifully and give such sweet homage to my friend. You're an amazing man and I love you so much, Nathan. Come home to me now!"

I realized I said "home." Of course he had a condo here, but I was referring to my home. I truly wanted him to come home to me.

Nathan laughed. "The day after tomorrow—and yeah, it can't get here soon enough. You know, I hope you didn't think that sending that garden of flowers and having the fixture delivered and set for you was presumptuous of me. I know it's only been about two weeks, but Marisa, for me it seems I have known you so much longer. I feel…."

"Stop there, Mr. Nathan. I feel exactly the same. The thought of just a couple of weeks came into my mind too, but just as you said, I feel exactly the same. For some reason, this connection is powerful. It's a like a magnet pull."

"Yes, baby, it's like a magnet pull." We paused for a moment in silence listening to other's breathing.

"Well, that stone fixture, as you call it, will be done in no time, since it only needs to be set. So, baby, your home is complete now, as you say. I wanna say we're complete too, you know? I feel as though we're also somehow fixed in stone,

Marisa. From the beginning that I saw you, I somehow knew we were. Already set from eons old. I love you, baby."

Again, he said everything I wanted and needed to hear. "I feel the same. I love you, Nathan." I wiped my tears.

"It's crazy and it's wild, isn't it?" Nathan tried to lighten it up.

"Yes, but I love it. You make me crazy, you know. And it suits me. I'm just your wild, untamed gypsy. It's in my soul."

"Ahhh, exactly, my beautiful wild gypsy. Exactly. I love it!"

A knock on the door told me that the work was completed. Nathan and I said our goodbyes for now. I went out to observe the view from the entrance.

I gazed at the words. At the top was the name "MoonGlow" in a dark yellow color on a dark-gray slate plaque. Below were the words:

An enchanted abode of long ago dreams
filling evening's dance with luminous gleams…

The day was passing fast and I was glad, since that meant the weekend would be coming soon and my fine specimen of a man would be arriving. I imagined him driving up and getting out of his truck. I would be drooling at the window as I would admire his masculine face with his scruffy beard and anticipated kiss. I would skim over his body and lust for him. If I were not so somewhat proper, I would be naked and ready to devour him as soon I opened the front door. *Maybe someday, Marisa. Maybe soon.*

I went for a walk along the beach. I walked over toward the southern part this time. I noticed a woman who seemed to be walking toward my direction. I was right. She approached me with a beautiful white smile.

"Hi, I'm Terri…Terri Roberts. I live in the house up there. I know you are new here and I wanted to introduce myself. I've been wanting to meet you, dear. I've seen you walk the beach and at times have seen you and another lady out having a good time in the evenings, back about a couple of weeks ago. That's how I know you are the one who bought the house and my, my, I have to say you have done an amazing renovation of that home! I love the way it looks now. It seems as though what that dilapidated property that looked something awful for years had suddenly been transformed into a jewel of a place. Listen to me, I haven't even let you say a word. Where are my manners?"

"Oh, that's okay. I am just so happy to meet a neighbor, actually. I most certainly have been busy with a lot of stuff. Oh, my name is Marisa Bordeaux…uh, Landon, and I live alone. Well, I have my two cats, Charlie and Sugars, and…."

"Oh my goodness, you're an animal lover! I am too. So much that I help run an animal shelter here on the other side of town. You should come over and see it.

Hey, you may just want to volunteer once in a while. You are most welcome to do so. You would love it, dear. Plus, all our babies would love it too, as well as all of us, the volunteers of course. So you just have your two cats? No dogs? My husband and I have three cats and one dog. We are just busy, busy, busy. No kids. Never had any, so my babies are my kids. Oh, my husband's name is Bill. He's a realtor in this area. Oh, I know Stan was or is your realtor. Right? Bill and I know him and his wife well. Paula is her name. Have you met her? She's a sweetheart."

As she took a breath, I interrupted quickly, "Yes, I have known Stan and Paula quite well for some time now. They are both sweethearts. I would love to come over and see the shelter. Let's plan that. In the meantime, I really have to get back to catch up on stuff."

Before she could say another word, as I could tell she was anxious to do, I rattled some more stuff off. "It was so very nice meeting you. I've been wanting to meet some of my neighbors. I haven't had the time to do so just yet."

"Well, goodness, let's get together for lunch in town and then drop by the shelter. How about tomorrow?"

I thought since Nathan was not around and there was not much else to do except for my writing, I decided to agree.

"Actually, that would be great. How about noonish? I will drive up to your place and pick you up." I wanted to be the one to do the driving so that I could manage the time frame, since I had started back on my writing and I needed to discipline myself, which had not been a strong suit of mine since I had moved here. *Hell, I met Nathan. What would you expect? He is Mr. Fine Specimen of a Man!* I clearly was thinking to myself as Terri had started talking, but did not quite remember all that was said until I stopped dreaming.

"That's wonderful, new friend of mine. I am so looking forward to it. But you know, you have to promise me that you are going to give me the full presentation and viewing of your beautiful home. Promise? Ohhhh...and at night..." Terri placed her hand on her heart and let out a deep breath, "that house is absolutely glowing at night. What kind of paint did you paint her with? Oh, and especially when the moon is out. It's amazing! I just can't wait to see her."

She made me smile. My new friend, Terri, loved my home at a distance. Wait until she saw it up close.

Believe it or not, we did part and went our separate ways back to our own homes. As we gave each other a hug, I felt as though we had been friends for a long time. *Oh wait,* I thought. *Did we know each other in another lifetime? Is that why I am feeling this way? I am so much more aware of these feelings of "familiarity" now.* Of course, we all go through life meeting people and feeling akin to them at the very first moment. So maybe Terri and I were related or friends in another lifetime indeed. Maybe MoonGlow would reveal that to me some day.

I giggled with her as we said goodbye. I thought, *I like her. There's something about her. Here we go again.* I was laughing as I walked away. I sighed a joyful and fulfilling sigh. I contemplated this new friend of mine on the way back.

As I reached the boardwalk and stood looking up at my home, my MoonGlow, I thought about what Terri had said about my beautiful home. Yes, she was right. It was amazing at nightfall, especially when the moon was out...when my best friend, MoonGlow, appeared. Little did Terri know, though, that the moon was out every night in full view for me, showing off her glowlight and her majesty every single night, just for me. I guess I was special. No, I was just blessed. I was blessed for having this lovely home, my family, my friends, old and new here, and most of all, for Nathan...oh, most of all for Nathan.

As I entered my charming and curious abode, I began to think how other people, besides Terri, would view my home. I wondered about their thoughts, their comments, and even if they would dare to ask about the unseen inhabitants in and around this newly established beach vessel of mine. I smiled, for I clearly was convinced that nothing but complimentary thoughts would occur to visitors.

After I called Nathan and we talked about how much we meant to each other, I spent the entire afternoon writing. I had started writing a novel a short time before I had moved in. I was writing about a woman whose husband had died. Her son was in college. She moved away and bought a house on the beach. Her adventures began with her best friend who helped her meet the man of her dreams. Yeah, I was writing my own story. Fiction? Well, in a way. I was changing things up and making up along the way. It helped that this amazing experience was actually helping, too.

Twilight was coming soon. Nathan had called me a couple of times now. Texting was frequent. Everything about him was inviting and reciprocated. I loved him more and more every day, every minute, and every second as time went on.

I had started relaxing and drinking my wine for the very much anticipated evening. I gave Charlie and Sugars each a strong hug and several kisses. I started my ritual. I put on some maroon-colored lipstick and a little blush. It may sound silly, but this was always a part of the ritual before my elusive nights of mystical delights.

I pulled on a white camisole. A yellow flowered sarong wrapped around my hips and fell slightly above my knees. I was barefoot. My hair had been loosed and parted on the right side. It had not been cut or even trimmed since I moved in. It was several inches down my shoulders now and I liked it that way. Nathan had told me that he loved my hair and I thought about how he would take hold of it, lift it, smell it, caress his face with it. I had left it curly and wild today. I wanted tonight to be gypsy wild. I wanted it to be like the first couple of nights when I had started my adventure. I could not wait to spend time with MoonGlow and High Tide. I had missed them so much, yet I was with them only last night. Oh well, I was just a mere human. Time and timelessness were both elusive to me now.

I took my music and my soul along with me as I glided barefoot down the boardwalk and onto the sand. It felt good to feel the cool sand wrapping itself around my feet. The Great Liquid was still at low tide. Where was MoonGlow, though? As I waited for her, as I longed for her, I drank the wine. My thoughts went back to the man I loved. Maybe the two men I loved? I laughed.

"No one would believe me. My story would be too bizarre. Definitely, I would be labeled demented and crrrraaazy!" I began to swirl and dance the dance of gypsies long ago. Oh, how I wished Caroline were here to dance with me too, for my MoonGlow refused to appear. Why was that?

I continued the dance. I suddenly was startled with a piercing ring in my right ear. It made me lose my balance for a bit as I looked upward toward my right into the night sky. There she was. She had come with a glowlight, illuminating more than I had ever seen. Yes, she was the Queen Bee. She was the Queen Bee of the Nights, of all nights here and elsewhere. Because of her majestic size tonight, her countenance was ever so clearly pronounced, like never before. Her beautiful face was of no comparison to any other. Who was she? Why of course, I knew who she was. She was my friend, my best friend. She was my sister, eons old.

MoonGlow closed her eyes and blew me her kiss. Oh, how I loved her kiss, for I knew it was a kiss of love, a kiss of a special blessing and of a special promise. That special promise she had bestowed on me from the moment my father dedicated me to her…and from thence onward everything was set…set and written in her heart, which no one could or would ever be able to fracture or rupture. She would always be mine to keep. She would always keep her sentimental watch over me. She would always be my MoonGlow.

SENTIMENTAL PLAY

It was relayed to me that she meant to come at this time and in this special way of majestic glowlight for a reason. Before she commanded her own lover to come forth from the Great Liquid, she would take me to a special place tonight…a place of play and delight. It was time, she relayed. It was time to play for a while.

I started laughing and twirling as if a childlike trance had come over me. I was giggling, and the sounds were those of a child. I was unexpectedly taken by a swift and instant force, which seemed like wind projecting me to take flight into the "nights of lights and mysteries."

As I was carried by this unknown force, I felt helpless, and yet I had succumbed. I knew my MoonGlow was taking me there and she would keep watch. I suddenly felt my upper arms being held by someone. I was unable to move any part of my body due to the force I had succumbed to. For a moment, though, I could see behind me, without ever moving my head, who this someone was. It was a gargantuan creature, surely of some paramount control in these night skies. I was not afraid, though. I felt safe, for as I looked about I saw galaxies beyond galaxies. They were composed of zillions of illumined stars and glowlit moons. Shooting lights were flickering in colors indescribable in my human language. I felt myself being wrapped more securely. I felt safe and I felt a joy that seemed to me at that moment no one else but myself could have felt.

My being rested in this magnificent, beautiful winged creature as he led me further and further up into the heavens. I began to feel large drops of tears running down my face. They were not tears of sadness, but of extreme ectasy of utmost joy. I could taste the saltiness of my tears.

Quick as a lightning bolt, I was immediately placed on a starlit playground, as it was relayed to me. The playground had no ground beneath me, though. It was filled with the night skies of swirls and shoots of colored lights, rainbows, and distant fields of endless flowers. There were giggles of children about me, but I could not see any of them.

"You are in a place of play now that you may call 'The World of Sentimental Play.' We of old and we of ancient call it 'The World of Ancient Play.'"

I smiled and giggled again. I was a child again. I was one of them. I started to dance the dance, but not the gypsy dance, but the dance of the ancient...the dance of "sentimental mystical play."

Then they came. They were the "starlight children," as relayed to me. They came from every direction. They were skipping and dancing all around me and their giggles were delightful and welcoming. Their little bodies were filled with light as they frolicked. I thought of their light being remnants of the Great Light from our Creator. *Can God get any more awesome than this?* I thought.

I took delight in them and they in me. Their stardust glistened on my skin as they spun around and speckled my eyes with dancing lights. I knew and felt their love for me was pure. I laughed and surrendered without thought to their playful dance as I merged with my light-bodied friends. The play would continue. There were no expectations, no judgements, no questions. It was just a sentimental play filled with immeasurable love and joy never felt before.

After some immeasurable time, I knew I had to go. I saw the immense winged creature coming forward. His wings were glasslike and clear. There seemed to be liquid pellets—or maybe they were crystals—interspersed throughout his wings. He was beautiful and grand.

As he swept me up, my eyes began to mist again with large drops of tears. I did not want to leave. I was not ready. I could see my light-bodied friends signaling their goodbyes and blowing their starkisses toward my way.

As we left with lightning speed, I could hear lullabyes which seemed to be sung by the starlight children. So sweet and innocent were their voices, the tears would continue on my way back. What a delightful place I had been. I wondered why I was sent there? MoonGlow, do you know?

"In time, my mother, in time," I heard my Calissa say as I traveled back.

"Oh, my Calissa! Did you see me? Were you there?" My tears dried.

My feet landed on the cool sand. It felt good. I looked up at MoonGlow and smiled. She smiled back and blew me a kiss. "Thank you, my sweet MoonGlow." My sincere, heartfelt gratitude was given to her.

I began to wonder though why my MoonGlow had taken me to that whimsical childlike world of play without the power and spirit of her High Tide's assistance as she always had done. I would realize later it was to make known to me her own maternal reasons for doing so. She had wanted to share with me her own maternal feelings toward me and what was yet to be. What was yet to be was not relayed at this time. I would realize that in due time, as Calissa had always said.

I felt alive. I felt giddy. I found my wine bottle and began to drink again. "MoonGlow, ever so feminine and ever so flirtatious you are. Call forth your lover. I am ready for him to take me, too. Show him your playfulness and pull him forth. You know your lover can't stay away from you."

I thought of how her countenance and powerful radiating glowlight could hypnotize and illuminate even the darkest creature set upon this earth. Even in the darkest recesses and crevices where we hide our secrets and our shame, this MoonGlow beckons us to come out and play and dance and seek, even if for a few moments, the delights that only she can give to both lovers and loners.

"Who doesn't love the moon? I asked myself. "Everyone loves her," I shouted and swirled slowly around. I caught a glimpse of Terri's house. I saw a light and a shadow passing upstairs and wondered if she was watching me.

A powerful roar came out of the depths of the Great Liquid, which caused me to break my glance away from the house. The sound had set me unbalanced and I fell back. I felt a force from MoonGlow to keep me from falling. There he was. His liquid plunged out of his recesses and pulled forward. Was he angry? No, it was just because MoonGlow was in such a pronounced glowlight tonight that he could not but help feel the pull of her seductive charm. Oh yes, she was just that.

His liquid projectiles came bulleting forth in various directions. They drenched me and intoxicated me, more than the fine wine I had been drinking. He took me into him.

"Oh, what a flirt you are, High Tide. You are not of human form, but you possess a masculinity that causes the stirrings of my body as your pulling force takes me. A mighty magnet pull you are, mister. Yeah, you are."

I laughed as I was enraptured by him. My heart was soaked and drunken from his liquid. "How sweet to see you again," I relayed. "Why don't you tell me your secrets, High Tide? Do you envy me in any way, since I am human?"

I fell back and my extremities fell limp as High Tide took me into his depths. He took me into his recesses of his liquids. I began to feel myself projecting in a spiral vertical position as I was being lowered. I could faintly hear the voices of others. The books came along the way with their pages flapping in the water. *I'm going back*, I thought. I was ready.

1881 - SEVENTH ENCOUNTER

I was lying in bed. His warm body was behind me. Strong masculine arms were holding me while his mouth was kissing my neck. My eyes opened and I watched myself looking at the small dresser across the way with its smudged and dark mirror pressing up against a wall of dark green. I knew I was back. I was back with Daniel…my sweet Daniel.

I had turned around to face him. Our eyes met and we both smiled and kissed each other. He continued to hold me close to him. I felt safe. I felt secure. I knew we were in the brothel, but I did not want to see myself leaving that bed, that room, nor this place. I did not want to leave if it meant we had to get up, dress ourselves and go about our own ways.

"So Collette, we consummated our union, umm?"

As I watched myself smile broadly and happily, I remembered the last thoughts I had during my last encounter, "We would consummate our union." So we did and we did so willingly. We did so totally against Madame's wishes.

I watched Daniel as he got up from the bed. He was striking. His arms and chest were full and muscular. His legs were strong. He was mine, I thought. Just as Nathan was mine.

I wanted him. I could not resist him. I saw myself quietly tiptoe up to him while he was facing away, about to dress. I kissed his neck and then his shoulders. His breathing deepened and as he turned around, our mouths met as I lifted my right leg and wrapped it around his waist while he grabbed it. His other arm pulled me to his body as he penetrated me again. I knew this love of ours was real. I knew that this man loved me as much as I loved him.

It was relayed to me that we would see each other and be together every evening for the rest of the week. Nothing else was shown or relayed. How in the world did I get away with all of this? How did Madame not even suggest or question me about my goings-on with Daniel? Did she not see it? Certainly, the looks and the change in just myself would have given it away.

I had spent the week in a sorting-out mode. What was natural and familiar about the grand house and my work here now seemed uneasy and distant. I had fallen in love with Daniel. I had my thoughts on possibly and hopefully spending a lifetime with him. I wanted that. I yearned for that. Though I would terribly miss Madame, Annabella, and all the inhabitants here, I wanted Daniel more. I knew he wanted me too. This was a time to contemplate, and decisive conclusions were soon to be.

I saw myself entering the front door to the foyer. It was near the end of the week. I had delivered some clothes and such from the work I had continued to do for just a couple of days a week because of my duties at The Pink House. *My duties?* I thought. I had to laugh for a moment, for my so-called duties were only to tend to the needs of a very fine specimen of a man I had found here. Right here in The Pink House did I find that fine specimen and his name was Daniel.

Madame danced her way back into the foyer. "Oh Collette, my sweet dear, my number one money maker," she happily yet softly said under her breath so no one else would hear. She gave me a kiss on the cheek and a light hug. "How are you, my dear? So are you ready to see that client of mine again? He is treating you well, I hope? Of course he is. All my clientele are gentlemen indeed and treat my fine and best pretty pink ladies well."

No sooner had she that than the front door opened. Two policemen walked in and looked at Madame Mae. They did not even seem to know I was standing right beside her.

Madame looked rather surprised, just as I did. For a few seconds there no words from the two policemen. She stood there looking bewildered and asked, "So officers, why are you here, may I ask? How can I help you?"

"Do you have a lady that happens to be an employee of yours, named Estella Benoit, working here?"

"Why, yes I do actually." Madame appeared to be somewhat worried now. For whatever reason, I did not know, but I was about to find out.

"When was the last time you saw her, Madame?" I heard him say with a sarcastic tone when invoking her name.

"Well, actually I have not seen her in over a week, sir. She had left to visit family and was to have returned by now, but I have not heard from her." Madame took a deep breath and with one hand had tended to her hair as she did when feeling a little uncomfortable or unsure in some way.

"So this Estella has been an employee of yours for some time?"

"For several years now. Never has she not returned, though. She always returns. She enjoys working here."

The two officers looked at each other with raised eyebrows and returned their glances toward Madame.

"Ma'am, I don't know how to put this delicately, but we have reason to believe that we know what became of this Miss Estella Benoit." With a rather long sigh, he continued, "A woman's body was found near the river close to here. She was found early this morning, ma'am."

Madame gave out a cry and I took arm and wrapped my other arm around her. "Let us sit down, Madame," I said to her.

My thoughts came rapidly as I thought how Madame loved each and every one of us. Maybe she loved some more than others, but I knew she loved us all in her own way. I knew she loved Estella too.

I suddenly had glimpses of Estella with Madame. She was childlike, in a way, whenever she spoke with Madame. She would gaze at Madame as a child would gaze at her mother with love and contentment. I never knew of her background and where she came from, but I always sensed her as the "broken girl."

"How do you know it's her? How do you know if it's Estella? My Estella!"

Madame was crying. Her cries brought in a couple of the ladies. I could see Miss Nellie and Miss Ella peering from the dining room into the front parlor. They had taken out their handkerchiefs and placed them to their eyes.

Annabella ran in and sat on the other side of Madame. Tears started flowing from her eyes too, though she had not heard what had happened.

"What is it, Mother? What's wrong?" She looked at the officers and then at me. I thought for a moment that I had never heard her call Madame "Mother."

Madame could not say a word. Her cries were almost like howling sounds. She bent her head and refused to move, and said nothing. She could not speak. I knew then that Madame cared for Estella. I felt her love for her lost pretty pink lady who really meant so much more to her. I began to cry too and Annabella did the same.

After everything was discussed and we understood that identification was found on her, it was decided that poor Madame and Big Sam would go along to identify her body anyway. Annabella would go too.

I saw that I had stayed and remained in the parlor for a time. A couple of the other ladies were there with me. I decided to go out on the front porch and sit on one of the wide, cushioned chairs. I did not remember a time before that I had done so.

As I, Marisa, was watching myself, I could see a fixed glare in my eyes. Suddenly I was seeing through Collette's eyes. There she was.

Estella had come to her in spirit. She was more beautiful than she had ever been here at The Pretty Pink House. Even when she was all dressed up fit to kill, nothing compared to her beauty before me now.

"Collette, my beautiful Collette. I was taken. I had been with my client, the very powerful and rich Mr. Jim from up north of us. He had taken me on a trip with him. While returning, we had stopped to stay at a hotel. He wanted me to speak with one of his fine upstanding friends there and spend time with him. I did not intend to do so, but I spoke with him anyway.

"As Mr. Jim left for a while, this fine upstanding friend of his gave himself permission to get unacceptable with me. I fought him and so he beat me. He killed me, Collette.

"He quietly had me taken out of the hotel by two of his servants. They took my body away. I was taken miles and miles away from there. They ended up throwing my body into the river nearby here. Have they found me yet, my dear Collette?"

I was stunned. I could not move or speak for a while. When a jolt of some force pushed up against me and causing my body to throw forward a bit, I began to speak.

"Yes, Estella, they found your body. They found your beautiful body." As I cried my unceasing tears, so it seemed, I continued on to say, "Madame is crushed, Estella. She really loves you. She really does."

"Shhhh, shhhh, no more tears. You see, I am free now. I am going to the place of mending. You were right, Collette, I am the 'broken girl,' as you say. I need to be mended. I will go into the night skies now and I will be with those who love and mend. All is well, my dear. Do not fret."

Estella held out her hand to me. I saw myself reaching my right hand out to touch hers. I watched our hands touch and fingers intertwined as Estella finished, "We will see each other again, Collette. We are 'familiar.' We are akin."

I was not surprised by Estella's last few words. I had felt that familiarity the first time I had met her. I had felt that I already knew her. Was she with me again in the present?

I continued watching myself and observing my afterthoughts. It was relayed to me that in time Estella's perpetrator would be revealed and justice would be served. It was also relayed that Madame would never be the same. She would grieve for quite some time. Annabella would take over some of Madame's duties. Contracts would be revised and new rules and regulations would also be enforced for protection of Madame's pretty pink ladies. All would be well, I guessed. In time, all would be well.

I was taken back to my mother's bedroom. My mother looked weak and frail. Miss Isabel was there applying washcloths to her face and forehead.

I started to cry. I ran over to the other side of the bed and while holding her hand, I placed my head near hers, telling her how much I loved her. I could barely speak the words, for my cries were dominating and incessant.

I knew I had to tell her. I had to tell her something good and wonderful to allow her to have some peace. If she was dying soon, I wanted her to know that I would be all right and that something good was going to happen. Even though Daniel and I had not discussed that we would marry, I knew that this marriage with Daniel was inevitable. It was written. It was written in the night skies and I knew it was so.

"Mother, I met a man. A good and decent man he is. I know what you are thinking. If I met him at the brothel, how could he be so good?"

I told my mother all about Daniel and how he came to be at The Pretty Pink House. I told her how Daniel had not been one of those who frequented the house. She was told about how he saw me out with Annabella and followed me to The Pretty Pink House. I told her that he loved me and that I loved him. I told her we would marry.

She was happy. She let out a sigh and began to cry. The tears were of joy and relief now. Her prayers had been answered. My mother had suffered for many years for the choices she had made that were not acceptable when raising a child.

"Mother, do not worry. You did what you needed to do for me and for the both of us at the time. God forgives you. He forgives me, too. No more, Mother. No more worries. I am with Daniel now and there will be no others. I am with the man I love and we will have a good life."

My mother rested well after our discussion. The angels blessed her with a deep and peaceful sleep that late afternoon and through the night.

As I entered The Pretty Pink House, it was business as usual—or so it seemed. Madame was in the foyer at her desk. It had been a couple of days since the news of Estella. She was a businesswoman indeed. It was time for work and so she was back to normal—for the night, at least.

I saw myself then in bed with Daniel again. We were talking and we were making plans.

"You need to know that I truly love you. I know that we are meant to be together and have a life together…a family together. I love you, Collette. Will you marry me? Will you do me the honor of being my wife?"

I started to cry. I thought, *Here I go again, crying too much.* I was humbled and I was baffled. Why would a woman like myself who was tainted, it seemed, have a fine man such as Daniel be smitten with the likes of me?

"I love you so much, Daniel. I want to marry you. Yes, yes of course, I will marry you! I just feel bad for Madame. She has done so much for me and my mother. She has taken good care of us, and then there's Annabella and…."

"It's all right, my love. I need to tell you something." He then sat up in the bed.

"I have taken care of everything and I will continue to do so. You have told me about your mother. I want to provide the best for her as well. I want to meet your mother. As far as Madame, Annabella, and the rest, as you say…."

"Oh, Daniel!" The tears began to flood. I was so overwhelmingly consumed with his love for me. I felt so undeserving. I was doubting myself that I could ever be a lady of fine standing with someone as himself. How could I possibly ever measure up to having a man of his stature being proud of me as his wife? I told Daniel my feelings after I had regained my composure. He assured me of his love for me as well as understanding the circumstances which led both my mother and me to surrender to a life such as this.

Daniel held me tightly in his arms. I felt his warmth and his love for me. He said the words I wanted and needed to hear. He assured me that everything would be all right.

"I love you, Collette. You know, once the soul tastes the sweetness of the extraordinary, then the ordinary just will not do. You, my beautiful lady, are the extraordinary that I have tasted."

I then remembered that Nathan had said similar words when we had talked this morning. I remembered. Of course he would say such words of old. For this man with Collette was Nathan's soul, and Collette was my own soul.

I stood motionless in timelessness it seemed as I watched Daniel and myself stare into each other's souls, dreaming of a life together again. Again? I was not at all surprised that we would begin a life again and that we had lived other lives together, even before this one. Everything made sense now.

It was relayed to me that during this time, Daniel had continued on to inform me that he had a made a business deal with Madame. He would not elaborate to me about the deal, for in those days business was never discussed in detail to those not partaking. Things were quite different in that time period. I trusted him, though. I knew his love for me was genuine and it was deep.

I started to remember how jovial Madame had been before we heard of Estella's death. I had wondered why she was not revealing any suspicions of my time with Daniel. Now I knew. Daniel had taken care of everything, as he said.

Even so, I looked at Daniel and admitted that my feelings about leaving Madame, Annabella, and all at The Pretty Pink house would not be easy. I loved everyone here. They had become family to me. Madame Mae had been a surrogate mother to me. Annabella was as my sister.

Yes, they may had been broken too, just as Estella had been the "broken girl." I was broken. My mother was broken. We were all broken. For surely we must have been, for who would succumb to this shameful life, as the fine upstanding women of New Orleans would call it. Selling flesh for money was unworthy and a distinct aversion to society. Why would anyone succumb to such a life? Why would anyone do so? Well, I could give a hundred and more reasons why any poor soul would do so.

I, Marisa, saw a light coming forth toward my right peripheral visual field. As she came closer, I smiled with utmost delight.

"My Calissa. I have missed you. I always miss you. You come to me now when I am in such sorrow. Thank you, my sweet daughter." My tears drenched my face.

"My sweet mother, I love you. Do not cry. This was part of your life. There is a time and place for everything both good and evil. We choose always. It is up to each soul to decide their destinies and the lessons we must learn. In the end we all choose Love. It is the Law."

"The Law?" I asked. "You are right, my daughter. I choose Love. I will always end with choosing Love. Please return to me frequently. If you can that is. If it is permitted, that is. I miss you so."

"I love you, Mother. I am always here with you. I will never leave you. It is written in the light bodies."

Calissa faded from my view. I thought I would try to remember that she was always with me.

And so it came to be that Daniel and I would plan to marry. It was relayed to me that within the next several days, Daniel would meet and spend time with my mother. There were many tears shed again for my mother's transition to a place beyond this world. She passed away happily and at total peace, though. Daniel and I were there with her, as well as Miss Isabel and Madame Mae herself. I would hold her hand and stroke her pale face as she went on her way. If it were not for my valiant and loving Daniel, I do not believe I would have been able to carry on with this life of mine.

After my mother was buried in the cemetery, the priest at the cathedral married Daniel and me in late November. He was twenty-three years of age and I was nineteen years of age. We were one now. We were akin in every way.

The next few days were difficult in every way. I, Collette, had worked as a pretty pink lady for less than five months. It seemed much longer, and I do believe it was because the inhabitants had become as family to me. I would no longer be a part of that life anymore, though. I was sad that I had to leave New Orleans. Why could we not just stay here? I had to say goodbye, but I would go where my husband would go. My heart wanted this more than anything.

It was not relayed to me the conversations with the family. Maybe it was just too painful. My thoughts went to Madame and all the pretty pink ladies, except for Estella, whom I believed was now in a better place, a realm of "love and mending," as she had said.

I thought about Big Sam, my sweet lovable and polite Big Sam. Miss Nellie, Miss Ella, and Miss Isabel were in my heart too.

But most of all…most of all was it was Annabella. How could I leave Annabella? My thoughts wandered back to the first time I had met my sister, Annabella. Yes, she had become a sister to me, and I had become one to her. Just a glimpse of my saying goodbye was relayed to me. Yes, it was much too painful to view. What would become of Annabella? I would find myself praying for her to meet a nice gentleman and marry someday.

So the day came. The day to say goodbye for a while. Daniel promised me that he would take me back here to New Orleans for visits. I would again someday see my family…yes, my family.

So Daniel and I came to be. We came to be husband and wife. And we would go to live our lives elsewhere. We moved to Charleston, South Carolina on November 29, 1881.

2010

I awoke in my bed. My arms flared up. I sat up and touched my chest. I felt as though I was drowning. I could not breathe. As I looked out my window, I could see the starlight children coming toward from their world of play. They blew me their star kisses. I felt them upon my face and mouth. I began to swallow their stardust. I was able to breathe again.

I smiled at these fantastical illumined children of the skies. I remembered their love for me was pure, untainted, and ever so welcoming. Oh, to be suspended in their world of play, their world of suspended timelessness would be a delight again, I thought. For to be as childlike and merry as they were, surely no harm could come my way for all eternity. Their home was no place for any harm or melancholy. Their home of Sentimenal Play would be unquestionably a most welcoming completion after this world, with its innumerable karmic woes. With no hesitation, I would choose to reside with these little bodies of light in their playground of light itself, if it were possible.

I lay in bed thinking of my meandering into that life of 1881 again last night. How happy it made me feel that Daniel had rescued me. He came to me and saw the beauty in my soul before he had ever met me in that lifetime. For you see, he had met my soul once before, or maybe twice, or maybe more. We were "familiar."

But why my experience of drowning as I woke up this morning? Did it have something to do with my fear of the Great Liquid since childhood? Somehow, I knew I needed to be informed of something. Maybe something yet to come. I wanted to forget these thoughts for now, though.

Chapter 11

A TIME OF COLD LIQUID

It is a blessing…that familiar feeling.

It was Wednesday morning now. So the three of us went our merry way downstairs to the kitchen and again relived our usual morning ritual. I did my usual stretching and meditation on the veranda. I prepared coffee for myself. I then prepared breakfast for my darlings, Charlie and Sugars. Lastly, I prepared a little breakfast for myself.

I had felt a little drab for some reason. The drowning sensation continued to bother me. Also, the loss of Estella, and then saying goodbye to all my family back in New Orleans.

I had to adamantly tell myself aloud, "Now Marisa, stop it. Just stop it. This all happened over a century ago. It is done and it is over. You got your man, though. Be happy. You will soon know the rest of the story."

Did I really want to know the rest of the story? I believe I did. I wanted to know about Calissa's birth and her life. Was she happy? Were Daniel and I happy? "Oh, but I don't think I want to know how we died."

I called an energy healer in the area and made an appointment to see her. I felt drained and I had not had my chakras rejuvenated in quite some time. I needed to take care of my soul today.

Nathan sensed I needed to hear his voice. He called just in time.

"Hey, my Marisa. How's my baby this morning?"

His sexy, throaty voice made me swoon. I wanted him here with me now, and then forever. "You know I love you calling me baby, don't you? You're making me swoon. I think I'm actually going to faint."

His manly laugh made the swooning even worse. "Well…you are my baby and I love that I can make you swoon. Wish I were there to catch you. I'd make sure you wouldn't faint from swooning so much over me, cuz I'd take you in my arms and hold you tight against me. You'd be safe with me, woman." As he continued the smile I knew he had on his face at this moment, I imagined his arms around me as I closed my eyes.

"I miss you so much, so much, so much. Will I ever see you again?" I softly and seductively laughed as I lifted my hair and allowed it to fall in its own place across my right shoulder.

I heard him laugh a bit. "My beautiful Marisa, my baby, yes, yes, you're gonna see me again on Friday. I promise. I miss you very much too, you know?"

We talked for the longest time, it seemed. I knew I had to get things ready around the house for Terri. I wanted it to be picture-perfect since I knew she was anxious to see this stunning home.

That did not matter, though. I would have spent the entire day just talking to Nathan, even if I had to cancel my lunch and visit to the animal shelter.

"I can't wait to love on you. I want you so bad, Marisa."

"I want you like crazy, Nathan. Let's get naked like really soon when you get here." I laughed, and he laughed right along with me.

After our talk had ended, I stood up and lifted my arms high above me with my head falling back, took a few deep breaths, and did a few stretches. I looked at the cats, as they both were staring at me, wondering what was going on. They had seen me do my stretching and yoga poses before, but something was different. I somehow was different. Charlie seemed to shake his head humorously and pranced off.

I quickly showered, got dressed, and sprinted around sprucing up the house. Everything looked to be in order. "Damn, what a absolutely beautiful home you are, my MoonGlow. You make me so proud."

As I drove up to Terri's house, I could see her through her front window. She waved without hesitation and flashed that gorgeous white smile of hers. As I had said before, I liked her. I already knew we would become great friends.

Her house had an oversized window which nearly reached up to her ceiling, overlooking the ocean. It was magnificent. Large stone stairs stood proudly before her house. It was a two-story, painted pale turquoise, with white shutters. It simply looked gorgeous. I actually loved it. It was perfect to be setting on a hill before the majestic view of the ocean.

"Well, well—welcome, Marisa, to my home, my dear new friend." She danced her way out the front door, but stayed at the top while I walked the mile-long stairs, as it seemed at the time. "I call her Sea Dance."

"Oh, I like that, Terri. How beautiful she looks, and definitely I would dance with her all right."

"Ohhhh, you're a dancer, too? I love to dance, especially once I've had a drink or two—and you?"

"Oh, that's me, all right. But I'm always ready to dance no matter what." I lifted and swung my arms. "If you only knew, my dear, if you only knew." Suddenly, I was thinking of inviting her to an evening of adventure. But why was I thinking that? Hmmm? Maybe she was a lot like me. Just maybe she was.

Terri proceeded to show me the rest of her house. It was indeed magnificent. Very light and bright it was. Very welcoming was her home.

She then introduced me to her cats and her dog. Her cats all came over as she called them. I thought how amazing that was. They were three of different colors. One was pure black, the second was a gray and white tabby, the third was a calico.

"Okay, this is Eeny, Meeny, and Miny. My dog here, a mutt actually, so mixed and sweet, we really can't tell quite what he is. Now he's my real baby, Moe."

I suddenly burst out laughing so hysterically that I ended up feeling so very embarrassed. Yet, so much was my uncontrollable laughter, that I could not even begin to apologize for my outburst.

Then there it came. Terri began to bellow out her laughter too. It reminded me a lot like Caroline's.

Damn it, I thought. *We both are going to ruin our makeup.* We ended up having to wipe our eyes.

"I am not offended at all, Marisa. Believe me, everyone who comes to meet them the first time does exactly the same. They all start laughing hysterically. It's okay. It's okay. And don't ask me why I named them as I did. I don't really know. I just thought it would be cute and so I did. Yes, it's hysterical, isn't it?"

I continued to laugh some more. I just could not help myself. There was something naturally funny about her pets' names, and something naturally funny and lovable about Terri.

We managed to hug it out, dry our eyes, and settle down for a bit. Terri was totally delightful. Not only did I get such a blessing of buying and moving into my dream home along with my friends of old to keep me company, and then Nathan, the new man of my dreams, I had also met an amazingly beautiful new friend, who happened to live right next to me.

We drove into town to a nice casual beach restaurant overlooking the ocean. We sat at a covered table outside. We acted like old friends. It was so easy to just sit and talk with Terri. I never had many of these occasions with others, because I always felt people were judging me for being so different in the ways I viewed life and such. Terri was just like me. She was eccentric in her own way, too. We were akin.

After our delightfully easy and carefree lunch, we drove over to the animal shelter. Terri and her friend, Cathie, had started the shelter several years ago as a nonprofit charity, and fortunately had numerous volunteers who ever so willingly offered countless hours of providing not only the necessities, but the love and devotion needed to care for these homeless dogs and cats.

The shelter was located on the other side of the town and was a simple structure. It was nicely kept outside as well as inside. As Terri and I entered the premises, a couple of the volunteers were in the front living/office area. I could immediately guarantee I would be become a volunteer myself, and possibly make a set of new friends here. Somehow I knew these friends would be genuine. I already knew Terri was a sure thing.

"Cathie, here is Marisa, whom I had told you about. She's the one who bought the house next to me…the house which stood alone for several years. Can you believe it? But as I already said, it looks like I will be the fortunate one to see first the unbelievable transformation, as you know!"

Cathie had been smiling and held out her hand immediately to mine, saying, "So nice to meet you, Marisa," right after Terri had said "Cathie, here is Marisa…."

"I heard you did an amazingly beautiful job on renovating that house. I would love to come see it too sometime. It looks stunning, just from Terri's view at her house."

I humbly thanked her for the compliment as I looked at both of the ladies and said, "Of course. As a matter of fact, I will invite you all over soon some evening. I promise you will be enchanted."

"Ohhhh, enchanted? I like that!" Cathie seemed to have a unceasing smile and laughed readily at everything that was said. She had a contagious way of making myself and probably everyone immediately feel joyful, I must add. She went on to tell me that she had a young son in college too. Her husband was chief of surgery at the nearby hospital. I thought it was no wonder this shelter was so nice and well kept. They did have the means of keeping it quite meticulous, it seemed. On the other hand, they did have fundraisers a couple of times a month, along with the adoption days.

After my visit, I drove Terri back to her house. I told her I wanted to spend time writing and that I had scheduled myself disciplined times for doing so.

"Why don't you come by tomorrow early evening before nightfall, of course, and we'll have drinks and appetizers? I can show you my enchanted abode then. Oh, and also my enchanting cats."

"Oh, would I love to come by? Of course, I would. That seems like fun. I can't wait."

Terri and I gave each other a hug. "Yes, I now have a friend right next door. It seems as though I'll be making other friends too." I smiled and thought how happily my life was turning out. Most of all, though, I was ecstatic about having that fine specimen of a man, Nathan…my Nathan…he was mine now.

After I spent an hour with the energy healer, I felt rejuvenated. I thought, *My chakras seem back on track.*

I spent the rest of the afternoon writing, into early evening. I had no interrupted thoughts, no moments of being unclear about what I was writing. It was as if some force had propelled me with profound and welcoming "aha" moments. These kinds of moments never ceased to amaze me, as I sat humbly in awe.

Nathan and I would send each other our love notes and sometimes naughty notes during a needed break every now and then. This carefree afternoon had filled my heart with a joy of that sweet "familiar" feeling of days of old. That feeling belonged to me and to Nathan, and we had shared it many ages ago.

Just as I finished my writing for the day, there went the doorbell. "My, a third time now since yesterday. That is unusual." I laughed out loud as I looked at my two surprised-looking cats. The two of them always seemed to get excited whenever the doorbell would ring at my old home, but now it had not been frequent at all since I had moved in. But yesterday was totally out of the norm. I had never seen those two cats in such a frenzy, wondering, "What the hell?" As doorbells were ringing, and flowers were being sent in the multitudes, my cats really saw some action. It was good for them, I thought, to get out of the everyday norm for a bit.

I peered through the curtain door. My jaw dropped. As I opened the door, there she was! Caroline had surprised me and indeed it was a delightful surprise.

"Surprise! Here I am!" She threw her hands up as if she was everything that anyone would want to see. Well, I most certainly did want to see her, even if nobody else did.

As I just stood in shock, she told me she wanted nothing more than to surprise me for once in her life and just show up, "like in the movies," she said. "I always wanted to know what that was like…just showing up totally unannounced and see the expression on that, well, somebody's face. Uhhhh, how's it going, dahhhling? Are you going to invite me in or what?"

We both started laughing hysterically. Oh, how I loved hearing that laugh of hers in person now. That loud bellowing laugh was the most contagious of all laughs. Yes, it was the best surprise ever.

"Oh, I see you got your MoonGlow name stamped out there. Looks totally awesome…love it."

As we brought in her belongings and settled in the front room, she said, "What the hell? Oh my goodness!" Her eyes glared at me while her hands had rested on her hips. "Are you kidding me? Well, I know for sure who sent these to ya."

Yes, she was astounded by the flowers, the many many flowers, but she had not seen the veranda yet, so I had to laugh.

Caroline told me that she had taken a few days off to finish some of life's catch-ups, as she always called it, and wanted to come over to surprise me.

"I am only here for tonight and tomorrow night. I know, I know, your Mr. Fine Specimen of a Man is coming back to his little sweet darling Marisa so she can have some of him…and take hold of that good stick of …."

"Stop it! Caroline, you are so so bad. For goodness' sake!" I turned all shades of red indeed.

"Oh come on, Marisa," she said, laughing even louder. "I'm your best friend. Tell me—what is he like in bed? Tell me everything. He's gotta be good, girl. He is so fine."

"Oh my goodness, you are incorrigible!" I screamed aloud, so emphatically that the cats scurried off. "Well, look what you've done now. Even the cats think you're a little too much."

Caroline belted out as I just for a moment appeared puzzled, "Okay, that does it. Where do you keep it?" But then I knew exactly to what she was referring. "Where's the liquor? Oh I remember now." She went directly to the liquor cabinet to select what was best for the evening. "This will get you talking. Oh yeah, in no time at all."

She peered over at me as she lifted her brows and broadened her smile with those pearly whites.

"I surrender, dahhling. For sure, I am all yours. But let me have a chance to get lit up quite a bit before I spill the beans on that ever so hot and sexy Mr. Fine Specimen of a Man."

"Well, all right. But first let me tell you, something." She gave a deep sigh. "I'm also here to go on an adventure with you tonight and possibly tomorrow night—if you want me to, that is?"

Did I want Caroline to go on an adventure with me tonight and possibly tomorrow night. Well, "Hellllll yeah!" I was ecstatic.

We both did our clinging our arms together thing, and spinning around and acting like the wild-gypsy-ass girls that we were. My Caroline was coming with me tonight. She had told me on her last visit with me that she had been shown what she needed to be shown. She was telling me now, though, that she really had not completed her knowings. Something or someone had prodded her to come visit and come see...come see what else she needed to see.

As Caroline settled down in her room and freshened up, I went ahead and made the ever-dependable nachos for the evening. Caroline asked for them. They were simple and yeah, always good with liquor...any liquor.

I am not quite sure I remember everything I divulged of my sexual rendezvous with Nathan, but hopefully not too much. I felt some things were sacred and must be kept to myself and Nathan. What? Whatever. I did tell her all about Terri, Cathie, and the shelter. She was happy that I was making friends and would soon be starting to volunteer.

Caroline and I were quite boozed up as we headed down the boardwalk. She wanted to stop and just admire my house. "It's amazing the luma...the lumino... the luminous...ity, the...." We both started to laugh.

"Yes, I know, I know what you mean. It is quite a sight to see. A sight I had been waiting for all my life, you know."

"Okay, let's go down and party. Don't want ya to start any of that crying shit now. We gotta get to MoonGlow, get to dancin' and flirtin' with that man of hers so he can show us some really good shit tonight."

I had to laugh. Her voice had that southern drawl, thicker now than ever. She always did this when she was drinking. So we marched on down the boardwalk and onto the soft warm sand.

Caroline asked me again to repeat my "southern belle thing." So I did and as always, we laughed.

We began the dance as the music blared. Our gypsy souls came forth as our hair went wildly into the wind, and as our eyes would try to catch a glimmer of her majesty's appearance.

As we were waiting for my ever so lovely MoonGlow to appear, I looked over the Great Liquid's horizon. My head was spinning. I felt flirtatious and thoughts of Daniel came to be, for I knew I would be going back into time. I could hear the whispering voices coming forth. They were coming from the recesses of the Great Liquid where they lay hidden.

"Oh great spirit of High Tide, reveal more to me tonight, as I shyly look your way before your masculine physique. Given that I am highly skilled and experienced in the 'art of pleasing pretty,' as Madame, herself, would say, I would presume you want to take me somewhere."

Caroline continued her swirls and lightly took sections of her hair curling them around her fingers, then releasing them to the night skies. I had taught her well. Or was it my MoonGlow who taught her well? My mind wandered again to a time long ago.

There she was. MoonGlow came forth to us. She would remember and recognize Caroline and appear in full glory to my friend also. She lowered her eyes, her lips pursed. A slight pause ensued before she blew me the kiss. The kiss was sweet and loving. Yes, MoonGlow loved me. My beautiful friend and sentinel loved me.

I thought of my MoonGlow and our differences in nature. As a human woman, I was able to flirt, tease, dress and please and even touch to arouse my lover, but my poor MoonGlow could do her flirting and teasing only from afar. She, in her majestic being, chose High Tide to be her lover, although she could neither touch him nor hold him. Only from her place where all mankind can see and adore her, can see only dream of the art of seduction as we humans can partake in such delight.

"But MoonGlow, are you jealous even a little bit? For as you summon your lover, High Tide, do you even feel for a moment a bit of jealousy as I and Caroline will be taken by him into his depths? We will be swallowed by him and he will be swallowed by us. Are you jealous at all, my beloved MoonGlow?"

Why would I say such a thing? I wondered That was cruel. It was the liquor, of course.

MoonGlow's light began to illumine as if ten times over. It startled both

Caroline and me. We stepped back a bit and held hands. Her light began to settle and I could see a glimpse of her smile. It was a smile of love and understanding. I knew she understood the limitations of us mere humans. She knew our weaknesses…at least, my weaknesses.

"No, no…you are not jealous, for we are keeping our night vigils with you, sweet sister. We keep spellbound with your free spirit as we dance the dance with you, dear sentinel. We will ever so seductively dance the dance of wild gypsies that you taught me many moons ago. Free-spirited wild sisters are we, am I right? So why would you be jealous? You have taught me well and I have taught Caroline well. I am grateful indeed. No boundaries will I cross. I will never let you be disappointed in me."

A brusque whooping sound came forth from the Great Liquid now. This particular sound I had not been familiar with, since my journeys with High Tide. He came forth with piercing liquid pellets shooting toward Caroline and me. A sting-like sensation was felt, but just as quickly, he bathed our bodies drenching us with his healing salty balm. We were under his spell again. I was ready to take flight and once more Caroline would be attending. We would go together into his deepest creviced recessed bowels…where secrets lay hidden in liquid.

COLD SLEET…

I was placed on the sand. I realized I was naked. I stood there looking about. MoonGlow was not to be found, yet there were the other ones. The seven moons I had seen before were scattered with only faint glowlight. The constellations could not be seen. They were hidden by dark oppressive clouds. Then the rains came down. They deluged the beach, drenching everything. Sheets of ice pellets began to hit my skin. I lowered my head to protect my face, and I began to run. I ran and ran. I was freezing. The ice pellets were painfully stabbing and stinging my skin as though innumerable needles and pins had chosen to target me and only me.

I cried to God, "Why, why are You doing this to me? Please help me! Please have mercy!"

I had become tired from running. I was drenched with the freezing rain and my skin stung from the ice pellets. As I stopped and lowered myself upon the sand, I curled my body in an upright fetal position. My arms and hands covered my head.

I cried out to God again and to Jesus and Mary, "Please save me!"

The sleet of ice-cold pellets ceased at once. I felt a soothing warmth placed on my right cheek. It was a sweet kiss from my MoonGlow. A blanket of warmth immediately followed onto my skin, as its slight electrical energy made my arms and legs begin to twitch. Master Sun was coming up on the horizon. It was daybreak.

To my right I could see MoonGlow with only a delicate glowlight, knowing she would soon fade for her brother's commanding reign for the day.

I stood up and noticed my hair was dry, and a clean white robe had I donned.

"Thank you." I looked up into the great heavens and realized my lowliness and my nothingness, as I turned around and began to walk back.

I was lightheaded from the ordeal I had just experienced. I began to contemplate and try to make sense of what just happened. I came up with very little sense, but realized that we are all here for a purpose. We souls are here to advance and to move on, and at times we must suffer and accept what comes. It is the law of karma that we reap what we sow before we can get past this massive veil of illusion. I looked up into the daylight's soothing and warm rest.

"God, my Father and Creator, have Your Karma take pity on me and on all us lowly broken humans. We can be obstinate and difficult, yet we can be loving and giving. So please, have mercy. Remember, You created us and we are Your children."

1882...EIGHTH ENCOUNTER

It was the end of February, 1882 now. Daniel and I had settled in Charleston, South Carolina. I was standing outside in front of a grand three-story home. I suddenly had thoughts of a similar home in New Orleans, The Pretty Pink House. I realized I was looking at my present home...my home with Daniel, and the grandeur of our home had me more spellbound than Madame's had ever done. I could not stop staring at what was actually my home, Collette's home. My, had she, or I, had moved on up, as they say?

Daniel's father had died after Christmas, before the new year began. I thought it odd how the both of us were left orphans now. Neither one of us had living parents now. Yet, life has a way of being good to us humans at times, such as bringing Daniel and me together at the right time.

How sad it seemed, though. I thought of our having Calissa and her not knowing any of her grandparents. I was thinking of my mother too, and how I wished she could had been here with me in Charleston to see how her daughter had turned away from the life that she never wanted her to live. She would be happy for me and Daniel. Surely, she must had been able to come visit me at times in this earthly life. Surely our light-bodied friends from above would had taken her back here for visits.

Although there were no grandparents for Calissa, Daniel did have a sister. She was several years older, married, and with two sons. Her name was Elizabeth Howard (married surname). Her husband was named Robert and her two young sons were Robert, Jr. and Adam.

Elizabeth was a kind woman. In time, she would know my history, but she accepted me anyway. It was relayed that she would become like a true sister and friend to me.

After the death of his father, Daniel had taken over the business at just twenty-three years of age. He was an old soul, though. How strange I was thinking that. At twenty-three he seemed wiser than most men twice his age, more mature and more settled. Although his dad's brother would help oversee their businesses and properties, if need be. I began to get teary-eyed thinking how wonderful my life had turned out…or so it seemed, anyway.

We both had moved into the family house. Our house was located on a corner lot in downtown Charleston. While I stood before this grandiose house, it was quite an elegant façade of three stories, old Victorian. Its stone structure was of a pale rust color with bold cream shutters enveloping the windows. Along with a wrought-iron fence to keep the abode private, there were two large magnolia trees standing proudly on either side, along with an angel oak tree on the side street. Wide stairs leading up to the grand veranda had dark-green rails with decorative metalwork, which just added more to the elegance of the outside appearance.

Tall white pillars stood prominently at the top of the stairs, displaying the veranda on the first and second floors; both wrapped around to either side of the house. Various chairs and small tables for family and guests to sit and take pleasure on visits filled the spaces. I stood in awe of this majestic home.

I was immediately taken inside to a large foyer and saw to my right an over-sized living room. Before entering, I glanced over at the staircase. It was unusually wide, with rails of a pewter French antique color displaying stunningly decorative engraved metalwork.

As I looked into the living room, I saw myself, Collette, placing fresh flowers in a large blue flowered vase on a table near a window. The room seemed of English and French décor. The large windows displayed from ceiling to floor were set with thick, massive green curtains opened wide and pulled aside for the day. I could see through the window the carriages and people scurrying along their way on nicely dirt-paved roads.

After I, Collette, completed the flower arrangement, I returned to a desk to continue writing letters, it seemed. I watched myself stop at times, taking a hand-kerchief to dry my eyes. I was incredibly sad. It was relayed to me that I was writing letters to both Madame and Annabella. Oh, how I had missed them. Oh, how I had missed my family.

"Yes," I said to myself, "they were my family."

It was then relayed that Madame had contracted tuberculosis, which was known as consumption in those days. She had become too ill to work. She would seclude herself in an upstairs room. Miss Isabel would be taking care of Madame now, as she had done for my mother. Annabella had taken charge of The Pretty Pink House. She was now known as Madame Camilla for the Jolie Maison Rose. She was twenty years of age now. Although she was quite young, her mother had taught her well. I knew she could run the house just as well as her mother had done.

The front door opened. "Where's my beautiful and loving wife? I want to see her and give her a long-overdue kiss."

It was my Daniel! Oh, and how handsome he looked. He looked regal in his fine clothes. I ran up to him and actually threw myself into his arms. He kissed me while he swung me around. The tears came as he asked me what was wrong.

I watched us walk over to the couch to sit and explain to Daniel about the letter I had received from Annabella. As we were discussing the matter, I peered around the room and noticed the sparkling crystals on the high ceiling chandelier. The walls were covered with a velvety paper with pale-pink flowers. Framed pictures of family, young and old, filled the room. A piano was at one end. Dark maple furniture was covered with cream upholstery embellished with delicate scattered embroidery. I seemed to be more enthralled with the décor than with what was going on.

I was then removed and taken to an upstairs bedroom. It was our bedroom. Daniel and I had retired for the evening.

Daniel walked over to me as I was taking off my jewelry and staring at myself in the dressing-table mirror. I saw him standing up behind me and looking at me with that masculine need of his. He was shirtless and I all I could see were his muscular shoulders and arms moving upward as he began to breathe heavily. While he continued to stare and lust over me, he put his arms around my waist to bring me closer to him with a force that made me expel an audible moan. He unbuttoned my high-collared blouse and started to kiss my neck. I continued to moan in my ecstatic delight.

He began to undress me as we watched ourselves in the mirror. He was still standing behind me, as I saw him looking at my naked body. I saw his longing. I saw his desire. He made me begin to swoon with panting desire for him…for my husband. He grabbed my body and turned me around to face him. He unpinned my hair and started grabbing and fingering through my hair like a madman. I, too, was mad, as we both became wild with our shameless animalistic lust. He was all over me…and I was all over him.

He picked me up and gently threw me on the bed. No need to bring down the covers. There was no time for such a senseless act. His body was hot, his breathing was deep and manly. He kissed me with fierce passion. He kissed me all over. My body surrendered like never before. We were one in unison. Every movement of our bodies relayed to me that our union was complete. Our union was passionate and fixed.

I remembered then what Nathan had said about us being "fixed in stone, Marisa…I somehow knew we were fixed." Never before had I experienced such a surrender and such as a love as this. Daniel was my Nathan. Nathan was my Daniel. How wild can that be, pray tell?

So at this moment in time, Daniel was mine. I was his. We were each other's.

We woke up the next morning in each other's arms. We had not even had dinner.

"I love you, my dear Collette. Never has there been a more beautiful woman than you, and never will there be. We are fixed now…fixed in bodies of light."

I smiled as I caressed his face and asked him about the bodies of light. As we continued to talk, I, Marisa, was completely in shock, yet giddy at the same time. I could hardly believe what I had just heard. We as souls, I guess, stay the same in some ways as we travel through our lifetimes, and in some ways we change. I thanked God then that Daniel seemed to be the same in my present life.

Then there she was. My sweet Calissa. "Oh, you came to me, my lovely daughter. Oh, how I love you. Oh, how I thank you for bringing me here."

Calissa smiled. "I love you too, my mother. As you are being relayed, many chapters are told in this lifetime as other lifetimes. Many chapters are also untold and those chapters are torn from the books, for not everything will be relayed to you, Mother. You will be given what you need to know in due time."

At that moment I did not know what to say. I took it as it was given to me. I understood that what I needed to know would only be relayed.

"My dear mother, when we souls are released from our earthly bodies, only then are all these mysteries truly understood, but then again, when we return to another body, chapters are hidden from us again. Only the Creator guides the light workers of ancient to reveal accordingly for purposes known to Him alone."

Wow, I thought. *How profound was that?*

Calissa then blew me a kiss. "Can't I just spend a little more time with you, Calissa?…just a little more time?" I pleaded.

She laughed. "For you, Mother, I will come back soon and I will spend more time with you."

That was all I needed to hear for now. She promised me more time with her, and that was enough for now.

Time had passed. It was now the end of April, 1882. It was relayed to me that Daniel had promised me that he and I would travel back to New Orleans soon. He needed to go there on business and this time I would tag along.

I would get to see my family. "My family!" I gleefully said.

I thought of how I would be allowed to view myself being excited, yet sad, to see Madame, Annabella, Big Jim, Nellie, and all the others. Oh, I thought how excited I must have been just knowing I would see them all again.

In the meantime, Charleston's society was about to have its annual Society Party, as it was relayed to me. It was the party of all parties, shall I say. The wealthy, the prominent, the successful from the northeast coast to the south, from Texas all across to Charleston would attend. These were mostly men who were merchants, traders, landowners, politicians, lawyers, and bankers. Of course, they would bring their spouses and not their mistresses. What made me think of that, now? Hmm, I wonder.

I began to think whether any of these fine, upstanding prominent women of Charleston knew my history. I thought whether I had noticed if any of their fine, upstanding husbands ever looked familiar to me. This information would not be relayed to me. Yet, I would get a glimpse of this party. Somehow, I just knew that would be so.

The day came for the Society Party. I had an elegant light-green silk dress on. My hair was in an updo with ringlets falling softly to the sides of my face. I smiled to myself as I looked in the mirror. I looked very pretty, I thought. I most certainly was worthy enough, or so I thought.

Daniel had donned a dark suit nicely cut with satin lapels. A vest opened low showing his white linen shirt. He looked so handsome and irresistible that I could not understand why we were actually going to go to this dance. You know what I mean?

Our carriage awaited us outside as I stood on the grand veranda looking about. I could not fathom for a moment how I actually ended up having lived this life. Was it really so?

I was suddenly taken to the grand party room. I did not know what kind of building or residence this was, but here we were.

People were busy talking and walking and greeting and mixing. It seemed very busy indeed. I saw myself chatting with Elizabeth and her friends. Daniel was off chatting with his comrades.

Daniel's sister, Elizabeth, and two of her lady friends were just walking away from me when I noticed several women from a distance looking my way. They were staring at me with darted glares. I sensed then what was about to happen. Two of them looked familiar. They were from New Orleans. They had known my mother and me. I began to think about whether I could or would ever be accepted into their society because of my upbringing, because of where I had been.

I watched myself walk over toward the fine, upstanding women. I then decided that I, Collette, did not need their approbation after all. I smiled and said to myself, "You just go, girl. Give them hell, Collette."

Not a one of them had a smile on their faces. I looked directly at two of them. "May I please have a word with you both?" I ever so politely said with a southern drawl along with an obvious fake smile.

Both stood there with their upturned noses and glaring eyes, saying nothing. I then said, "It would behoove you both if you excuse yourselves for a bit, believe me." I noticed my eyebrows had raised and now I was also without a smile.

As the three of us excused ourselves and walked out of an entrance into another room which seemed to be a foyer, one of the ladies commented, "We know who you are. We know who and what your mother was in New Orleans, too."

I smiled at them both with a sarcastic grin and slowly said, "Well, I know who the both of you two fine, upstanding women are also. Let me tell you something first. A good friend of mine once explained to me that all women are whores in some way. We all give up most of our dreams so we can be taken care of and then end up caring for our husbands and such. You see, maybe I had been a whore back then in old New Orleans, but at least I worked for my money. It looks as though you two never have nor have ever needed to do so. You should never judge a person until you've walked in their shoes. Then again, you could not even fathom that." I lifted my hand to touch my curls as I got myself ready for the big spill.

"Let me tell you something. I see that all of you fine, upstanding women in New Orleans think you all are so much better than me, my mother, and all the rest at the Pretty Pink House. Well, it might please you to know...then again, maybe not...that your husbands are quite the opposite."

They both stood there with their mouths open, ready to leave. I grabbed the arm of one who looked the oldest and the worst. "I do believe that you and your friend here and the others inside need to know a few things. Your husbands that you think you have a lovely marriage with...well, they have been known to frequent Madame's house many many times. Oh yes, indeed! I can tell you all about your husbands' indiscretions and oh," as I started to laugh, "their behavior...well... it would be a shame that all your pretty, fine and upstanding comrades could end up privy to all this knowledge. Now would it not be so? You see, when women like yourselves do not precisely know how to please your husbands, well...then they frequent lovely places like Madame's Pretty Pink House. You see, your so-called gentlemen prefer pink. That would be us pretty pink ladies."

Before either could get in a word, I stepped closer in and continued, "You better believe that I would, without even a moment's thought, let it be known to everyone from here all the way past New Orleans, up the Mississippi and throughout the northeast of all your husbands' infidelities. For you see, I have nothing to lose if you ladies decide to ruin my reputation."

I grabbed the older lady's arm again. "If you or any of your other lowlife, pompous bitches do or say anything to destroy my marriage, hurt my husband's business, Madame's business, or any of the pretty pink ladies back home, I will bring down every one of you, including your own husbands and your entire families. For if you choose to do such an unkind thing to my people, my family, I have nothing to lose, you see. Everyone will go down...and I mean everyone. You ladies have nice evening, and may you have a most pleasant evening with your husbands later on tonight, if you know what I mean."

They stood frozen in shock, and visibly shaken. I continued to smile and with that sweet southern drawl accentuated, "Now before you go on your merry way, do please close your mouths, ladies. It is not exactly ladylike, you know."

I, Marisa, was shocked. I could not even compose a thought as I heard myself berating these ladies. I was proud, though and with utmost satisfaction, I relaxed a bit and now thought, *Kudos to you, Collette. Wow, I was a true bitch back then! I stood up to those bitches and I stood up for my husband. Yes, I do believe I am proud.*

I saw myself walking ever so pretty and confident as I made my way back into the grand party room. I could see Daniel now and he politely excused himself to his comrades and walked over to me.

"Did I tell you that you are the most stunning and most beautiful woman here tonight? You are my lady, my love, and everything I have ever wanted." As he kissed me, he wrapped one arm around my waist and the with the other took hold of my hand. We began to dance. We danced and we danced.

I smiled with pleasure as I watched myself and Daniel dancing and being ever so much in love. I looked over to right when my peripheral vision noticed an oncoming light. There she was, my Calissa.

"Oh Mother, how pompous they are when they, themselves, have lived tainted lives, unaware except in the recesses of their own souls. There is always uneasiness deep inside their hearts, I assure you, Mother. In the deepest of our recesses there is such uneasiness whenever a thought of judging another occurs. For we are all broken. In the many lives we live, we are broken in some way. We are here to learn to never judge another."

Calissa said her piece and then she was gone. I knew she would back soon, though, and spend some time with me as she promised.

Some time had passed again. Daniel and I were in New Orleans. It was the end of June 1882 now. I had just turned twenty. We were there for Madame Mae's funeral. She had died a week before. I was saddened I had not made it back for a visit to see her. My heart was deeply broken.

I saw myself back at the Pretty Pink House. The funeral was over. It was not relayed to me my arrival, nor the participation at the funeral. Maybe it was because of the deep heartbreak I had experienced. I know that I had gone to visit my mother's grave too, and that added even more pain upon pain.

As I observed myself hugging Annabella, my heart was inundated with such melancholy, as if I were reliving all the sorrow again. It was as though I could not take it anymore. I had started to breathe rapidly and felt faint. I stepped back and decided to view no more.

A few days had passed before me now. I was no longer permitted to experience the agony and sorrow. "Thanks be to God," I said aloud.

Annabella and I were sitting in the third parlor at The Pretty Pink House now. She was smiling now. She was twenty years of age, like myself. She was sharing with me all the things she had not shared with me in her letters.

"What? You're getting married? Oh, Annabella, I am so very happy for you, my sweet dear sister!"

Annabella was getting married to a frequent client of hers whose wife had died a year ago. He had become quite smitten with her as naturally he would, of course. He was older, thirty-eight years of age. He was successful and lived in Alabama. She would be leaving New Orleans. The Jolie Maison Rose would be managed by one of the ladies who would become the madam. Annabella would still own the restaurant/bar and land that her mother had bequeathed to her. Her new husband, Harold, would have his own people make certain that Annabella's businesses were run properly and that all remained in order.

I was so elated for Annabella. I had been so worried for her since she had no other family left. Now, I could rest assured for it was relayed to me that Daniel and I had met this gentleman, Harold, and we were assured that he would be a good husband for my Annabella. Besides, she could be a bit closer to Charleston since she would be residing in Alabama.

We stayed in New Orleans for two and a half weeks. We had been blessed to take part in the nuptials two days before we left. Before the nuptials though, Annabella had something to tell me. "I am pregnant, my sister!"

My heart melted. Annabella and I cried. My, my how things had changed, and all for the better, except that her mother, Mabelle, would not be here. Although I felt she had been here in spirit for the wedding of her precious daughter and would be for the birth of her grandchild.

My Annabella is an "honest" woman now just like myself. I laughed for thinking such a thought.

Daniel and I arrived safely back in Charleston. All seemed to be well. Even when I happened to run into one of those fine, upstanding women, all seemed to be well. As I viewed myself and watched my almost constant smiles, I knew I had fallen more and more in love with my Daniel. He was a good man. He was a handsome man. He was a successful and upstanding man...and he loved me, the former pretty pink lady from The Pretty Pink House.

It was mid-September. The summer's heat was still hovering. Yet as I looked through my window, I could see the autumn coming soon. I loved the autumn season the most. "Come, autumn...come along and bring along your cool brisk evening breeze, and cover my world with your tapestry of your mosaic hues."

Toward the end of November, 1882, it was presumed that I was pregnant now. I was pregnant with my sweet Calissa.

Chapter 12

A TIME TO CHOOSE

"It is fixed. It is written."

s I opened my eyes, again I felt as if I had been gone a very long time. Yet it had only been several hours. I looked over at my phone to confirm this anyway. It was now Thursday morning. As the fresh morning breeze sung its way through my window and onto my face, I thought of Nathan.

"It's Thursday and I will see you once more tomorrow." So captivating was this thought that I felt fully awake, alive, and ready for the day.

As I quickly got up and Sugars began to follow me out the door, I reminisced about the travel I had last night. I contemplated the tremendous sadness and anger, yet there was such tremendous joy that I had experienced with Daniel, and now… yes now, the next time I would view myself with my loving daughter. This kind of joy seemed inescapable, for it was consuming and inundating my heart and soul, as if High Tide had drenched me with his mighty soothing balm. Yes, his soothing balm had coated me, penetrated me with a love and calm so effective that I remained in a trance for some time before beginning my day.

"Guten morgen, dahhhling." Caroline danced her way into the bright morning ambiance created by Master Sun, himself, as she clung on to Charlie.

"Wow, you were in some deep thought there?" she said, as though she wanted a definitive explanation of what my thoughts had been.

"Oh Caroline—come, let's sit on the veranda for a bit, please. But yes, let's get our coffee and bagels first, my dear. I have so much to say and catch you up on." I had started to dance my way now around the kitchen.

It seemed as though we could not get to the veranda soon enough. It was still early and Nathan would be calling me soon, but I needed to elaborate on everything that I had viewed last night and especially about being pregnant with my sweet Calissa.

As I rattled off everything to Caroline, I finally got a clue about the expressions she was exhibiting. She would maintain her smiles and nod often, occasionally with a "Right, yes, you are right."

"Okay, what is it? Do you already know all this?"

Caroline took a deep breath and then slowly she expired. "Marisa, I know everything. Do you remember when I was about to leave last time, we discussed how I had the knowledge of what I needed to know at that time. I knew I would be shown more in time though. I would come to know what you know right now… and then some, Marisa."

Being somewhat baffled, I leaned back in my chair and stared out at the Great Liquid. "You know everything, don't you? Tell me, do you know more than I do right now?"

Caroline had elucidated—without any hesitancy—and without any holding back every bit of knowledge of this past life I had encountered so far. I had already come to know of things that I had suspicions about and had envisioned my own conjecturing of every why, what, and how question I had from the very beginning of this sojourn. Although I had been willing to travel on, at times I was engulfed with distinct trepidation.

Caroline knew it all. She was given more knowledge than I on the first go-round during her last visit. Last night, she was given even more.

"I was given the knowledge of how and when your travel in that particular past life will end. I mean when the 'viewing' will end. I don't understand why I was given this, nor why the higher ones," as she looked upward into the day skies, "decided to play it out this way."

"You were there with me, weren't you? You were Annabella?" I stared and waited for Caroline's answer.

Caroline smiled as she waited for my smile before she spoke. "Yes, I was Annabella. I am your sister…your best friend. We have known each other for a very long time. A very long time, indeed."

I took immeasurable delight with Caroline's answer and reached out to hold her hand.

"You must also know then that Nathan is Daniel?"

"Yes, I do. Listen, Marisa. As I said, I know when your sojourn will end. I cannot tell you anything else. You need to see this through yourself. It is written already."

I started to laugh for those words were "familiar." A lot of things were familiar now. We began to get excited and more carefree about what had happened and what was going to happen. Caroline took delight in knowing that I was taking delight about Calissa's impending birth.

"Oh no! Nathan. I…I…."

"Go ahead." She motioned me to go answer my phone. I had left it upstairs, silly me, again.

"Hey , most beautiful woman in the world. Most certainly that would be you, Marisa."

"Hi most handsome man in the world and most certainly that would be you, Nathan Gregory Rinn."

I could see him. I could see him standing there. He would have a day or two-day- old beard. His hair would be loosely combed back and full. His hand would be holding his phone to his ear and I would be ever so captivated just by his hand holding his phone. I would watch his mouth open and close, wetting his lips from time to time. I would watch him blink his eyes and I would stare into those crystal-blue dancing eyes of his.

Really, Marisa? You do most certainly have it really bad. Yet, I had surrendered to being infatuated with every aspect of Nathan's being, but most of all, I loved every aspect of his being, too. There was nothing that I did not love about Nathan. On top of all that, I had known this unbelievable man for maybe two weeks? But not really. We had known each other like forever. He loved me and I loved him. That was all that mattered. We knew we were akin. We were "familiar."

I could not wait until tomorrow, it seemed. I wanted my Nathan here with me now. "I will see you tomorrow evening. I will hold you, and love on you, tell you you're beautiful and that you're my baby. I just may not let go of you at all."

"Then don't. Don't ever let go of me, Nathan."

Late afternoon was approaching. I had given Terri a call earlier and told her about Caroline's surprise arrival. I asked her to join us for a happy hour at the Sea Bay Bar and Grill. The plan included heading back here to my house afterwards so she could see my house as we had planned to do so. Terri immediately complied and said she would be delighted to meet Caroline, and especially to see my house.

As late afternoon approached, Caroline gave Charlie a loving hug and kiss while I repeated the ritual of doing the same with Sugars. We decided to take my convertible and lower the top as we drove off to pick up Terri. We saw her opening her front door as soon as we approached, flashing that stunning white smile of hers and waving as if we had all been friends forever. Well? That might not be a far-fetched thought there.

I was not at all surprised how Caroline and Terri hit it off. It was as if they had known each other forever. Well, there you go. I was right.

We enjoyed the late afternoon, telling each other things we did not know yet about the other. Oh, womanhood—it is such a treasure when you share your stuff with other women. We discussed our past, our work, our marriages, our dreams, our kids (furry kids too, if not human). We talked somewhat of our hopes and dreams and fears of growing older.

Oh, to find that bond with other women, even if it is only with one, is beyond priceless. And it was fun to be silly, to be girly, and to know you could say whatever you wanted with my two friends. *Wow*, I thought. *How did I get to this point in life of feeling actually "happy"?* I could not answer that question without thinking of my Nathan too. Mr. Fine Specimen was in my life too and that made it all the better.

I even found out that Caroline had a new guy in her life. His name was Bryan, a cardiologist. They had just started dating, but she seemed smitten with him. I was happy for her. I was happy she was not alone now.

Finally, we decided we had enough of the drinking. We were ready to get back to the house. Well, actually it was Terri who was really ready. There was something peculiar about how excited and enthralled she seemed to be about viewing my home. Anyway, that pleased me.

After I had parked in front of my house rather than driving into the garage, I had looked through the mirror seeing how fixed her gaze was as her mouth had dropped opened.

"This is truly unbelievable. To think that poor old broken and lonely home is now such an engaging sight to behold. Simply amazing…and surely somewhat bewitching."

As she giggled and then gasped again, I was pleased and thought aloud, "Okay, I'll take that. Thank you."

Caroline and I walked with her all around the outside and periphery before ever entering. I wanted Terri to have the deluxe tour, especially for someone as excited as she was.

"Ohhhhh, MoonGlow!" Terri seemed to be viewing something beyond what I could see, it seemed. Even Caroline noticed something unusual about her.

After being amazed at the flowers almost as much as Caroline had been, Terri completed only maybe a third of viewing the inside. She looked toward the stairs and then back at me. "This lovely abode of yours is not haunted, Marisa. It's just mystical."

I suddenly felt as though her words had struck me like a lightning bolt. She seemed much more than just a new friend I had met a couple of days ago. She was "familiar."

"I know, Terri," I said, exchanging smiles, "just as you know, too."

"I have known and felt this abode of yours is not haunted and that no spirits dwell inside here." She hesitated to continue, but then she looked at me. "But they do elsewhere. I want to go. I want to go with both of you this evening. You are going, right?"

Caroline and I were both speechless. There were no words spoken for a few seconds.

Terri continued after no response, "I saw you both on a couple of nights. I stayed and watched from my balcony. I saw the lights and the spiral crystals which formed a water-like tunnel. You both were being summoned."

I was delightedly surprised as I looked over at Caroline. She was not smiling, but remained with that look of being puzzled as she continued to look at Terri.

"A new sister has joined us!" Caroline had snapped out of her trance and reciprocated the smile that Terri had shared.

"Yes, a new sister we have," I softly agreed.

The questions for Terri suddenly overwhelmed me, as they seemed to come freely and unexpectedly, "But tell us, what happens once High Tide takes us into his domain? Do you see this happening? And how do we come back? Where are our bodies while we are gone?"

"Well, actually you seem to just diasppear. I don't see either of you after the tide comes. I just know that something mystical is happening."

Late afternoon turned into early evening quickly. The three of us chatted and discussed many of our encounters. Not once did Terri show the slightest doubt about what Caroline and I had been experiencing. Terri just seemed to take in all in as if she could not get enough. Yeah, she was a sister of ours indeed. She was one of us.

Terri had called her husband, Bill, to inform him that he would be spending the evening with us. We went through our usual ritual of deciding on an appetizer, liquor, and music. What a silly bunch we were!

As we walked the walk down the boardwalk, Terri turned around to look at MoonGlow. She did the same as Caroline had done on our first journey. My home was a stunning sight to view on an evening full of the night lights.

Caroline and I did not need to teach Terri the dance. It seemed as though she already knew our spirited gypsy dance from watching us from her home. As she lifted her arms, she reached for her hair to be flung in the quick brisk wind.

I broke the dance for a moment and beckoned the two to come together with me. As our hands met and toppled upon each other, "A new sisterhood has begun, girls. Gypsy girls, wild, untamed and unabashed, we are one," I declared.

"Ohhhhh, where does that wind come from?" Terri broke the connection and we looked upward to our right.

There she was. In resplendent beauty, the night queen had taken her seat among the illumined bodies of light who were destined to reign with her. Our MoonGlow had made her magnetic presence before us. She pulled us into her sphere as we helplessly, but willingly surrendered with the night's menagerie of concealed worlds unseen by the human eye. How charmed we three women were to have been favored to dwell and experience this foreign existence so covert to so many. Yes, we were charmed to have revealed this night...what is hidden...hidden in liquid.

The three of us bowed our heads and curtsied in reference to MoonGlow's majestic presence. This time she would appear to all three of us. I was not special anymore, it seemed. Even so, I was happy that she acknowledged and loved my sweet new friend as well. I felt her maternal love as her beautiful face appeared and heard the gasps of my two friends, as I continued to stare and be mesmerized by my MoonGlow's presence.

She blew us her kiss. This was the kiss that I longed for and have always received without any hesitation from her for many many years. We reciprocated with our own kisses blowing in the wind, hoping they would somehow reach her soft cheek.

Not a word was spoken among us. It was as if each of us was in our her world now in the night skies' abode. Each was basking in her own delights.

Then the heavy and foreboding sounds of the Great Liquid reconnected us again. High Tide's presence was coming forth as we all seemed to shudder. Terri positioned herself between me and Caroline. She was shaking, though not a word was spoken still.

Caroline and I grabbed hold of Terri. I stood on her left and Caroline on her right. Yes, I knew how intimidating this massive liquid could be. I still felt intimidated at times. His presence commanded a unique reverence—ever powerful, yet inviting.

"Terri, look up at our MoonGlow," I said to her, as I knew that just peering at our sweet Sister Moon, she would provide a sweet calm, a sweet repose. I knew certainly that Terri would surrender to the moment if she looked up.

His masculine presence had us standing without reserve. We seemed to be ready for whatever he had planned this evening. I felt I needed to speak for all of us.

"Take us, High Tide, into the depths of your bowels, where lie hidden the secrets and sins of our own lives, as well as others. All are held and all are hidden. Let us taste your salty balm as it soothes us in curious, fantastical, and unexpected wanderings, sometimes pleasing and sometimes not so."

We were unexpectedly taken up into the night skies. With great speed and distance we flew past zillions of projectile crystal liquids of varying shapes and colors. We were saturated with the massive liquid. It felt as if his inviting balm had permeated every cell of my body and soul.

The Three Doors

We stood motionless, as we could now see three doors standing in front of us. We knew instinctively that the door before each of our presence was the one already chosen for us.

I hesitated as my hand took hold of the large handle. Voices came forth, but as usual they were muffled. Then clearly, "Have you chosen the right door? Have you chosen the door to love? For you see, love is the greatest of all. Love is the greatest of all there is."

I hesitated again. I was afraid. I knew that I wanted to chose the door to love, but I remembered I had no choice but to choose the door before me.

As I opened the door, I heard a sweet voice, "Mother, you have chosen well. You have chosen love, my dear sweet Mother."

Calissa appeared to my right. She was enveloped in a bright white light. Her crystal-blue eyes shone prominently and they seemed to be projecting rays of light. The light was full of love and acceptance.

My lovely Calissa, will you be with me as I proceed? You had told me you would be spending some time with me. Do you remember?"

"Yes, Mother, it is time. We will spend some time together."

The World of Ancient Gardens

I could no longer speak. I just smiled and took hold of Calissa's arm as she directed me to a path of unknown pavement. It glistened with sparks of golden crystals, such as I had never seen or dreamed of before. The left of the path was filled with endless fields of garden patches, various kinds of trees, some of budding flowers, and plentiful leaves. Streams of constant flowing waters were audible and soothing.

It was relayed to me that this was the side of Trees and Streams. We walked for a long time in this ever peaceful sanctuary. Calissa and I were talking and smiling, and even laughing at times.

We then stepped over the wide crystal path onto the right side. This side was filled with flowers of various kinds. There were miles and miles it seemed of endless prisms of colors unbeknownst to me. With each step it seemed to cause the stepped-on flowers to just burst back even more beautiful than before. Nothing was harmed. The space above was filled with butterflies, hummingbirds, and bees. It was relayed that all were carrying out their assigned duties. The sky was a luminous bluish color with rainbows doubled and tripled in parallel unison.

Again, Calissa and I walked for quite a long time, enjoying this other sanctuary known as Hummingbirds and Butterflies. "You get to choose, Mother." Calissa continued her smile. "You get to choose which side you want to visit for a while when it is your time."

"You mean I get to come here at another time? Oh, you mean whenever I leave the earthly realm?"

"Yes, Mother. Whenever it is your time. You will have your time here. It is written. You see, many choose to come here after their time spent in the purification realms is completed. They come to here to contemplate, rest, and bask in this sweet delight before moving on to better and higher realms."

I contemplated then how anything else could have been "better and higher." This was heavenly already. I thought I would never judge anymore. I would never judge another person on their status of the soul's enlightenment.

"How long do I travel there? I mean in the earthly realm. How many more times?"

"Until you are ready, Mother. Until you see. No one could even begin to comprehend the order of this universe. No one can even imagine the endless beauty and joy that our Creator has ordered for us in our due time."

Calissa and I hugged and kissed each other goodbye for now.

I was back on the sand with my girls. We stood there and surrendered to High Tide's mighty summoning. We were taken...

1882 - 1900————NINTH ENCOUNTER

It was the first part of December when Daniel and I received the news that Annabella had given birth to a beautiful healthy boy, named David Edward, on the 27th of November. We were so happy and thrilled for her. Yes, my Annabella was happily married with a son. She had a famly...a real family and a good normal life. No offense to her mother, Madame Mabelle, for I truly did love her. I was just happy that both of us turned out just fine and that we both were very happy.

I was almost three months pregnant now. Although it was still early for confirmation, Daniel could not be more thrilled. He seemed to be more loving and attentive than ever before, if I could even imagine he could be more so. I watched myself happily setting up a nursery with the help of one of our servants. I could only imagine how I must have felt, knowing earlier times of hardships and settling into a lifestyle considered shunned and unforgivable.

Time went on. Calissa Marie Ryan was born on June 23, 1883 and somewhat postdue. She was born healthy, though, with dark hair and beautiful large eyes which would become like Daniel's, clear crystal blue and with dancing lights. I watched how Daniel held our baby girl and gazed endlessly upon his precious daughter. He was in love with her, as was I. We had set our bond and our love in stone now...or I should say fixed in bodies of light.

Daniel would say to me as he finally lifted his gaze from Calissa, "We are fixed now, my Collette. The three of us are fixed now in bodies of light...now and forever." I would begin to cry because of the unbelievable and amazing love that I was feeling and that I possessed for my husband, Daniel, and my daughter, Calissa. Yes, we were absolutely "fixed."

The three of us were walking along the shoreline one evening. Calissa had just been baptized in the Catholic church. She seemed to be around two months old now. Daniel had us stop along some boulders a slight distance from the great liquid. We sat as I watched Daniel gazing up into the night skies toward his right.

There she was. It was our illuminous glowlight of ancient past. Our MoonGlow had come to us even then in 1883. I was stunned as Daniel recognized and acknowledged her presence as if she had been a dear friend of his for a while.

I watched myself acknowledge our night sky's ancient and benevolent presence. I had known her too for a while. Daniel lifted our sweet Calissa up toward our MoonGlow as she reciprocated with lowing her eyes and blowing the kiss of her many nights. Now, Calissa had been dedicated to her, the same as Daniel and I were also.

Time continued on. It was not relayed to me much of Calissa's growing years. It was relayed though that the so-called fine upstanding prominent ladies of Charleston had started to treat me well and even included me in their charity work and events. Yes, I, Collette Marie Duprey-Ryan, the former pretty pink lady, was now considered one of these "real fine" ladies. But of course I was. Since my performance and threats at the Society Party, how could they not accept me? Oh brother.

The years flew by, as earthly years do. It was relayed to me that the year was May 1900. Calissa was sixteen years of age now and would be turning seventeen next month in June. She was ready for the social life of parties and meeting people other than those of her young age. She was a lovely young girl, or should I say a lovely young lady.

It was a lovely day in June. I was in Calissa's room. Yes, the room looked exactly as it did the first time I met Calissa in my journey. She was now standing before the mirror as I brushed her hair, took strands and curled and pinned it up as they did back then. I would leave ringlets to fall softly around her face. She looked beautiful. She was my beautiful daughter.

I was in a large party room now. People of all kinds were parading and laughing and being their cordial selves, as people usually do at these parties. I was with a small group of familiar ladies chatting when I glanced over to the right.

Daniel and Calissa were walking toward me. He had his arm around her, looking at her as a very proud father would. He glanced over at me and gave me his familiar wink and smile. I shyly smiled and with a coquettish downward look, I began the "art of pleasing pretty" (oh, how I missed Madame). Even now, I thought,

Daniel and I still flirted. How enticing that was to me. At that moment, I could feel our strong and passionate love…that endless passion that some people just are fortunate to have and behold.

Daniel and I watched as we saw a young man about the age of twenty-eight take a fancy to our daughter. Calissa seemed to have taken a fancy to him also. They spent the rest of the evening dancing, chatting, and laughing. I felt sad for some reason. Was it because she seemed to be too young? No, she was seventeen and that was the way it was in that period of time. There was something else, but I was not privy to that at this time.

It was relayed that Daniel knew of this young man. The young man's name was Andrew Wilcox. His father was a longtime associate and friend of Daniel's father. They lived in Mississippi, but Andrew had been here in Charleston for quite some time now on business per his father's request.

Daniel knew Andrew also, but not well. I was introduced to Andrew eventually during the party that night. As time went on, he and Calissa would fall in love and marry in September, 1900.

I thought about how strange it was that Daniel and I had allowed Calissa at seventeen to marry. What was it about Andrew, though, that made me feel uneasy? He seemed like a nice man, very handsome, and he was very loving and kind toward Calissa, but the uneasiness would continue to baffle me.

I was taken away from that moment. I watched myself come out of a clothing store in town. It was early evening. I was about to hop into a carriage that had been waiting for me. As I looked back and past the store, I eyed an older black lady. She motioned me to come to her. I was hesitant, but some force seemed to guide me to her.

She was a voodoo priestess from New Orleans. I had seen her at Madame's a couple of times. Why was she here in Charleston, though?

She smiled at me. Then some kind of a laugh expelled from her mouth for just a second. She was glaring with sad dark eyes now.

"That man will bring you sorrow. Your heart will be broken into a million pieces. Rootworks say so." She continued to glare.

"What do you mean? My husband and I love each other dearly. He would never…."

"It is written in rootwork," as she held up her hand and fixed a long, pointed, gray cracked nail at me, "No, no, not him." She shook her head and looked past me and beyond, "That man." She continued to point past me. "That man will bring you deep guttural sorrow."

I could not speak a word. She fled from me. It was relayed that I would not see her again. I pondered as I watched myself dry my eyes and was escorted to the carriage. I watched myself continue to cry.

2010

I woke up in my bed. I had been sweating. I was drenched. I looked over and out the window. It was barely daybreak. I jumped out of the bed and quickly peered out to my right to see if I could see my dear, sweet friend. She was still there. She looked at me with a soft, pale, loving glow. She blew me a kiss and began to fade, as I blew one back to her.

"Thank you, God, for allowing her to see me this morning before I begin my day."

I reflected on last night, "What did that voodoo woman mean? Daniel and I are fixed. Nathan and I are fixed. Who was the man who would bring me such sorrow?"

I thought of Caroline still being here. I thought of Terri being with us. I grabbed Sugars and hurriedly but quietly went up to Caroline's door. "Come on in, my perpetual friend."

I walked in. Caroline was smiling. "What a ride, huh? You're toward the end of that journey, you know. I do believe tonight will be the end, don't you think?"

I was saddened. I began to feel that Caroline was correct. It would be the end tonight. Yet, Nathan would be coming in. It was Friday. *How could I continue my journey tonight?* I thought.

"You're leaving me today, my bestie." Caroline reached out and grabbed me to give a most consoling hug.

"For heaven's sake, you're gonna have Mr. Fine Specimen of a Man with you tonight! You don't need me anymore. Hey, where is Terri? We need to talk with her and see what's with her before I leave, girl. I wanna know."

We immediately charged to the kitchen and I gave Terri a call. "So you called, friend. I didn't know when I should come over. Shall I come over now for a bit? Got some stuff to share."

"Well...yeah, you better...and hurry!" I said with a slight quiver.

As the three of us sat on the veranda, drinking our coffee and nibbling on croissants, we told Terri to start, since she had never ever experienced anything as we had. Or had she?

Terri began to tell us of her journey. She was taken to the year 1881. She encountered all of us as we were during that period of time. She was not a part of our lives, though. She stunned us by saying that Estella had been her mother. Estella was four months pregnant when she was murdered.

"I know about my mother, Estella, and her life, but I am not to share any information. You see, my mother in this present life passed away a year ago. I have been very heartbroken since that time. She and I were very close, as if one and the same."

Caroline and I did not interrupt with even one word. We looked and listened intently as Terri continued on. I felt such a kinship toward her, especially after she had told us about knowing Estella. My heart was racing with sadness, excitement, and delight. I was saddened by Estella's death, but delighted that Terri was soulfully akin to us.

"My mother appeared to me one evening on the beach as I was looking out from my veranda. I walked down to greet her. It was relayed to me that she had been Estella Benoit, whom you both know. I was given all this information and then some while I was on my journey, you see." She began to cry a flood of tears.

Caroline and I held her tightly for a while. We shared our own stories and knew the three of us were really akin to each other now. We were sisters. Our souls were bonded and fixed.

After we said our goodbyes to Caroline and watched her leave, Terri looked over at me and said, "One more thing. My mother said that you, Caroline, and I should remain close as sisters now, since we know who she really was."

"Naturally, of course…and always we will." As I gave Terri a hug, she perked up, realizing I would be getting ready for Nathan's arrival this evening.

"Now don't do anything that I wouldn't do." She gave me wink. "Which means you just do everything, girlfriend."

I felt exhausted as I went back into the house. "Whew, babies, it's been a whirlwind," I said, as my sweet Charlie and Sugars stared at me.

I called my cleaning service to come over and give the place a good clean. I needed to rest up and fantasize about how I would please my man this evening. I wanted to spend the time daydreaming and not cleaning.

Nathan called me, "Is the coast clear, beautiful? Can I talk dirty to you now?"

I laughed. I was ecstatic as always to hear my man's voice. So I gave him the go-ahead to talk dirty to me since my friends had gone. We spent some time being playful and silly before the cleaning crew arrived.

"Get ready, mister. You're not going to even know what hit you."

I spent some time going through my lingerie, wondering what would be best for me to wear tonight. It had been a week and the time could not get here quick enough even though I felt I needed more time for decisions. I was hungry for my man…really hungry.

As the evening approached, the sun had cast a soft glint of Master Sun's color through the front room's curtains. I lit various candles around the room, along the niches on the stairway, and in the bedroom. I even laid rose petals along the way up to the bedroom. "How romantic this is. Surely Nathan won't mind my plucking these for the occasion." I said to the cats, "Okay, don't get too excited by the petals. Let's call it a day, shall we?" I had the cats say good night to me as they reclined in their respective beds in the laundry room. I was ready.

I had my makeup just perfect. My hair was pinned up loosely—to be easily undone, of course. I was wearing some sheer lace lingerie, and black stockings with black pumps. I looked at myself in the mirror and then thought, *Oh, what the hell. Naked it is.*

Nathan text me a message, "Arriving in 5. Be ready, baby."

I hurried with my black pumps to the door and waited. I was breathing heavily. It had been only five days, but it seemed like five months. Insisting that I not start thinking again of my journeys the last couple of nights, I pictured Nathan before me. I saw him looking at me, looking at my womanly body and knowing he was lusting for me.

There he was. He pulled up. He was in a light gray t-shirt and jeans. He had a scruffy beard and his hair combed back as I wanted. He was the most handsome and most desirable creature I had ever seen. And he was all mine.

Of course, he had flowers in his hand. I had to laugh, "Oh, my Nathan. You shouldn't have."

As I opened the door, he froze in his steps. He looked at me. Up and down he looked at me. He lusted for my naked body, as I knew he would.

He threw the flowers on the table near the door. With force he grabbed me around my waist and pulled me to him. He was hot. As we kissed and exchanged our wetness, he put his hands on my body. His hands were all over me. His being was all over me.

"Hey," he said with a moment's laugh.

"Hey, yourself," I replied in a moment of deep pants.

"You're just way too beautiful tonight, way too hot." He looked toward the stairs for a moment.

"Come with me."

"Nice." He looked at the string of rose petals trailing from the front room and up the stairs to my bedroom. "You thought of everything."

"You really haven't seen anything yet, mister."

As Nathan held me tight to his body, his wet kisses soaked my neck and shoulders. I started to swoon. I swayed and felt weak, like an animal surrendering as prey. His body's potion had cast the spell, and without any hesitation it commanded me—I was a prisoner tonight and forever.

I tasted the sweat on his shoulders and chest. It intoxicated me with a fiery and unbridled submission. A total surrender we both passed to each other as our breaths and rhythmic movements flowed in unison while our bodies synchronized to that total submission of longings and passions. They were "familiar," yet new and inviting as if for the first time.

"We fit," I said under my breath.

"Yes, we fit," as Nathan looked into my eyes and we both could see each other's soul. The souls of two people who were ancient and ever new.

"Never go away. Never leave me, Nathan. I love everything about you."

"Never will I leave you, my Marisa. Never. We are fixed. It is written."

He said it. "It is written."

The night passed. We would awaken again and again. The candles flickered and danced their dances. Nathan and I would blend and merge and fade into each other, as we would bask and soak in our love. We knew we had become as one.

It was early morning when I opened my eyes again and peered over at Nathan. He was on his stomach, facing me. His shoulders and the nape of his neck and scruffy beard made me desire him again. I longed for him. I hungered again. His magnetic pull was much too forceful. I was like a huntress staring and getting ready to devour her prey, but only to sustain and cherish her prey for just a bit before the devouring, as the "art of pleasing pretty" had taught me. Man, do I love this man!

"Good morning, beautiful. I know you're lusting after me again."

We laughed as he pounced up on all fours and cuddled me, nipping at my ear and neck, as though he would be the one to devour and not I. That was all right with me.

"I'm so in love with you, Nathan."

"I'm so in love with you, Marisa. Forever have I been and forever will I be. I have found my treasure again."

His words seemed to confirm that he knew we had lived another life together. At some point I would need to speak with him of my experience.

After we merged again, we went downstairs. As I let the cats out to roam and be fed, Nathan blew out the candles that continued to flicker, and cleared up the strewn petals.

We sat on the veranda having our coffee and breakfast. The early Saturday morning air was nice and cool. The waters of the Great Liquid refreshed our souls as we listened to its soothing sounds of its healing balm. *What a beautiful creation*, I thought. To think that a massive liquid, a powerful liquid, an intimidating liquid could draw one to be soothed and healed. I thought how much I loved the ocean, and yet I was much afraid to enter into it, other than when in that spiritual state as High Tide, himself, takes me deeply into his abode. I still wondered why that was.

As we finished our breakfast, Nathan moved himself closer to me and gave me a kiss. "I think it's time that we talk about something. It concerns us. It concerns something that we are both familiar with. Something that we both share."

He said that word, "familiar." Somehow at that moment, I just knew.

Nathan began to tell me of everything that I had thought he already knew. Of course he would because he was Daniel. We had shared a lifetime together in the late 1800s. We were "familiar" and we were fixed in this lifetime again.

He told me that he knew who I was the moment he saw me at the intersection the day I first viewed my home. I was a little surprised about that, but oh so elated to hear it. He said it was him on the Carpet Ride and in the Pebble Story. He said he already knew about our lives together, of Calissa, of Madame and the pretty pink ladies. He knew everything. Yet, I did not know everything. I still had yet to view how our lives would turn out.

"We're going together tonight, Marisa. You and I will be together when High Tide takes us."

Chills filled every inch of my body now. Nathan knew everything. We would go together. The ecstasy of knowing all this overwhelmed me so that I thought for a moment I could not contain.

"Tonight will be the last night on this journey. Oh, there will be others, but this particular journey will be completed," he said with his crooked smile and his dancing blue eyes. "Everything will be fine, Marisa. Just remember, that life is over and has passed now. This is our life now. At this moment in time, we are back together again."

I started to cry, as my man's strong arms held me and I knew that all was well. The tears came of those with joy and those of sadness. I felt not all was well, nor would be well on this last journey. Nevertheless, my Nathan would be with me. That alone would suffice.

Chapter 13

AND SO IT CAME TO BE AGAIN

"Return to me, for it is written."

*A*fter our time again spent in merging our love and passion, Nathan and I decided to get out of the house for a bit and spend time diverting our attention from tonight's journey.

It was a lovely day filled with hints of cool breezes as the beginning of autumn was at hand. Nathan drove my convertible as we enjoyed the feeling of surrender to this beach life I had finally settled into now.

"I love the way the wind catches your hair, how it dances, and how it falls in layers across your face. You're so beautiful, my Marisa." He would glance over at me mesmerized as he drove along the coastal road.

"How did I ever get so lucky, so blessed to have you as my man again?" I lifted my hands toward the universe above me. I laughed and hollered out, "Thank you, thank you my MoonGlow and all you heavenly light beings out there," as I blew them kisses.

I reached over and put my arms around Nathan's shoulders and mounted kisses on his neck. We laughed as I now had to wipe off the multitudes of lipstick marks.

We spent some time shopping and browsing. We had lunch at a bayside outdoor restaurant. As I noted that Terri had text me asking how things were going, I replied that it could not even for a moment get better than this. I would talk to her tomorrow for a bit to catch up. I was not about to get into what Nathan knew and of our plans for this evening. Yet, I somehow knew she would see us together this evening as she would watch from her veranda. I know she would be happy too that we were together and could not wait to hear about everything.

After we arrived back at the house in late afternoon, I received a call from

Zach. How delighted I was to catch up on how he was doing. He seemed to be very happy with his classes and also with spending time with his girlfriend, Ashley.

I then decided it was time. I wanted him to know about Nathan. I went on to tell Zach about how I met Nathan, what kind of a man he was, and that we were together now. He seemed genuinely happy for me.

Nathan had come into the front room and heard me talking about him. As I continued to look at him, he whispered to me if I would like for him to speak with Zach. I wanted him to do so, but I thought about the daughter he had lost and would never speak with again in this lifetime. Or would he?

Nathan's conversation with Zach was easy. It seemed as though there was nothing awkward and I was happy to see that. I thought that the two of them would hit it off, naturally. A part of me felt sorrow for Nathan.

The early evening came quickly. Since we had a late lunch in town, we decided to just do the same as Caroline and I would do most of the time. I made some nachos, poured us some wine, and sat on the veranda while waiting for the time that we would present ourselves to our beautiful MoonGlow. Yes, Nathan, knew MoonGlow too, for back in 1883, he as Daniel, had dedicated our Calissa to our sweet sister moon.

The winds came even before we had reached the shoreline. As we walked along the boardwalk, we looked back together at my abode, MoonGlow. She was glowing and stunning. Even Nathan had to give a "wow."

As our feet touched the sand, we both looked over to our right. There she was. MoonGlow was striking as Nathan and I gasped and soaked in her presence. The spell had been cast many many moons ago, I thought. MoonGlow had chosen us to drink her potion and have our hearts drunken with her wine as she has done for lovers many times. For such a long time, she had concocted her potion to perfection, and now, we seemed to be her most blessed and pleasing fruition of all her endeavors.

As she batted her eyes several times, she finally blew us both the kiss that settled everything. That kiss would define and fix our union. It was settled indeed.

As her glowlight increased and lit the night skies with zillions of whimsical lights while dancing their dance, it brought me back to the first night I had driven here to see my once abandoned and forgotten abode. It was gloriously alive now, though. It was alive and it was magical and mystical.

"Yes, my dear old friend, my MoonGlow, you have taken care of me. You have watched over me and you have kept me afloat." For a moment, I thought the word "afloat" had been a strange word to say.

Nathan had reached out to hold my hand again, as we both stood motionless as MoonGlow began to turn a color of bright light pink. "She's showing us her love for us."

Nathan reciprocated, "Yes, and she's confirming the love we both have for each other, too." He gave me a kiss.

As we continued to hold hands, the Great Liquid before us began its clamoring blusters of its hidden rumbles. We watched with fright as we saw the cocooned fetal beings bursting upward out of the waters. From above the light beings vertically descended upon the waters and shot upon these helpless beings the healing balm of liquid filled lights. Various projectiles of their healing lights were dispersed and scattered among these fetal beings as well as all who lay hidden beneath the liquid. All that was encompassed in the Great Liquid seemed to be blessed upon with this healing balm that the Great Liquid possessed and was bestowing.

The beings began to peel off their cocoons. They had been released, but appeared weakened. They began the ascent as the benevolent creatures of light held them and began to spiral upward into the galaxies through their liquid tunnels.

"Where are they being taken?" I heard Nathan ask.

In a millisecond Nathan and I were taken with great force. High Tide had consumed his prey. We belonged to him now—at least for a while.

1901-1902...TENTH ENCOUNTER

It was late November, 1901. I was standing in the large sitting room at my house in Charleston. I could see family sitting around. My Daniel was there discussing business with Calissa's husband, Andrew and Elizabeth's husband, Howard. Calissa, Elizabeth, and I were near the front window enjoying our tea and watching the goings on outside the window. I believe it had to have been a Sunday.

I heard Calissa talking about Annabella's son, David. It was relayed to me that Calissa and David, who were just months apart, had remained close friends. We had visited Annabella and her family in Alabama during the years, as well as she had visited us here in Charleston. I was saddened when I suddenly thought of Madame Mabelle again and all the others back in New Orleans. What had happened to everyone else? This, I did not know.

I looked over at Daniel. I watched Andrew as he seemed to take over the conversation. He seemed somewhat overly self-assured and rather pompous. I still felt as though there was something not quite right. I actually did not care for him. I thought then that I wished Calissa and David could have ended up together. My heart felt this would have been a blessing for all.

I reluctantly was taken aback at the meeting with the voodoo priestess. I felt an uneasy sickly feeling now as I glared at Andrew and wondered if he was "that man."

Finally, an announcement was made. My Calissa was pregnant. She would be due in late April, 1902. I was overjoyed. Daniel and I would have a grandchild. I then remembered Nathan had told me that tonight would be the last of my journey here in this time period. Would I get to see my grandchild, though?

Daniel came into our bedroom. He looked as if he had been through some terrible experience. His hair was uncombed. His eyes were red. He was broken…very broken. Something dark…very dark and evil had him so disturbed. He started to cry as he fell to his knees.

It was February, 1902 when my daughter's body had been found along the shoreline. My Calissa was eighteen years of age and had been pregnant seven months. She had been beaten and drowned. I did not know the particulars, but Daniel was called out when she was found. It was relayed that her husband, Andrew, had been dealing with a friend of his father's who was quite unscrupulous with his business and Andrew had made a few fraudulent dealings. It was relayed that he and his cohorts would be punished for his role in this, and justice would be served. I thought how could there possibly be a worthy punishment to atone for the murder of my lovely daughter, Calissa, as well as my grandchild.

I watched as Daniel could hardly speak the words, as he would stop with his own bellowing cries of grief. I could not say a word. I saw myself fall to my knees, bending over to grab my lower abdomen. My cries were the most frightening guttural moans of utmost despair. They seemed to be unceasing, uncontrollable, and unending. The tears I saw myself shed would have filled an ocean, it seemed.

I, Marisa, started to cry too. I felt as though I had fallen to the floor as well. The tears came as it did during the travel to the Place of Tears and then again through the Cold Sleet.

How and why did this happen to my sweet and innocent Calissa? She had never become what my mother and I had. She was pure and she was kind and generous.

Karma is indeed a bitch, I thought. *She makes us pay every penny until our fetters are white as snow. Amends have to be made for our wrongful choices, our selfish choices, even if it involves the innocents.* "It is the Law," as Calissa would say.

I, Marisa, was walking along the sands again. It seemed to be early evening. The night skies paraded their bodies of light. No MoonGlow was in sight. I had grabbed my lower abdomen and started to moan and cry again. I was holding on to my womb.

"My womb," I heard myself say. "My womb where I nestled, nourished, and rested my sweet baby girl. My womb, which was the safest place my sweet daughter had ever been, had ever lived. And so, my daughter's womb had been the safe haven for her own child, too."

I knew that a woman's womb had always been the safest place for her baby. Never would there be a safer place. When the time would come for a woman's child to leave such a sacred and safe haven, the woman would forever be submitted to a life of worry and concern for her child's safety, always thereafter, neverending.

"Mother." I looked around. I started to turn around in circles to see her, to find her. I knew it was my Calissa's voice.

"Calissa!" I threw myself onto her and covered and held her as we both dropped to the sand. The massive tears came again. The guttural groans and moans bellowed out to the Great Liquid. I could see my tears flowing from the sand and into the oceans. *My own salty balm*, I thought. *My own healing balm I am giving away.* I knew somehow that everything suddenly made some sense. My own tears were being shed now not only for myself, but for all mothers who had ever lost children. My tears were finding their way to reach them. They were leaving me to go to those who still lay hidden…hidden in liquid. Those mothers who needed to be healed, to be soothed, to be cleansed and were deeply hidden in the deepest recesses of the ocean's bowels.

"Mother, do not fret. All things are passing on this earthly realm. Here I am now, yes? I am here with you, Mother, right now."

Calissa had been holding me tightly. It looked as though the roles had been reversed. I had become as a child and my Calissa was holding and soothing me now in a loving, maternal way. I wondered then if she had been able to hold her own child in the netherworld, since she had never been given the opportunity in this particular lifetime.

"You know, sweet Mother, one lifetime in the earthly realm is not just one book full of chapters. One lifetime is actually a series of several books with their multiple chapters of living and experiencing different lives within the same body. For you see, lifetimes are continuous, flowing and constant, whether in the present body, another one, or in our higher self. Everything in the universe is a constant and moving flow. There is no death. The soul never dies. Let me take you for a moment."

Calissa continued to hold me as we shot up into the night skies through prisms with a matrix of unknown colors and shooting lights. The endless stars and glowlit moons gave away their secrets as we sped past them, for I knew for sure where we were heading. We sped every so quickly as I suddenly heard the familiar laughter.

"The starlight children!" How delighted I was. There they were as I watched their continuous dance of play, giggling and sprinkling their stardust on each other and all the souls who would come for a visit.

A few had danced their way up to me and started to play with my hair, which had become tangled with their glistening dust. I could see Calissa playfully dancing their dance and looking over at me to take delight in this World of Sentimental Play.

We stayed and danced for quite a while, it seemed. Although here in this space, time is suspended. There is no sense, reason, or rhyme of time.

Calissa had taken me back to the sands again. We stood on the beach. I felt all was well now. She was here and I remembered that death is not real. We never die. We just transcend.

"When we come here as humans, we can change some things because of free will, but there are those already declared "fixed." It is written in the bodies of light. You will come to understand more of what I have spoken. That is all I can relay now."

"I love you forever, my Calissa." As my daughter reciprocated, I knew we would see each other again.

I was on the sand. It was relayed to me that it was now June 9, 1902. I had just turned forty. It was early evening. As I gazed into the realms of the night skies, I looked over to my right. There she was. My MoonGlow, ever brilliant and ever captivating as always. She immediately blew me the kiss. I saddened and started to cry again. My sweet sister moon knew that my daughter and grandchild were gone now.

I lowered myself to the sand and lay there filling my body and soul with my anguish. I drenched myself again with my tears. No consolation could I feel. I could not pray. I could not holler out to the heavens for mercy, for relief, for any kind of reprieve of the hopelessness that had consumed me. Not even my MoonGlow could soothe and comfort me. There was nothing…nothing to keep me here. Not even the man I loved so dearly, my Daniel, could be enough for me at this moment.

Where was my Daniel at this time? Oh, how he must had been suffering too. Why were we not together consoling and loving each other? Why were we not sharing this horrific loss in our lives together?

I stood up. I began to take off my wrap and my shoes. I looked out across the Great Liquid before me and up into the endless starlit night skies.

"Take me. Take me, Lord, and have mercy on me. I need to see my babies."

The Great Liquid began to tower and come forth. As I walked into the massive liquid domain, I felt my body being pulled into his depths. Into the darkest recesses of his bowels did I go. His liquid filled me as I struggled to breathe. I struggled as my limbs thrashed against the thick liquid. Just as quickly, though, I began to settle.

I went limp and I allowed myself to just be. An amazingly luminous light hovered above me as I saw flying toward me the familiar magnificent winged creature. As he was great in size and of great strength, yet with the gentleness of a dove, he lifted me out of the Great Liquid.

As I humbly surrendered to this benevolent vast creature of flight, I bowed my head. "Let it be done to me accordingly." I was placed upon the sand. I molded into my fetal position and lay there for a time cocooned. The winged creature suddenly swept me up and into the Great Liquid I was submerged again. This time I was to be consumed with the healing balm. His healing solvent drenched me, consumed me, and cleansed me. I felt at peace. I felt loved. I felt safe.

Then the secret was revealed. It came to me. The fear of this Great Liquid I owned and had held on to in my present lifetime was because of the path I had chosen in this past life. I had chosen to take my life because of not being able to bear the death of my sweet Calissa. I had broken the law of the universe…the law of life. "So it let it be done to me accordingly."

I watched myself floating to an unknown area in the depths of the liquid. I was outstretched now, no longer curled in a cocoon. I felt submerged in timelessness.

Then there they were. Calissa and my granddaughter were merging toward me. Dancelike movements were shared in flowing unison. I heard melodies of the celestial light beings above coming upon us through the liquid. Light beams of warm, pale colors struck upon us. The Great Liquid soothed and bathed us as we continued the dance.

We merged together, facing each other, while our fingertips touched and kissed our souls. The touch was magnetic and electrifying. I felt the forgiving and unconditional ancient love that we had always shared…the ancient timeless love that always existed. It was a goodbye for us now. We separated. Calissa and my granddaughter soared upward out of the water, as I had begun to spin into the depths of the Great Liquid. I cocooned myself again into my respective position. It was time for going into our designated worlds, separating ourselves for the time specified for healing and refreshment. The time would be allotted for a while, or was it for a moment? There is no time here in this space, I thought. Only timelessness resides here.

I was placed upon the sand once more by the magnificent winged creature. "Had I been abandoned now?"

There she was. "Oh, MoonGlow! Come get me, please." I was happy to see her in her ever-glorious glowlight. The light from her was warm and loving—and yes, her pinkish hue was ever present. She blew me her kiss of her undying love for me and all seemed well.

High Tide came forth with a gentleness not seen before. His mighty arms were outstretched and wrapped gently around me now. As he took me away, I saw MoonGlow shedding tears for me, which I had never seen her do. I had gone limp and surrendered to my fate, as High Tide took me into the deepest recesses of his bowels where always lay hidden the secrets and sins of all humanity.

I thought about the World of Ancient Gardens. I wondered, *Will I go there now?* No, I was not ready.

I had committed irreverence against the law of the universe…the law of life. I would need to make atonement. It was relayed to me that because of the enormous grief and mental anguish of my daughter's death, the sentence would be lightened.

Two angelic beings appeared. They looked familiar. Yes, they were the two angelics who appeared to me near the beginning of my journey.

"Am I to return to the Place of Tears?" Oh, how I remembered the innumerable and endless tears of sorrows I experienced. The endless tears from the healing salts that were much needed. I remembered that it was a purgatorial realm within the veil of illusion. Would that moment in time that I had previously spent suffice so I may never need to go there again?

No, it would not. Look what I had done to Daniel. He lost his daughter and then he lost me. Where was my Daniel now? Where was my love? How and why would I do this to him?

The two angelic beings swooped me up. I was taken into a darkened realm where lay hidden countless mansions filled with beings and unrecognizable life-forms. I heard voices and whisperings, incomprehensible to the ear. Known and unknown faces and glimpses of past, present, and future lives—all intertwined and mishmashed together—flew past me endlessly.

Then just as quickly, there was no sound, no faces, no mansions. I was sent to one of countless Cities of Healing. It was a city of being "fixed up." I saw myself in a hospital bed. The two angelic beings were clothed in white robes now. They hovered over me, placing their warm light-projected hands over my soul in various places. I felt myself drifting off into the most restful sleep of all sleeps. It was another time. It was another dimension…a dimension of healing. For how long? I did not know. Did I rest for many moons…for many ticks and tocks…unrelenting and forever? Or maybe it was set and written…and so it would come to be again.

Nathan and I woke up suddenly and together we were in my bed again. We looked at each other and began to hold each other as if nothing could pull us apart, nor did we ever want to try.

"It's okay, Marisa. I love you. It's over now. That life is over."

I did not say a word. I was still in a fog. I still had questions, but I could not question at this time.

"I got through it, Marisa. I suffered much from my loss of you and Calissa, but I got through it. I never married again, but I died a few years later from heart failure. It was natural, but I somehow think it was because of the grief."

I started to cry and say, "I am so very sorry that I left you." Even though I knew it was ages ago, I needed to feel the cleansing of my tears. Nathan waited patiently to have me do so, for he knew all about the healing effects of our tears. As the tears faded, we fell asleep.

When we awoke again, it was still early morning and still the night skies were present outside our window. "Let's go." He took my hand and we playfully bounced off the bed and ran downstairs, like a newly married couple childishly parading.

MoonGlow was still beaming her glowlight upon us, as well as upon all the endless encompassing creations of lands, realms, and galaxies unseen. The kiss of her love was felt warm and welcoming upon our cheeks, as we reciprocated with ours. Though it was the beginning of autumn and the evening temperatures would normally be cool, our MoonGlow's light irradiated the sand and water tonight with inviting warmth as a gift for Nathan and me tonight.

"May I have this dance with you, my lady?" Nathan bowed and kissed my hand.

"Why Mister Nathan, you most certainly can." I curtsied and ever so coquettishly, tossed my hair, lowered my head, and smiled. I did so in the manner just like Madame Mae had taught me…just like a pretty pink lady would do naturally.

With one arm he held me tightly around my waist as our bodies pressed against each other. We danced as Nathan would grab and lift my hair and smother me with his wet kisses. I would soak in his delights and bask in our evolving rhythms as we found ourselves naked and filled with passions ever ancient and ever new. We fell to the sand and made love as we merged and faded into each other's beings.

I felt the waters rising up from my feet and taking my body as Nathan led me into the Great Liquid. I was no longer fearful. For the first time in this lifetime, I had succumbed to the waters, not by having High Tide take me while under his trance, but by Nathan's love for me, eons old.

As we played in the water, as we merged in our liquids, we knew we were fixed. We were not perfect, but we had found each other and we would move on together now. MoonGlow had brought us here. My ancient glowlight had forever been my sentinel and friend indeed.

As Nathan and I headed back to the boardwalk, we both took a look at the abode named after our MoonGlow. She was glowing, of course, and she was stunning.

Nathan ceased our steps for a moment. "Always dance with me, Marisa."

"Always we will dance and always we will do so together." As I stared into his crystal-blue dancing eyes, I saw myself being led off to another lifetime. To another lifetime again I would be shown after the healing had taken place…and we would come to be again.

CPSIA information can be obtained
at www.ICGtesting.com
Printed in the USA
FSOW01n0321070217
30461FS